"If you're going into the mountains, you're not going alone."

period turned then, sending heat and sparks sizzling through her. One of his powerful arms wrapped around her and pressed her to his chest.

Alison looked directly at his black-as-night eyes. Somewhere in those depths she could have sworn she saw hot burning coals.

"Damn," he whispered, just before he kissed her.

The weakening in her grew as he deepened the kiss. Beyond any shadow of a doubt she knew she'd never felt this degree of longing for any man.

All she wanted was to enjoy this new experience of feeling utterly safe, utterly cherished, by a man who looked like a lethal weapon.

"Tell me I shouldn't have done that," he murmured.

"I can't," she answered on a mere breath of air.

"Oh, hell," he said. "I'm in trouble now."

DEADLY HUNTER

BY
RACHEL LEE

Published in Great Britain 2014
by Mills & Boon, an imprint of Harlequin (UK) Limited,
Eton House, 18-24 Paradise Road, Richmond, Surrey, TW9 1SR

© Rachel Lee 2013 (Susan Civil-Brown)

ISBN: 978 0 263 91419 1

46-0114

Harlequin (UK) Limited's policy is to use papers that are natural, renewable and recyclable products and made from wood grown in sustainable forests. The logging and manufacturing processes conform to the legal environmental regulations of the country of origin.

Printed and bound in Spain
by Blackprint CPI, Barcelona

Prologue

Cleaning guns had always soothed him. The smell of the oil, the focus required to disassemble and reassemble small parts, the rubbing motions as he worked the oil into them.

He had them all out tonight, a collection of a dozen different weapons, everything from small pistols to his semiautomatic AR-15 and AK-47. Running his rags and oil over them focused him on his new mission.

It was a good feeling to have a target again. A very good feeling. There was no longer any reason to contain his rage, no longer any reason to hold back. He'd be in and out, and the remains of the target would be carried away by woodland animals, leaving no trace.

Then he could carry on with life again. Only then.

Chapter 1

Darkness fell early on cold winter nights in Conard County, Wyoming. Allison pulled into her driveway, feeling the weight of the frigid night air even inside the warmth of her SUV. She sat for a bit, reluctant to get out, to once again feel the sting of icy air in her nostrils and lungs.

It was a silly reaction. After all, she'd grown up around here, the winters rarely held any surprises, and the cold was the least of them. But for the moment she decided to enjoy the blast of heat from her car vents before dashing up to her door and stepping into a house that would be even colder than the car.

She believed in conservation and saving energy. During the days when she was at work, her computerized thermostat turned the temperature down to sixty. Right now it would be pushing the house toward sixty-eight, but wouldn't have quite made it yet, given how cold it was today. Later, at bedtime, it would turn down again until morning.

Which meant she wore a lot of fleece indoors, and thick mohair socks, and even had a heavy blanket to wrap herself in for sitting around and reading in the evenings. Plus, the house itself, being older, managed to remain drafty no matter what she did with weather stripping and insulation.

She needed new double-paned windows, but those were far beyond her budget right now. Instead, she had to settle on insulated curtains, and while they helped, they didn't quite stop the drafts.

And this was ridiculous, she told herself. Burning gas with her car needlessly just to avoid going inside and wrapping herself in layers of warm clothing. Wasteful. Bad for the environment.

Nearly giggling at herself, she flipped off the ignition and sat listening to the engine tick as it cooled down. Man, it wasn't like this was Antarctica or anything, and the trip to her front door wasn't that far. What had gotten into her?

Just as she reached for the door handle, a truck pulled into the driveway next door, not six feet away from her. Her new neighbor, a man she had barely glimpsed in the two weeks since he'd moved in, apparently kept so much to himself that the only gossip about him so far was that he kept to himself.

A strange thing around here.

Well, she thought, this was her opportunity to at least say hi. Climbing out quickly, watching her breath blow frosty clouds in the muted light from his truck and a streetlamp three houses down, she looked up and waited.

For a minute she wondered if he was waiting inside his truck to avoid her. Cold began to snake its way into the neck of her jacket, and she moved her purse strap so she could pull up her hood.

At last he climbed out. Tall. Lean, even in his layers of winter clothing. He glanced her way just briefly, and she almost caught her breath as she saw the narrow scar that slashed his cheek. He had just started to move toward his own door when she called out.

"Howdy," she said cheerfully. "About time we met. Welcome to town, neighbor. I'm Allison McMann."

He froze, still mostly turned away from her. The hesitation was perceptible, and she began to wonder if he was going to say anything at all.

"Hi," he said shortly, then trekked toward his door without another word.

Okay, Allison thought. *Have it your way.* Turning, she hurried up her steps, slipping on ice she thought she'd gotten rid of. Then, like some crazy cartoon, she cartwheeled backward. All of a sudden she was lying on her back, staring up at the starry night sky, her laptop case and backpack in the snow, her purse wrapped across her chest.

"Well, dang," she said to the stars. She *never* did this. That would teach her to hurry.

"Are you okay?"

Just as unexpectedly as she had fallen, Mr. Inscrutable was squatting beside her, looking down at her. Even in the lousy light she could see chiseled features and dark eyes. He had bone structure an actor would kill for.

"I think I'm fine," she said. "Well, except for my pride. Despite evidence to the contrary, I almost never fall."

"So you're a mountain goat?"

Was that humor? She looked at his face but found it as unreadable as everything else about him.

"Not exactly." She started to push herself up, but his hand on her shoulder stayed her.

"Take it slowly. You can't always tell, and it sounded to me like you hit pretty hard on the pavement."

"Yeah. Pavement I salted just last night so I wouldn't slip and fall. Go figure."

"Must have missed a spot."

She pushed up again and was grateful that this time he didn't try to stop her. In fact, he didn't offer unnecessary assistance, either. He just remained there, watching.

When she was sitting upright, she wiggled her shoulders and untangled her purse. "I'm okay," she repeated.

"No wooziness?"

"Not a bit."

"Okay, then." He stood, grabbed her hands without asking and pulled her to her feet. He dropped her gloved hands as fast as he had seized them, and stepped back. He watched her almost clinically for a few seconds, nodded to himself then bent and retrieved her laptop and backpack.

"There you go," he said, passing them to her. Before she could thank him, he was trotting toward his door again, as if he couldn't get away from her fast enough.

"Thank you," she called after him. She didn't even get a grunt in return.

Realizing she was getting colder by the second, she headed for her own door, more cautiously this time. No more pratfalls, she warned herself. Especially not in front of that guy. He seemed almost as cold as the winter night.

Thanks to her longer-than-intended sojourn outside, the house didn't feel quite as cold as usual. Checking the thermostat, she saw the temperature had already reached sixty-six. Stripping her outerwear and hanging it on pegs by the door, she headed to her bedroom in the back for what she thought of as her "grungies," old, comfortable sweats and socks and a sweater if necessary. She'd warm up making her dinner, then settle in with grading the latest chemistry test.

In the kitchen, she flipped on the small TV to listen to the weather while she cooked. This cold wave was extreme for this early in the winter, arriving more than a month sooner than usual. Tomorrow she had fieldwork to do and figured unless something happened overnight, she would have to dig out the snowmobile suit she kept for the coldest days of the year. She never went snowmobiling, but the one-piece suit had other uses, including protection from the wind.

This damn job was going to be tough enough as it was. A rancher had recently lost two cows to a deadly toxin, one that had been outlawed years ago and had the ability to spread far and fast with little control. The state had asked her to take some soil and water samples to try to identify the affected areas. Given the toxicity of the chemical identified in the dead cows, this was going to be dangerous.

Still, it had to be done, and she'd just have to be careful, wearing protective gloves and booties over her winter gear. All of which was going to make collecting the samples awkward, but there it was. This compound had to be tracked and the source cleaned up as swiftly as possible. The spring thaw would only make things worse.

With these thoughts running in her mind, she broiled a chicken breast and tossed a small salad. Inevitably, though, her mind returned to the stranger next door. He'd been quick to help when she had fallen, but was otherwise utterly unfriendly. She hadn't even learned his name.

His face suggested he might be a hunk, but the scar on his cheek looked as if he'd been slashed with a knife. He might also be bad news. He could be hiding out from the law for all she knew, although with a face as memorable as that, he wouldn't be able to hide for long.

The lights had been turned on next door two weeks ago, so she assumed that was when he moved in. In all that time, tonight was the first glimpse she'd had of him, although his truck seemed to be gone an awful lot, so he was doing something with his days.

But given this town's penchant for gossip, people had been amazingly quiet about this guy. They noted he'd moved in, but nobody knew a thing about him. If he had a job somewhere, someone would have mentioned it.

He was well out of the norm in a number of ways, and it made her curious as hell. None of her business, of course, but it was impossible not to think of the lines she'd heard in so many horrible news stories: He kept to himself. He was a loner.

She giggled at the direction her imagination had taken and poured coffee to take into her home office with her while she graded those tests.

Despite all the technological advances, giving an in-class test meant that she had to pore over chicken scratchings. In a couple of hours, she would feel nearly blind and probably have a splitting headache. Such was the price of teaching Chemistry I and II at a community college. A small price overall, she decided, as she picked up the first test.

She liked her job. And she had to stop wondering about the stranger next door.

* * *

Little more than thirty feet away, the stranger next door stood in his unlit back room and stared out an uncurtained window. Agitation crawled across his nerve endings, and he faced that fact that not even six months had been enough to ease the constant pressure and stress he lived with. It was as if his mind and body had simply forgotten how to relax.

He'd moved here for the wide-open spaces and the clear sight lines. A strange way to pick a town. Well, that and the fact that he knew Seth Hardin a bit and Hardin had always spoken well of this place. But he hadn't even let Hardin know he was here, although he heard the guy was currently on station with his fiancée somewhere out there. No point in introducing himself to Hardin's family hereabouts. He might not stay long.

He might not be *able* to stay long. Questions about his past simply couldn't be answered. His whole adult life was stamped "classified," and it was hard to talk around those things without inadvertently giving something away.

He had his cover story, but it didn't fit him somehow. He'd rather say nothing than lie needlessly, anyway. It was beginning to strike him that all he'd done was exchange one covert life for another. How did you build on that? He had six months of public history and a childhood. The rest was best forgotten.

Hell, maybe they should have filed him in the warehouse with all his mission debriefings.

The thought amused him, but not for long. Something about that encounter with his neighbor earlier had seemed to cast his current existence in high relief. Was he always going to live in the shadows?

It hadn't been so bad when he'd shared those shadows with the other guys in his unit, but now he shared them with no one, cut off from friends who could no longer talk to him about what they were doing, and cut off from everyone else because he couldn't say where he'd been or what he'd done.

He wasn't feeling sorry for himself. He'd made his choices. But it sure got irritating at times. Even the most casual of conversations felt like a minefield. He'd probably get used to it, though. He'd gotten used to a lot worse.

So he had some decisions to make and some learning to do. First off, he could have handled that encounter with the woman—Allison—with a minimum of common courtesy. Damn, it wasn't as if his name was classified. Would it have been so hard to say, "Nice to meet you. I'm Jerrod"?

Except that it might have been taken as an invitation to get to know him better. So he'd been rude. Not even helping her up after she'd slipped could make up for his cold response to her friendly greeting.

Time to learn to get through those simple courtesies without keeping his guard so high that he failed at the smallest aspects of daily life.

It wasn't as if he didn't know how. During his service, there had been plenty of opportunities to practice the social graces, at least to a minimal extent. Certainly the academy had drilled them into him. But then covert operations had kind of drilled them out.

Still, it was no excuse. What was going on inside him? No longer in uniform, he was feeling like some kind of sham. Because at heart he was still a long way from being a civilian.

He sighed and pressed his forehead to the icy window glass. When his career came to a close, thanks to shrapnel lodged near his spine, he hadn't dreamed that he'd feel so much like a stranger in a strange land. Or that he'd be so ill prepared for a so-called normal life.

His old normal was no longer normal, and he needed to get his act together. Traipsing around the countryside all day, every day, might ease the need for action, at least a little, but it wasn't moving him forward in any useful way.

He had a lot of years ahead of him, and he needed to do something worthwhile with them. If worse came to worse, he supposed he could return the call from the CIA, but did he really want a covert future where his ability to act would be hemmed in by pretending to be a diplomat? Was he even certain that he would do any good? At least what he'd been doing for the military—well, damn near all of it—had sure as hell seemed necessary.

The CIA was a whole different can of worms, one he wasn't sure he wanted to open. At least in his former capacity, he hadn't usually needed to lie and gain the trust of people who shouldn't trust him at all.

There it was again, that whole lie-and-trust issue. Kind of late, he thought almost bitterly, to be developing moral qualms.

Or maybe not too late. Not too late to want to do something productive rather than destructive. The only question was what would satisfy him. What did he feel equipped to do that didn't involve sniper rifles and C-4?

Maybe he just needed to take it in small steps. One little thing at a time.

He glanced at his watch and saw it was only eight

o'clock, still early, although the winter had made it dark as pitch out there.

Maybe he could rectify one small rudeness. Just a small step, but a right step.

One foot in front of the other. That had gotten him through more than he cared to remember. One step at a time.

The ringing of her rather sickly sounding doorbell startled Allison. Her friends seldom dropped by unannounced and solicitors were rare on cold winter nights.

She dropped her red pen, tossed her reading glasses on the stack of papers and walked to the front door, rubbing her neck as she went. It hadn't taken long for the first seeds of eyestrain to start making themselves felt from her forehead to the back of her neck. She wondered at the tension, then decided she was probably more worried about tomorrow than she wanted to admit, even to herself. Tracking down a poison so dangerous that many countries had declared it a chemical-warfare weapon would be no picnic, no matter how carefully she collected her samples. One slip might be her last. Unfortunately, she was the only one available with sufficient expertise to do this. Her fault for taking training with a decontamination team while she had been in graduate school. Curiosity had led her to this point.

She opened her door and felt her heart skip a nervous beat, even as her jaw dropped. She didn't know what she had expected, but certainly not the enigmatic guy from next door who had barely answered her earlier greeting. Up close like this, she saw that while he was lean, he was also larger than she had thought, and both the porch and hall lights cast his harshly angled face in high relief.

For the first time, she realized he looked dangerous. But as the wind whipped snow into her door, stinging her face, she knew she couldn't stand at the door like this for long. He might be wearing a parka, but she sure wasn't. Should she let him in?

"I wanted to apologize," he said gruffly.

She blinked as snow crystals melted on her face and made a quick decision, possibly a stupid one, but time would tell.

"Come in," she said. "I'll freeze standing here."

He hesitated, as if he considered his purpose here completed, but then gave a slight nod. She stepped back, letting him in and closing the door against the frigid night and blowing snow.

She wiped her sleeve across her face to get rid of the wet, then caught sight of herself in the hall mirror. Her grungies. A great first impression. But as she raised her gaze again, she met eyes that looked about as black as a starless night, and just about as cold. A little shiver passed through her.

"Coffee?" she asked.

Again he hesitated. "Sure. But I only wanted a minute of your time, not to disrupt your evening."

"Anything that takes me away from grading papers is welcome." She didn't know whether she was being brave or brainless, but manners were deeply ingrained.

She almost waved him into the living room, then changed her mind midmotion. Living rooms were too comfortable. They invited people to stay. She wasn't at all sure that would be a good thing, so she led him into the kitchen. Coffee tasted the same at a table.

Behind her she heard him unzip his parka, but when she turned around as she reached the coffeepot, she found he hadn't removed his jacket. He pulled out one of the chairs at the round oak table and sat on its very edge. A man poised to get the hell out...or to move quickly.

"How do you like your coffee?" she asked.

"Black as hell and hot as Hades."

She blinked. "Okay. I'm not sure it's that hot, though."

He closed his eyes for just an instant. "Sorry. I've been living too long among guys. I guess I could have phrased that more politely."

"It's okay." She quickly filled two mugs, getting a fresh one for herself rather than trotting back to her office. She sat on the opposite side of the table from him, as far away as she could get. Unsure about this visit, she, too, sat on the edge of her seat.

"So why should you apologize?" she asked.

"Let me start at the beginning. Hi, I'm Jerrod Marquette. Nice to meet you. Sorry I was rude when you said hello earlier."

"Nice to meet you, too," she said, although she wasn't absolutely certain about that yet. "Allison McMann. Or did I tell you that?"

"You told me, which makes it even ruder that I didn't respond."

Since he seemed to be making an effort, she sought for a way to make one herself. "Well, maybe you weren't too happy to be greeted, but you were sure fast to the rescue when I fell. Thanks for the concern."

He shrugged one shoulder. "It was nothing."

"But it would be something for someone who isn't too keen on meeting the neighbors."

He looked away from her, his gaze growing distant. "Training. Instinct. All of it."

"All of it? Which all?"

He lifted his mug, drinking several sips, saying nothing for so long she wondered if he would say another word.

But then he surprised her. "Military training," he said finally. "Nothing I want to talk about, even if I could. But…" His gaze came back to her. "You know, it's a devil of a time trying to become a civilian again. Sounds crazy, I know."

"I didn't say that." And a picture was beginning to form in her mind. She wondered how far from the truth it was.

"Regardless, you wouldn't think I'd have lost the common courtesies. It's just that…"

Again he trailed off. She decided not to press him, but to let him say what he chose and avoid what he chose.

He sighed and drained his mug. "Too many years of secrecy. Invisibility. Being in a new place brings back habits. I can't explain more than that."

"I think I get it. At least some of it."

"Nobody who doesn't do it really gets it. But that's the way we want it."

"What do you mean?"

"We do what we do so civilians can remain innocent."

It was as if he sucked the wind from her between one breath and the next. She felt an unexpected piercing pain for what must have been required of him to make a statement like that. Before she could think of a word to say, he was starting to rise, preparing to leave.

She felt a desperate urge to not let him go, though she didn't know why. Yes, he was attractive, but what she was feeling right now touched her in a much deeper way. She needed to do something. Say something. Give him the very welcome he seemed to want to avoid. But how?

"Have some more coffee," she said quickly.

"I shouldn't. You were grading papers."

Man, he didn't miss a thing.

"Consider it my excuse not to go to bed with a pounding headache."

For the first time, the very first time, the stone of his face cracked just a bit. One corner of his mouth tipped up. "You'll still have to get the headache eventually."

"Sunday will be soon enough."

She was relieved when he walked over to the pot and poured himself more coffee. He returned to the table and sat. "I should ask about you."

"Sure. I'm an open book." Only as she saw his face darken a shade did she realize how that had sounded. She spoke swiftly to cover the faux pas. "Nothing really interesting, no secrets, no jaunts to exotic and dangerous places. I grew up here, went to college and came back here to teach at the community college. Chemistry."

This time he settled back into the chair, looking less likely to take flight. Although she got the feeling he didn't quite uncoil. She wondered if he even knew how.

"Do you like it?"

"Mostly," she said.

"But not grading papers."

"It's the lousy chicken scratches. I think computers have killed the fine art of handwriting."

"So why not let them use computers?"

"Because computers give them access to information. Every exam would essentially be an open-book test then. I do it sometimes, but other times I want to know what they really understand."

He nodded briefly, then drank more coffee. "Great coffee, by the way."

"Thank you. But not hot as Hades."

Again that faint flicker of a smile. "Not quite. But hot enough."

A silence fell, but it didn't feel as tense. Still, she decided to fill it. "The big thing in my life right now is the state has hired me to find out how far a toxin has spread. A few weeks ago, a rancher lost two cows, and tests show it was a horrible poison."

"What kind?"

"The kind that is outlawed because it's so dangerous. Well, it was until the USDA allowed it to be used in a few states for coyote control. But to give you an idea what I'm dealing with here, a number of countries have labeled it a chemical-warfare weapon. And the way it spreads is incredible. It doesn't just stop where it's applied, which is scaring the ranchers and hunters."

For the first time she realized how intimidating it could be to have this man's full attention. Those black eyes had looked at her before and seemed attentive enough, but now they lasered in on her. They made her think of his comment about black as hell. She had to fight an urge to pull back, knowing that he would see it and not willing to make him feel like a pariah without reason. At the same time, she felt an unexpected and unwanted tingle of sexual arousal. Dang it.

"Tell me about it," he said. "What exactly is it? How does it spread?"

"Its name wouldn't mean much to you or to most people who don't raise livestock. It's applied to bait to kill animals that eat carrion. Unfortunately, that doesn't just mean coyotes. Well, it's bad enough if it stops there, but it doesn't. The contaminated animal can take hours or days to die, wandering away from the bait. It becomes toxic itself, so wherever it dies, it can contaminate the ground and water, and if anything eats it, it'll die, too."

"Damn."

"Yeah. So they found the bait—at least, they think it was the bait—and only two cows have died so far. They think the cows must have licked some snowmelt or eaten some contaminated grass that was under the snow. Regardless, once the toxin was identified, we had to get into high gear because we can't be sure what appeared to be the bait wasn't simply an animal that had eaten the original bait. The spread could be big and getting bigger."

"So what do you do?"

"Take soil and water samples to try to figure out the impacted area. At the very least to let the ranchers know whether their grazing land and water is safe, but also to try to home in on the dangerous areas."

"Does it break down? Disperse?"

"Everything does, but you wouldn't believe how little of this stuff it would take to kill a grown man. In theory, it's supposed to be used only in livestock collars. So, for example, if a coyote bites a collared ewe on the neck, it'll get a fatal dose of poison. But there's enough poison in that one collar to kill six grown men or twenty-five children. If collars get lost or punctured, the poison gets into the environment. And by the way, if a collar is discarded, it's supposed to be buried at least three feet deep in the ground."

He nodded. "Okay. But if it's lost…"

"Yeah, if it's lost, the poison can leech into the environment. And even if it doesn't get lost… Well, I painted the picture of what happens when an animal gets poisoned. It wanders away, dies an agonizing death and something else eats it. And there isn't any known antidote."

"That could be bad."

"It *is* bad. It's the cascade effect that makes it so awful. If it killed just once, no big deal. But it doesn't. So until the poison dissipates to safe levels—and even sublethal levels can cause brain damage and so on—you've got a big-time problem that's spreading randomly."

"I can't think of a worse scenario. Do you think you can trace it back to its origin?"

"Probably not. I wish I could. If someone wasn't using it in an authorized collar, then they're breaking the law in a lot of ways. Law enforcement is looking into that part, but without any success so far. But I'm sure *I* won't get that far, and it's not what I'm out there to do, anyway. I'm just supposed to take samples for the state to identify any areas that present a threat. I hope I don't find a single one. Maybe it's all dissipated now. Maybe it was an isolated incident. I hope to God it was."

"Helluva problem."

"Yeah." She propped her chin on her palm and sighed. "If the weather settles down, I start tomorrow. Slowly circling out from where the dead animals were found. With any luck I'll be able to tell at least one rancher his grazing land is safe."

"But others?"

"That's the question. Was that bait the primary kill? Or have other animals died and spread the poison? I guess I'll find out."

"Why is this stuff even still in use?"

"Because it works." She straightened and threw out her arms. "They use it in Australia, New Zealand and Tasmania. To get rid of rodents and other vermin.

They've had some unexpected consequences, but they got the dose calibrated to do the job without killing too many other things, like the birds. The problem is these collars aren't low dose. And someone using it illegally would probably overuse it. People have a hard time grasping just how little of this poison is needed."

"That seems to be a common human failing," he remarked. Then he rose, went to the sink and rinsed out his mug.

"Thanks for the coffee. See you around."

She stood to walk him to the door, but he moved fast and by the time she got to her small foyer, there was nothing left of him but the blast of cold that had entered when he opened the door to leave.

"That was fast," she said to the empty house. She wondered what was riding his tail.

"Military," she murmured to herself. That probably explained a whole lot more than she could even imagine. But at least he had tried to be polite. She gave him marks for that.

It probably hadn't been easy for him, either, judging by his initial response to her greeting.

A glance at the clock told her it was still early. Back to grading papers. It was only as she sat at her desk with fresh coffee that she realized something.

That man had gotten her motor running for the first time in years. For all he was a cipher, he'd still kicked her hormones into overdrive and she didn't know why. Like she needed that? In fact, it was the last thing on earth she wanted from any man.

She squirmed a little in her chair as her most feminine parts insisted on reminding her that she was a woman with very real desires. They happened. It only mattered what she did because of them.

Right. With any luck, the chicken scratchings on the stack of papers in front of her would drive him right from her mind. And her rebellious body.

Chapter 2

Usually, walking and jogging over rough countryside for hours on end made Jerrod sleep well. That night he didn't sleep well at all, and he wasn't sure why.

His thoughts kept straying to that pretty brunette next door, her soft sherry-brown eyes, her bright smile, her nicely curved body. She may have thought her assets were hidden beneath those baggy sweats, but whether she knew it or not, those loose clothes enhanced her appeal. It was almost like playing peek-a-boo to watch her move. There was something to be said for not flaunting it.

Was a woman getting to him? It wasn't as if he'd been doing without sex for very long. Sex came easy to a man like him, especially when he'd still been in uniform. He also knew that he could do without it for long periods. He wasn't a kid anymore.

He'd been attracted to Allison. No question of that,

but maybe what was troubling him was that he'd been attracted to her in other ways than sexually. Something in her personality engaged him, even though they'd had only the briefest of conversations.

He didn't need that now, not when he was a long way from settled in himself.

If his life was a ledger, he wouldn't have known whether he was more in the red or the black. How would he? He seldom knew the real purpose behind much of what had been asked of him. He had been given mission briefings; sometimes he knew he was after terrorists, other times he just had to go on faith that his country needed this thing done.

That left him suspended somewhere between heaven and hell, he supposed. In purgatory. Regardless, things came back to haunt him—everyone got haunted to some degree—and they'd flash through his mind. If nothing else, memories goaded him to find a different way to leave the world a better place. Problem was, he hadn't found that way yet.

Maybe that was because he felt like he'd been through an emotional blender. He hadn't expected such an abrupt end to his career, although he was no fool and had known it was possible. If he'd expected anything, it was that he'd come home in a bag or box. He'd been wounded before and had recovered. So, idiotic or not, he hadn't exactly planned for an abrupt shift into civilian life. Truthfully, he admitted to himself, in his job neither he nor anyone else looked that far down the road. It was dangerous. You had to live for the mission and then for the next mission, and keep your focus tight.

Then, *boom,* every parameter of your life changed.

You went from fitting perfectly into a machine to fitting nowhere at all.

Interesting, really. A different kind of challenge, one he hadn't been up to so far.

But he supposed it was hard to go from a tight focus, where damn near every moment had been directed, to one where nothing was directed. It was like going from narrow tunnel vision to full vision. It was certainly a different way of existing.

He dozed occasionally, but sleep was fitful, more as if he was in a dangerous situation than completely safe in a house in a nice little town. It was okay, though. He'd learned to get a whole lot out of catnaps, just as he'd learned to take one whenever he got the opportunity.

He'd be fine in the morning.

And maybe he'd go over and offer his assistance to Allison. Sampling for a poison that dangerous didn't seem like something she should do alone.

Maybe it was time he reached out to someone. Just one person. It would be a big step out of the shadows that dogged him still.

Allison blinked in astonishment as she looked up from loading her sample case into the back of her car and saw Jerrod Marquette crunching through the snow toward her. A cup of coffee and suddenly he was no longer a loner? Uneasiness trickled through her.

She gave herself a mental shake, telling herself not to be ridiculous. If he'd moved in two days ago, she wouldn't even question his approach. He was a guy with a shell, as she had seen last night, but he'd done not one untoward thing.

"Good morning," he said as he reached her.

"It's certainly a beautiful one. Cold, though." Her breath was visible as she spoke, and she was grateful for her one-piece snowmobile suit. How much nicer if the weather hadn't gone crazy or she could just let this ride until the unusual cold passed. But the toxin couldn't wait.

"I was thinking how dangerous it might be for you to hunt this toxin all by yourself. Is someone going with you?"

She bridled. "I know what I'm doing."

"I'm sure you do. But if something goes wrong... Do cell phones even work when you get out of town very far?"

"Intermittently," she acknowledged. "Ranches are spread so far apart that it doesn't seem worth the cost to put in a lot of towers. But the lines of sight are good until you get into the woods and mountains, so...intermittent."

Reluctantly, however, she admitted he was making a good point. She'd been thinking in terms of wandering ranch land, shoveling away a little snow and drilling contained cores of about six inches of dirt. No big deal. But he was also right about being out there alone. Any accident could cause serious trouble if she had no way to call someone.

"I guess I need to get a radio," she said finally. "To call the sheriff if I need help."

"Good idea. Can you get one this morning?"

"I doubt it. I don't know how long it will take, and while we're standing here that toxin could be spreading."

"Okay, then, how about I tag along? I'll bring my own truck if you would be more comfortable, but if you twist an ankle or something, I can be there."

She studied him, thinking he didn't look quite so much

like a devil in the bright morning light. But every bit as attractive, even bundled up as he was.

"Are you a born caretaker or something?" she asked.

"Not exactly. Or possibly. What I know is, I almost never went on a dangerous mission alone. The smallest team I ever went out with was three. The average was six."

"Backup?"

"And rescue."

"Dang," she said. Mostly because he was right and she should have thought of it herself, persuaded one of her students to go along or something. No, she'd just been hot to trot to get those samples. "You know, I have to talk to the ranchers before I go out on their lands. They'll know where I am."

"Okay, then. Stay safe." He turned and started to walk away. For the first time it occurred to her that he might need something to do himself. Everything about him seemed to be at loose ends, though she couldn't exactly say why she sensed that.

"Jerrod, wait. I'd appreciate the company."

He turned back, nodding shortly and giving her a small smile. "You've got it."

But she made him take his own truck. She was *not* ready to get all cozy with this guy, no matter how much her hormones awoke when he was around. Even though her conscience *did* twinge when she considered the waste of gas and the pollution of unnecessarily taking two vehicles.

No, she thought as she backed out of the driveway, this was the wisest decision. If he got bored, he could leave. She wouldn't feel pressured by him being stuck with her. And she'd have her own escape route if she needed it.

She wasn't ready to trust yet. No way.

But thinking about Jerrod as she drove out to the Madison ranch where the initial incident had occurred, she wondered if she was being too distrusting. Yes, she had little to go on, and how could she be sure he really was ex-military? How could she be sure he hadn't spoken a pack of lies to her?

But she'd met a few con men, and as a rule they were smooth, charming talkers. He hadn't tried any smooth talk at all. Quite the contrary, he hadn't done a damn thing to win her over. Instead, he had struck her as a box full of tightly locked secrets. Everything about him screamed, "Watch out!"

Hardly the way to put anyone's fears to rest.

So she laughed off her doubts about him. Military vet, probably still struggling to make his way back to this life after one so very different. There were more than a few around this county. The adjustment to coming home always seemed far harder than the adjustment of arriving in a strange land. She'd even heard that from people who traveled for long periods of time.

She wondered if anyone had studied that adjustment issue. It seemed odd, but hadn't she read that Peace Corps volunteers also had reentry problems? She seemed to remember she had.

By the time she reached Jake Madison's place, she thought she had settled the issue, in her own mind, anyway. Until given some evidence that Jerrod wasn't trustworthy, she'd let it lie.

The wind bit at her as soon as she stepped out of her vehicle. Jake knew she was coming and why, so she wasn't at all surprised when he stepped out onto the porch, warmly dressed and ready to go.

"You sure picked a fine day for this," he remarked.

"I didn't pick it. It picked me."

He grinned and started down the steps. "I've even got my horses in the barn. Are you sure you should be out?"

She spread her arms. "I came dressed."

He glanced toward the truck. "Who's your compadre?"

"My neighbor, Jerrod Marquette. He seems to think I shouldn't be out doing this alone."

"Well, you shouldn't. But I didn't intend to leave you alone. Nora will be thrilled that I can come back as soon as I show you the site. Then the two of you be sure to stop in for something hot to drink. You're going to need it."

She noted that Jerrod didn't get out of his truck. Jake noticed, too, glancing that way again, but quickly turning to his own truck parked alongside the house. "I'll lead the way. Damn winter came early, didn't it? Ground is already frozen."

"How are your stock doing?"

"Unhappy, but surviving. We're spending an awful lot of time checking on them."

A minute later, Jake pulled away from the house, leading the small convoy across his rangeland. They had to stop a few times while he opened gates to let them through, then waited while he closed them.

Jake had a decent-size ranch, but they could have gotten to the problem location faster on a galloping horse. They weren't driving on a road, and Allison bounced up and down, her seat belt locking up frequently but preventing her head from hitting the roof of the car. Small mercies, she thought.

At last they came to what she would have guessed to be the farthest reach of his range, judging by the stream that still rippled and sparkled in the sunlight and the almost abrupt rise of the ground toward the mountains just beyond it.

An area was surrounded by yellow tape, and no cattle were in sight anywhere.

Jake climbed out and walked back to her as she exited her vehicle. Jerrod finally decided to emerge from his truck and she made introductions. The two men shook hands and exchanged measuring looks.

Jake got right to business. "Sheriff Dalton roped this off. It includes where we found the dead animal that might have been coyote bait, and the spot where my cows died and a considerable piece around it. For safety, I moved my stock to a different pasture."

"Those pin flags? What are they?"

"The red one is where we found the bait. The yellow ones are where we found the cows. They didn't get very far, but you could see where they convulsed and vomited before we got this fresh snow."

"Damn," Allison whispered.

"What?" Jerrod asked.

"I get that cows don't move far very fast usually, but this toxin affects the nervous system and brain. Most animals when they're exposed will run crazily, have seizures, try to bite at themselves. In short, I would have expected the cows to travel farther."

Jake looked at her. "You think the toxin was that strong that it killed fast?"

"They had to be eight hundred or so pounds?"

"They're Angus. They both tipped the scales close to a thousand."

"Damn," Allison murmured. "That was a lot of poison."

"Did you get results from the state lab?"

"Only as to what kind of poison. They haven't given me concentrations. I guess I need to call them Monday. I'm also wondering how they could have gotten so much of it. A little meltwater.... " She trailed off, trying to imagine it. "Given what cows eat, this is weird."

"Scary, too," Jake said. "I'm still amazed my dogs didn't get into the bait. They should have found it irresistible."

"Given that the poison is odorless and tasteless, yes, they should have. Maybe the cows' reactions were so fast they moved away."

"They sure moved the rest of the herd away." Jake shook his head. "Well, I'll leave you to it. I'd like some answers, but I'm not expecting them overnight."

He nodded to her and Jerrod, climbed back into his truck and drove toward the ranch house.

Allison stood looking at the roped-off area, feeling utterly creeped out.

"Maybe," Jerrod said presently, "you should have a whole decon team out here."

"It's crossing my mind. I'm trying to think of all the ways that quantity of poison could have wound up here. A single bait? It seems a reach. Maybe someone was screwing around out here doing something they shouldn't have been doing and spilled a bunch of the stuff. I told you how little it takes. But in terms of its effects on those cows, I'm thinking it was more than a teeny bit."

"Yeah. Enough to kill five or six men?"

"Or maybe cows react differently. I need to talk to someone after I get done here. The thing is, that poison usually takes a couple of hours to start working. That makes it even stranger that the cows and the bait were found so close together. They should have wandered away before it hit, even if they were grazing normally."

"Unless the supposed bait was still wandering itself when it got here."

"Which opens up a whole other can of worms. Where had it been? Where did it find the toxin? How far had it come?" She shook her head. "I'm going to get my gear. Maybe you should stay outside this circle."

He didn't look as if that sat well with him, at least insofar as she could tell from his stony facade, but too bad. She had the gear to protect herself, and he didn't.

Five minutes later she had disposable decon boots pulled up to her knees and big rubber gloves over her hands that reached up to her elbows even over her snowsuit. Then she picked up her sample case, corer and a shovel and headed for the circle.

Given what she had just learned, this was no longer looking like such an easy job. If the quantity of toxin was truly large, it could be all over by now. Some would have broken down, but she wondered how well. She had no idea how it reacted to the cold. She understood that fungi in the dirt would break it down, but how active were they near the surface now that it was so cold? Either way, she needed to be extremely cautious that she didn't carry the toxin out of this area in any way.

So many variables right now that could make everything worse.

She ducked under the tape, then reached back for her supplies. It was going to be a long morning.

Jerrod watched her work, pacing around the outer edge of the delimited area. He figured he could help her if he had the protective gear, and he decided to ask her if she had any spares, and if he could help in some way. He got her concerns about exposure, but it was a lot of work for one person, he thought as he watched her use the snow shovel to clear away the snow, then twist her manual coring tool into the ground, pulling up samples that were at least six inches long. She strained occasionally as she met a particularly hard piece of ground, but as the hours passed she piled her small core samples, carefully labeled according to some grid system, into her case just outside the ring.

And everywhere she drilled, she added a blue pin flag. Eventually, the place was fluttering with flags. She made her way back to the edge of the tape. "Can you get one of the big trash bags out of the back of my car? I need to ditch my rubber gloves and boots."

He brought her the bag, watching the caution she exercised in removing the boots and gloves and stuffing them into the bag he held open. "Please seal it," she said.

So she was worried she might have picked up contaminants. Great. He looked around again, wondering if it had ever crossed her mind to consider that someone might get upset if he or she thought Allison could track the toxin back to its origins. Then he remembered she had said that would probably be impossible. Given the way this crap spread, he supposed she was right. It all depended on whether the guy who'd done this understood that.

"What now?" he asked as he stood holding the tied-off bag and she bent to pick up her gear.

"I'm going to take a few samples outside the perimeter, then I want to go downstream and take some water samples."

He looked at her, thinking that even after all that labor

she was looking cold. "You should have brought a thermos of coffee. You're chilled."

"Rule one when dealing with toxic substances. Don't eat or drink."

"Bad enough you have to breathe, huh?"

She surprised him with a laugh. "Maybe. But I think the snowfall took care of that."

He felt his lips twitch, wanting to join her laughter. The feeling surprised him. "Well, I've been standing here, too. I'd hate to spread it. What's the likelihood I'm carrying some of this stuff right now?"

"Low. You're uphill." She waved her arm. "Just a couple more samples farther out, then we'll drive along the stream."

Her competence made him feel comfortable. He liked being around people who knew what they were doing, always had. The fact that he was the tyro here didn't bother him. He was learning.

And even in that snowmobile suit she looked tempting enough to eat.

He watched her study the terrain, keeping his mouth shut, refusing to insult her by speaking. He was a capable judge of terrain himself, extremely capable, but she didn't seem to need his help at all.

The back of his neck prickled. Moving slowly, he turned to scan the area. Someone was watching them, someone he couldn't see. He knew it as sure as he was standing there.

But who? A hunter? Someone who wanted to keep an eye on Allison's activities?

But then the feeling faded. Probably just a hunter, he told himself. Although given that everyone by now had probably heard of the poison, he was surprised that any-one would want to hunt in the area.

"Have they warned hunters?" he asked.

"You bet," she answered, then marched away toward the stream's edge where she took a few more ground samples. Then they were off, bucking alongside the stream.

It struck Jerrod that while he was of no real use, this was still the most useful day he'd spent in a while.

"Damn, man," he said aloud, "you've got to get your act together soon."

The daylight was fading by the time they got back to town. Allison had driven farther along the stream than he'd expected, and stopped frequently to take samples from the bank and the water. By the time she was done, the back of her vehicle was loaded with samples and she'd used quite a few pairs of gloves. He guessed the next time she went, if she did, she wouldn't have any trouble giving him some protective gear so he could help. She also skipped stopping back at the ranch house for a hot drink. It *was* getting late.

"Want me to help you unload?" he asked when they had parked. He crossed the small space between their two driveways easily this time.

"Nothing leaves my car until the state comes for it. Why don't you come in for some coffee? And I think I have some lasagna I can heat for the two of us."

It would have been smart to say no, but instead, a different word popped out. "Thanks."

Being with her all day had been easy. No reason to think another hour or so wouldn't be just as easy. Nothing about her was pushy or intrusive.

He paused once again and scanned the street. That

made twice today he'd felt watched. The uneasiness began to creep along his nerves again, a feeling he usually only had on missions, but a feeling that had too often been his companion since he'd returned to civilian life. Like some kind of training he couldn't shake.

But the street was quiet and growing dark, and this was a safe little town in the middle of nowhere. It was as if his brain was trying to take him back to places he no longer needed to go. Not at all. Or as if he couldn't let go of an adrenaline addiction.

Yeah, that was probably all it was. Imagining things because he was used to a whole different kind of life, one full of threats. Years of training he couldn't quite shake.

He blew a disgusted breath and followed Allison into her house. This adjustment thing was too much. Ridiculous.

Hell, he'd even lost his sense of humor, although he supposed the kind of black humor he and his team had often indulged in probably wouldn't fly well with civilians. But he clearly remembered it, remembered how often they had found reasons to kid around. It was a great way to break tension.

He hadn't laughed since he'd wound up in the hospital the last time. Man, he needed to shake himself up good. Rattle his head until it settled into this new world.

Inside, he found Allison in the kitchen. Evidently she was still cold because she hadn't even unzipped her suit yet. He needed to get one of those for himself, if the past few days were any indication of what he could expect here. A parka and jeans weren't making it.

Assuming he stayed here, of course. He wasn't even sure about that yet.

"Grab a chair," she said cheerfully. "I may thaw by tomorrow."

"And here I am looking at that snowmobile suit of yours with envy."

"I can see why," she answered, running her eyes over him. He didn't miss the appreciative glimmer in them as he ditched his parka. Despite everything, he'd kept himself in fighting trim. His shoulders weren't quite as broad since he hadn't weight trained in a while, but all the walking and running, along with calisthenics, had at least kept his belly flat and the rest of him lean enough.

He held her gaze for just an instant, long enough to feel the sizzle himself, and wondered how it was that a woman bundled up almost like a polar bear could get to him like this.

The coffeemaker started brewing. "I'll be right back," she said. "I want to change."

Back into her sweats, he supposed. He could understand why. Even after the cold they'd endured all day, he could tell she didn't keep her house that warm.

Five minutes later she was back, this time wearing a sweat suit that looked relatively new, a gold one that emphasized the unusual color of her eyes. Peeking out beneath the sweats were fuzzy booties in an astonishing hot pink. He blinked.

"No fashion sense, I know," she remarked. She waggled a foot at him. "But they're warm. Very warm."

That was when he smiled, genuinely smiled, for the first time in a long, long time. "I like them. I wouldn't advise them if you don't want to be noticed, though."

A peal of laughter escaped her. "We need to get something straight."

"What's that?"

"I'm a flaky professor. And I like the flaky part. As well as the professor part."

"Nothing wrong with being flaky."

The coffee finished as she popped a frozen lasagna in the oven. It looked homemade, and the thought made him instantly hungry. She brought two mugs of coffee over to the table and joined him.

"There are some things I'm not flaky about," she said, continuing the conversation. "Like my work. There I have to be very precise. No flakiness allowed."

"So it bursts out other ways?"

Her eyes smiled at him over the rim of her cup. "Obviously."

"What happens now with those samples?" he asked. "Do you test them?"

She shook her head. "The state lab is sending someone down to pick them up. I don't know where they go from there. Could be Washington, for all I know. I just don't have the facilities in my lab to test for something like this. It's a community college with limited equipment."

"Given what you told me about this toxin, can I say I'm glad to hear that?"

"I'm not real keen on working with it myself."

"But you still collected the samples."

She waved a hand. "It wasn't the biggest of risks. I'll need to collect some more, though, attack a bigger area. We don't know where that bait came from. If it was a poisoned animal, there could be trouble elsewhere, like up in the mountains."

"You'd need more than one person to search up there."

"Well, I can circumscribe an area, guessing how far the bait animal could have traveled. Or how far something that ate some of it might have gone. That's a good starting point. I'll check for other carcasses, take a few samples as I go. Then we'll see. By the time I do that, I should have some information back from the lab. This is going to be a priority. Those samples will get tested as soon as they reach the right person."

He nodded.

She sighed and put her chin in her hand. "It's going to be tough, though. We're going to be relying a lot on hunters to report anything unusual." She closed her eyes a moment. "Enough of that," she said, snapping them open again. "If I think too hard about it I'll feel overwhelmed."

"But you're fairly certain you won't be able to source it?"

"Not likely. Now, if the bait were wearing a tag or collar..." She shrugged.

"Would someone have that kind of a grudge against Jake Madison?"

"Wow," she murmured. "That's scary to contemplate. It's possible, though. He's the chief of police, such as it is, and his fiancée's dad is angry with him, I hear, but to do something like this?" She shook her head a little. "Is this how you think?"

He pulled back. Tendrils of ice filled him inside. Before he could say anything, however, she spoke quickly.

"I'm sorry. That didn't sound like what I meant. You have to understand you're talking to a small-town girl here. We almost never have things go to that extreme. But you're right, it's possible. I need to think about it."

He relaxed again, muscle by muscle, and tried to do his part to smooth it over. Here he was enjoying a woman's company for the first time in forever, and he'd stuck his foot in it.

But it was still possible. Like it or not, this could have

been a directed attack. And if that was the case, Allison could be inserting herself in the middle of something that could be deadly.

He needed to gather intel, but how the hell was he supposed to do that? Nobody in this town was likely to share much with him. He was a stranger and a total unknown.

But he remembered that sense of being watched, both out on the rangeland, and then here on her street. He trusted that feeling. It had never yet failed him, and had probably saved his life more than once. He'd be a fool to dismiss it.

Allison might be wading into deeper trouble than she had any idea. He came from a world where such things were possible. She did not. Yet just being aware of such a possibility might make all the difference.

She sort of changed the subject then, as if she wasn't ready to deal with what he had suggested.

"So," she said, a twinkle in those sherry-brown eyes, "how miserable were you standing out there in the cold while I took the samples?"

"I've endured worse. But next time it would be nice if you'd let me help."

"That might be arranged."

"Good. I hate feeling useless."

She studied him, and after a minute he started wondering what she was seeing, other than that knife slash across his cheek. He liked to think he was impenetrable unless he chose otherwise, but he had the uneasy feeling that she might be able to see right into him.

"You're young," she said suddenly.

"Young?" The idea didn't fit his self-image at all.

"Agewise," she explained. "Not experiencewise. I can already tell you've probably had a lifetime of experiences

I'll never know or even understand. No, I was just thinking you look maybe thirty?"

"Thirty-three."

She nodded. "So you didn't want to stay in the military until retirement?"

"It wasn't a choice. Medical separation."

She drew a breath. "Wounded?"

"Yeah." No details. The last thing he wanted was sympathy. In life you made your choices and lived with the consequences. He'd made his.

"I'm sorry," she said. "And that probably sounds empty. But I am. I hope you're okay."

"Okay enough."

She frowned faintly. He wondered if she had any idea just how revealing her face was. He enjoyed the chase of expressions across it. "I suppose I can't ask what that means?"

"I'm walking and talking. That's okay."

She gave a little nod. "Fair enough. And you can't talk about any of it?"

"Not much. Most of my life is classified now."

"Well, that'll make getting to know you an adventure."

He laughed. He had to, because of the way she rolled her eyes.

"I can't play truth or dare with you," he said presently. "But I can tell you a few things."

"I'm all ears," she said drily.

"I graduated from Annapolis. I took some training at Quantico, and then some other places."

She perked a little. "Do you happen to know Seth Hardin?"

"I've met him a few times. Briefly."

"Aha!"

"What?"

"That explains why you wound up in the middle of nowhere. I was wondering. Okay. I won't bug you about the rest. I heard Seth say once that most of his life was redacted."

Another laugh escaped him. "That about covers it." He wondered if she realized that her eyes were devouring him and awakening a hunger in him. Probably not. He doubted she had any notion of how easy she was to read.

"SEAL?"

He shook his head. "I can't tell you."

Her eyes widened a bit. "You mean there are units nobody ever hears about?"

"I can't tell you that, either."

"I think you just did. Okay, I won't bug you, promise. Even if I die of curiosity. But if you're thinking of hanging around here for a while, you need to meet Seth's family. His father and a couple of his sisters would be just about the only entrée you need around here."

An entrée? That snagged his attention. An entrée meant intelligence, and he still wanted a better sense of what Allison might be getting into.

"Okay," he said. "Should I just go over and introduce myself?"

"You could, but Marge might overwhelm you. She mothers everybody." She paused. "I'll find a way for you to meet his dad. Tomorrow. He used to be a Green Beret, so I guess he'll understand what redacted means better than I ever could. He used to be the sheriff here and knows everybody."

Exactly the man he wanted to meet, Jerrod thought. Handed to him out of the blue. Funny how those things worked sometimes.

The aroma of the lasagna was beginning to fill the kitchen now, and his stomach rumbled loudly as if it couldn't wait.

Allison laughed. "Twenty more minutes. Sorry."

"I'll survive." He was pretty sure of that. He'd been surviving for a long time.

Chapter 3

Allison awoke Monday morning after the worst night ever. Well, maybe the flu had been worse, but last night had been something else. How many times had she wakened from barely remembered dreams that had left her aching with desire? Heck, she hadn't even done that in high school.

Jerrod Marquette was certainly getting to her, and doing it in ways she didn't want. The man had materialized out of nowhere, couldn't talk much about himself and gave her the distinct feeling that he might evaporate at any moment.

He certainly wasn't planted here, and to her way of thinking that was as big a problem as the secrecy imposed on him. She'd lost everyone in her life who had mattered to her, except some girlfriends, and she didn't want to risk any more. Jerrod struck her as a huge risk.

He certainly was as zipped up as anyone she'd ever met. Maybe more so. Seth Hardin came across as an ordinary guy, easy to talk to, with a sense of humor that sometimes bordered on the wicked. Nor was Seth the only other former special-ops guy in the county. Nate Tate, the former sheriff and Green Beret, seemed to attract them. Or at least if they wanted to hang around, he helped make it possible.

When she thought about it, she almost laughed and spewed her toothpaste. This county probably had more guys with a background in special ops per capita than any place other than a military base.

She rinsed the toothbrush, decided last night's shower could carry over because the house was so cold this morning and climbed into her warmest clothes for work.

"Climate change," she muttered as she looked at her thermostat to ensure it had readjusted itself for the day.

She called Nate as she climbed into her frozen car and tried not to hop up and down on the seat from the cold. Sheesh. At least her cell phone was warm as she put it to her ear, waiting for the engine to warm up before she started driving.

"Nate Tate," the familiar gravelly voice answered.

"Hi, Nate, it's Allison McMann. I have a rescue mission for you."

"Yeah?" He sounded interested. "And how are you doing? Collecting those samples?"

"I've got a bunch in my trunk, but I think I'm going to need to branch out to be safe."

"Probably." He sighed. "Damn fool thing to do. There are better ways to protect stock."

"Nobody can afford cowboys and herders anymore."

"So I hear. But they got paid squat even in my youth.

Just about enough to tie one on when they came in from the range. So what's this rescue mission?"

"I have a new neighbor."

"I heard."

There was nothing Nate didn't hear, so she wasn't surprised. "He seems okay. One of your kind of guys."

"Meaning?"

"He said most of his life was classified."

"Ah. And you want?"

"It'd be nice if he met someone besides me. Someone who gets where he's coming from. He seemed interested when I mentioned you."

"I'll introduce myself, then. He at home now?"

"His truck's in the driveway. I'm getting ready to go teach a bunch of bored students about the Avogadro constant."

Nate ripped out a laugh. "You're over my head already. Okay, I'll drop on over."

"One warning," she added before she disconnected. "He's the most buttoned-up guy I've ever met. Thanks, Nate."

She shoved the phone back in her pocket and felt some warmth coming out of the heater vents at last. Time to go to work.

Definitely time to put Jerrod out of her mind and settle down her crazy hormones. Man, if she had to get the hots for someone suddenly, why couldn't it have been one of her fellow teachers? Not some guy who wouldn't or couldn't talk about himself, a guy who would actually think of things like someone pulling this stunt with a deadly toxin because they had a grudge against Jake Madison.

That was so far outside her world it astonished her,

and it was also a world she didn't want to enter. Not even tangentially.

Oh, God, had she actually told him he could help collect samples next time she went out? She ought to be barring the barn door before the horse escaped, ought to be avoiding a situation with *trouble* written all over it in neon capital letters. One broken heart was enough for a lifetime.

Maybe she could just forget. Kind of space it, and just go off by herself on her next collection. Distance seemed like a great choice right now, the more, the better.

After debating whether to take the samples into her lab, she left them in the back of her locked car unless the state wanted her to do something different. She pulled out her cell again as she hurried toward the science building, calling her contact with the state.

"I'll just come down and collect them from you today," Dan Digby said. "Much safer than you handling them repeatedly."

"They're in the back of my car. Let me know when you get close."

"Will do."

Well, that solved one problem, but considering the rapidity with which she seemed to be accumulating new ones, she wasn't sure that was such a great thing.

When she got to her classroom the first words she heard was a young man saying, "Global warming is a crock. Look at how cold it is right now!"

Oh, boy, she thought. Here we go. She dumped her laptop case and backpack on the table beside the podium and simply waited as the students settled. Quiet came quickly enough.

"Who's heard of the Little Ice Age?" she asked casually.

A couple of hands rose tentatively, but nearly forty other students remained still.

"All right, let me do this quickly. It's more interesting than Avogadro's constant."

Laughs. They were attentive now.

"The Little Ice Age started in the Middle Ages and didn't fully end until late in the nineteenth century, just a little over a hundred years ago. I'm sure you've seen paintings of people from that era. Didn't you ever wonder why Henry VIII was always painted wearing so many clothes? Or how people could wear the kinds of heavy clothing they did back then?"

Now she really had their attention. "Well, it was because it was cold. It was so cold that summers were short. People couldn't grow the kinds of crops they once had. They were starving. It helped set them up for things like the Black Plague because the rats came into town for food."

"Wow," a couple of voices said.

"But we need to get to Avogadro, a very brilliant man, so I'll just keep this short. During the early stages of the Little Ice Age, when the climate was starting to change, the weather went through wild swings for about two hundred years. They'd get a couple of really cold years, a couple of warm years, back and forth like a pendulum. Give that some thought. But only after you think about Avogadro."

It seemed almost cruel to get on with her lecture, because she'd excited their interest and they wanted more. She kept a lid on it until after class. When students clustered around wanting to know more, she suggested they hit the computers and look it up.

"Do your own research," she said, smiling. "Don't take my word for it."

It was kind of amusing, though, to realize she'd sparked the interest of quite a few of them, and of course it had not one darn thing to do with chemistry.

Jerrod was surprised at the knock on his door. He'd been here two weeks and not one person had knocked. Well, he might have missed some friendly overtures because he'd been so busy spending his days out in the countryside.

He went to answer it and saw a tall man with steel-gray hair and a weathered face. The man smiled and held out his hand. "Nate Tate. Allison called me this morning and suggested I stop by and introduce myself."

"Jerrod Marquette. You must be the former sheriff?"

"That's me."

"I didn't expect to meet you so soon." He stepped back and waved the man inside. Tate looked around and Jerrod knew exactly what he saw: minimal signs of habitation, not even a chair to sit on.

"I've got coffee," he offered.

"I never pass on a cup," Tate answered.

The kitchen wasn't any better. If anyone lived here, the only sign was the hot pot of coffee on the stove.

"Roughing it?" Tate asked.

"Still haven't decided what I want to do."

"That can be a big decision sometimes. I was lucky. I made the decision before I went to 'Nam, and she was still waiting for me when I got back."

"That makes you a lucky man."

"I guess you weren't so lucky."

"Lucky enough, just not that way."

With no place to sit, Tate leaned back against the counter with his coffee. "Thick enough to stand a spoon in," he remarked after he took a sip. "So what brought you to these parts?"

"Your son, I believe. Seth Hardin. I met him a few times and he always had great things to say about this place."

"I should've figured my boy would be part of it." Nate Tate smiled. "He's liked it here since the first time he set foot in the county."

Which opened the door to some questions, but Jerrod didn't ask. He'd just met the guy. "I was out with Allison yesterday while she collected samples from the Madison ranch. It sounds bad."

Tate's face darkened. "Damn bad. I still don't get why the Department of Agriculture is allowing the stuff to be used again in some states. I get that it's in livestock collars. I get that coyotes can be a problem. I also get that this stuff is so dangerous it shouldn't be permitted. Those collars get punctured. They get lost. And yeah, the poison deteriorates eventually, but how far will it spread before it does? Boggles my mind to think that killing one coyote might result in some bear dying, or some wolf, or poisoned water...." He shook his head.

"Why do they put so much poison in the collars? Allison said it's enough to kill six grown men. Coyotes aren't that big."

"Sure kill," Tate said. "One nip, a little on a canine tooth, and the coyote will bite the dust. From that perspective, and only that perspective, does it make sense."

Jerrod nodded, taking a gulp of coffee. Hot and bitter,

it slid down his welcoming throat. "Nobody's worried it might kill their animals?"

"Some aren't, apparently. Most of the time a grazing animal wouldn't be affected, and since the coyote runs away he's not likely to poison anything else until he gets sick and dies. Then you get a case like Madison's." Tate shook his head again.

"Would anybody do that deliberately to Madison? Have a grudge that big?"

Tate's eyes narrowed, even as his lips stretched in a humorless smile. "Anything's possible. Thing is, though, around here you might have a grudge, but you don't mess with a man's stock. That's a killing offense in these parts."

"Really?" Apparently some of the Wild West still survived out here.

"You get caught at it, somebody might take the law into their own hands. We have some rustling problems from time to time, and no jury around here would convict a rancher who shot a rustler. Or someone caught poisoning a rancher's land or stock. No, you got a problem with someone, you'd best take it up with them directly."

"So it was probably some kind of accident."

"Probably. A bad one, though. If we ever found out where it came from, somebody would be paying for two Angus cows and maybe a little more, besides. I sure wish we could find out where it started."

"Allison doesn't think that's likely."

Tate sighed. "Mebbe not. Likely not. What little I know about that toxin gives me a real bad feeling, and the way it spreads makes it almost impossible to trace." He cocked a brow at Jerrod. "So you went out with her on Saturday? You keeping an eye on her?"

"I thought she shouldn't be out there alone. In case."

"There're a lot of *in cases* out there. Especially when the snow covers things. From prairie-dog holes on up. I don't think cell phones work any too good out at the Madison place."

"I didn't think so. Which brings me around to something else."

Tate nodded. "She ought to have a radio. I'll stop by the office and talk to Gage Dalton. He's the new sheriff." Tate suddenly laughed. "Been a while since I retired, but he's probably always going to be the new sheriff. Anyway, I'll have a word with him. Chances are Allison won't get around to it."

He turned and dumped the dregs of his coffee into the sink. "I'll think on what you said about a grudge. Don't want to dismiss any possibility. In the meantime, you keep an eye on that young woman. I reckon you're good at that."

"It's not exactly something I've done before, but I get the basics."

Tate's gaze measured him. "Reckon you do," he said finally. "Who were you with?"

"Can't say."

"Like that, is it?" The former sheriff let it drop. "You need anything, give me a shout. And if you get to feeling sociable, I got a wife who loves nothing better than a guest for dinner."

When Tate walked out, Jerrod was left holding his card. He stared at it, figuring he had just found an ally who could help with intel.

So Tate didn't think it was likely someone had a score to settle with Madison. That was good to know, but it opened up some questions, like who and why? Just an accident?

It had been a long time since Jerrod had given much credence to accidents. Just like he wasn't ready to give credence to the idea that they'd never be able to find the person who was responsible for the poison. It might be difficult, but not necessarily impossible. And what if the person responsible for the release had something to hide? Say, some illicit stock of the poison that wasn't in collars at all. That would fit better with the idea of those cows ingesting some. In which case, somebody could have a whole lot of reasons for stopping Allison.

Remembering the way he'd felt watched out there, then later here on the street, he couldn't dismiss the possibility out of hand.

Of course, it was always possible that he was trying to act on training that had no place here in his new life. Maybe he wanted to believe this because it gave him a purpose again.

If so, he might be worse off than he thought.

Grabbing his jacket, he decided to head over to the college and see if he could find Allison. Just a friendly gesture, an offer to take her out for lunch. It seemed the least he could do after that wonderful lasagna the other night.

Or maybe it was because his whole body was humming like a homing beacon, dragging him toward her.

He snorted, but didn't fight it. She was interested in him, too, and she was a grown woman who could make her own decisions.

Whether he'd be good for her didn't even enter into it. That was her decision.

Besides, he'd all but promised to keep an eye on her.

* * *

Allison stood looking at the back of her sporty SUV with dismay. Somebody had tried to smash the tailgate window. Trying to get at the samples? But why?

They hadn't broken in, though. The car was still locked, the window was crazed with cracks and dented in at one place, but nobody had gotten in. So why?

It would be easy enough to take a swing at her car in the faculty lot. Even now, as lunch hour approached, there wasn't another soul around. There rarely was except in the early morning or late afternoon. Unlike the student parking lot, this one was seldom busy.

Well, if they'd wanted the samples, it wouldn't have taken much more work to get at them. Why would anyone want them, anyway? They might be dangerous, and it wasn't as if she couldn't just go out to collect some more.

Swearing softly, she pulled out her phone to call campus security. Dan Digby was going to be here shortly, and he'd be thrilled to find out that his trip had been lengthened by this. She probably wouldn't even be allowed to open her car until someone had gone over it.

Not that the campus had much of a security force. There'd likely be another delay as they called the sheriff. She sighed this time. Just lovely.

She shivered a little in the cold. She really hadn't dressed for standing out here long, but she didn't feel she could step inside a building. What if someone saw this as an opportunity to get into her car and look for money or something? They might get exposed to that toxin.

Security didn't keep her waiting long. Well, of course not. They generally had little to do on this small campus. Ben Herbert climbed out of the car, took one look at her and the window and said, "Climb in my passenger seat before you freeze. I called the sheriff."

"I thought you would. Has there been a rash of this?" she asked hopefully. It would be so nice to feel this wasn't directed at her.

"No," he answered bluntly. "Probably some stupid kid who did it on a dare, though. You wouldn't believe how much craziness happens on a dare. Maybe even fraternity hazing of some kind."

She liked that idea. She slid into his car, which was still running and blasting welcome heat. Even though she was wearing lined gloves, she held them out to the heater vent. Too much cold, too much snow. If this was the harbinger of the kind of winter it was going to be, everyone was going to wind up wishing they lived in igloos. At least the heating costs would go down.

A sheriff's car pulled up just minutes later. It was followed by a police car, this one piloted by the chief, Jake Madison. The deputy turned out to be Sarah Ironheart. Allison was almost amused by the fact that her broken window had drawn so much attention. That a broken car window could be such a big deal gave her some idea how little happened around here. Although on the same day they found the dead cows, they'd had that killer from Minneapolis show up and try to take out Jake's fiancée, Nora.

Crap, maybe things weren't as quiet around here as everyone liked to pretend, now that she thought about it.

She opened the door and leaned out of the car. "Don't touch anything inside the back of my car. I've got soil samples, water samples and a bag full of possibly contaminated gear in there."

Jake looked at her. "From Saturday?"

"Yeah. Dan Digby, from the state, should be here any minute to pick it up."

"He might have to wait a few," Sarah said. Holding a camera, she started taking pictures.

"I'm sure it's just a prank," Ben Herbert said. "We get all kinds of pranks here."

"Pretty expensive prank," Jake remarked. He looked at Sarah. "You want to dust or you want me to?"

She shrugged. "I'm voting baseball bat and not one fingerprint."

"You're probably right."

Which meant, Allison thought, they'd never figure out who did it. Oh, well.

Just then they were joined by Jerrod Marquette. Allison heard his step and turned to see who it was. She felt startled that he'd followed her here, but was glad to see him, more so because she hadn't even caught a glimpse of him yesterday. Of course, she had told him she would be grading papers on Sunday, so apparently he was respectful of her time. Nice.

"Hi," he said. He clearly had already taken in the scene. "I came to buy you lunch. Looks like that'll have to wait. What happened?"

"Baseball bat? Nobody knows. They didn't try to get into the car, though."

"Lucky for them if that stuff in there is toxic."

"I just warned everyone."

He squatted down beside her. "I'm sorry this happened."

"Me, too. But at least they didn't break the windshield completely. I can probably tape it and wait until the auto repair shop gets a new one in."

"Probably."

She glanced at him and realized his gaze was fixed on her. Immediately, her insides sparked in response. Boy, she was getting it bad. Not good.

"Why don't you scoot in and close the door so you can keep warm," he suggested quietly.

"I'm waiting for Dan Digby from the state."

"Do you know him?" He barely waited for her nod. "Then you'll recognize him as soon as he gets out of his car."

He had a point. "But what about you?"

"I'm fine. I ran over here. It warmed me up nicely. If I get cold, I'll run around the parking lot."

So she pulled her legs in and let him close the door for her. Then he went over and shook hands with Jake Madison, and was clearly introduced to Sarah and Ben. She wondered briefly if they'd be suspicious of him because he was a newcomer, but body language belied that. Finally impatient because she couldn't hear what was going on, she climbed back out into the cold.

They were beginning to collect a small crowd of gawking students as Jake dutifully covered the back end of her car with black fingerprint dust. She figured the students wouldn't be here long. The wind seemed to be growing more bitter by the second.

"Well?" she asked as she approached the knot of cops.

Jake looked at her with amusement. "You want a complete forensic analysis in ten minutes?"

"No, but a short one would do."

"Blunt object. And Ben's probably right about it being a bad prank, or some kind of hazing. Unless you gave someone a failing grade recently?"

He was serious, she realized. "Not recently. Whether they like the subject or not, no one is taking chemistry who doesn't need it for a reason. Almost everyone works hard. It's been a couple of semesters since I last failed someone."

Jake nodded and looked at Sarah. "It doesn't look angry."

She agreed. "Angry would have involved more than one heavy swing. I'd expect your entire tailgate and maybe other parts of the car to be involved."

"Unless," said Jerrod, "they got scared away by something."

Allison looked at him. "What's that mean?"

"Probably nothing at all."

But Jake and Sarah didn't take it that way. "That's a possibility. It happened since you got here this morning, right?"

"Some time in the past three hours."

Just then a car pulled into the lot. It bore the state emblem on the side and parked close before Dan Digby climbed out. A balding, slightly portly man of about fifty, he quickly pulled on a fur hat and looked around. "What the hell?"

"Vandalism," Ben Herbert said, stepping forward. He'd been quick enough to call the police, but apparently he wasn't going to relinquish all authority here. Allison felt a flutter of amusement run through her, despite her anger about her rear window. Watching men could sometimes be downright amusing.

Dan ignored Ben and came hurrying over. "Are you all right, Allison?"

"Of course. I wasn't here when it happened. And it really does look like somebody's bad idea of a prank."

"Hazing," Ben said knowingly.

Digby glanced at him and nodded. "Just so long as everyone's okay. But I suppose my samples are in there."

"Yes, they are," Allison answered. "You'd suggested that. Are you in a hurry?"

He flashed a surprisingly charming smile. "Only to get out of this cold."

"It'll only be a few more minutes," Jake told him. "We're almost done. Why don't you keep warm in your vehicle?"

"Because this is more interesting," Digby answered frankly. He pulled down the earflaps on his hat, then snapped the strap under his chin.

"Allison?" Sarah said. "Walk around your car and make sure nothing else appears damaged."

She did as asked, but didn't see one ding or scratch that she didn't recognize.

Jake shook his head. "Protocol says we should dust the entire car in case someone tried to enter it, especially the driver's side. But who'd be out here without gloves?"

"Skip it," Allison said. "Only a lunatic would pull his gloves off to try a car door latch. Not today. Can we get Dan's samples now?"

"Before we all freeze to death?" Sarah said with a humorous smile. "I think we're done. No prints. Of course, the cold isn't helping with that, either."

"I guess I'm going to find out if duct tape sticks at this temperature," Allison remarked as she opened the tailgate. Five minutes later, Dan Digby drove away with the samples, leaving her fresh core tubes to use, as well as additional sets of gloves and booties. The parking lot emptied out and she turned toward Jerrod, who was now bouncing from foot to foot to stay warm.

"I'm rescuing you," she said. "Climb in. At least you'll be out of the wind."

It was picking up again, as if the air wanted to snatch the last heat it could from them.

In the driver's seat, turning the engine over, she realized that she could hear the wind whistling inside the cab of her car now. Apparently some of those cracks had gone all the way through even though it was safety glass. Hell, she hoped the damn thing didn't fall out.

Given that the last temperature she had seen said it was about eighteen degrees out, she let the engine warm up again. "Guess I'm going to have to plug in tonight," she remarked.

"Plug in?" Jerrod asked.

"Engine block heater. I can tell you've never had a vehicle in a climate as cold as this."

"Not usually. Once I was inserted, I hoofed it."

That told her a lot, she supposed, or maybe nothing at all. "Back in the old days, when it got really cold, people would drain the oil from their cars and bring it inside, then put it back in the car in the morning. The block heater is a lot more convenient, but you can use an electric blanket under the hood, too."

"Things I never thought about."

The engine was starting to put out some heat, so she figured it was warm enough to drive. "It's kind of you to want to take me to lunch."

"Well, given a choice of eating alone or eating with you…" Then he laughed. She looked at him, wondering how to take that and then saw the heat in his gaze. Instantly, she blushed. He wanted her. Wow. Too bad he didn't have any idea what he might be getting into. She dragged her gaze from him, telling her body to shut up. She knew this could lead nowhere good. Maybe she should have refused the lunch, but the rudeness… She sighed and gave in. No way could she insult him by refusing his invitation. She was going to have to find another kind of armor. Trying to sound businesslike, she asked, "Where did you want to have lunch? It's not like we have an abundance of choices."

"The diner downtown is pretty good."

"Sure, if you can take Maude."

He chuckled quietly. "She doesn't bug me."

"She'd be disappointed to hear that."

The whistling from her back window worsened as she drove. She hoped it wasn't an omen. She hoped she was right, that no one would have a reason to come after her just for taking soil samples. That no one was stupid enough to think she could find out who had done this thing.

She hoped the uneasiness that Jerrod had inadvertently wedged into her life with his comment about grudges was unnecessary.

She hoped life wasn't about to change for the worse in a big way.

Chapter 4

At the end of the week, things started to blow up. At first it didn't seem so bad. Things had been quiet, her new window glass was on the way and the reports on the toxin levels in both the cows were reassuring. It appeared they had gotten a very small dose, and had died from effects to the nervous system.

A small dose was good. They could have gotten it from the meltwater or grass. The bait animal, if that's what it really was, was more severely poisoned, but consistent with what they expected to see if it directly ingested the poison in a larger quantity. The only problem was that the dead animal wasn't the kind of predator that would prey on a collared animal. It was a raccoon, and had probably fed on some other dead animal.

So while the news about the cows was reassuring, the news about the raccoon, which came later, was not.

Allison sat at her desk in her home office, rapping a pencil absently with the email opened in front of her. Raccoons were the world's great opportunists. Presented with carrion, they would probably eat, especially at this time of year.

Her doorbell rang just then. She looked up in surprise. Since their lunch on Monday, Jerrod had pretty much vanished, leaving her to wonder if she'd done something at lunch to turn him off. One thing was for sure, if he was going to run hot and cold like this, she definitely didn't need him. She'd already been rejected in a way that had left her permanently shredded, and if Jerrod was going to switch on and off, it would be best to avoid him. Dealing with her disappointment that she hadn't seen him again had been hard enough.

She forced herself to think about the job at hand and nothing else. The time lapse in the sampling was deliberate, to provide a comparison. With any luck, where she'd found traces of poison last time, they'd all be gone this time. It was important to know if the stuff was breaking down fast or slow.

Making her way to the door, realizing that she actually felt tired and not in much of a mood for company, especially after being ignored all week, she prepared an excuse even before she opened the door.

It was Jerrod, and something about the way he was standing smothered the ready excuse. "Come in," she said swiftly. The weather hadn't shown a bit of mercy all week.

He stepped in. "Thanks."

"Is something wrong?" she asked. "Come on, I was just about to make coffee." A lie, but an innocent one.

He followed her to the kitchen, not answering immediately. She heard the chair scrape, heard him sit. "Nothing's wrong," he said finally.

"That's good," she said and turned, but the instant she saw his face, she read a tension there that concerned her. "Jerrod? What is it?"

He started to shake his head then stopped. "Oh, hell," he muttered. "It's no state secret. I got a call from the father of one of my men. He died two weeks ago."

At once her heart went out to him. "I'm so sorry." Which sounded weak even to her own ears. He didn't say any more, just sat there studying the table. The silence seemed endless, and awfully empty, but what could you say to something like that?

Presently she said, "I made regular coffee but I can whip up some espresso if you'd like something stronger."

"Regular's fine. Thanks."

So she filled a couple of mugs and joined him at the table. Maybe he just didn't want to be alone right now. Finally she asked, "Did you just find out?"

"Yeah." He drummed his fingers, then seemed to give himself a shake. "It wasn't a surprise. He was badly wounded on my next-to-last mission. Nobody thought he'd make it this long."

"Well, it still hurts."

"For him it's probably a relief."

She waited, then asked, "Are you going to the funeral?"

"It's over. Apparently they didn't want me there, since I didn't hear about it beforehand."

That startled her. "You want to explain that?"

"Not really. I was responsible. They might hold me responsible."

"You mean they blame you."

"Same thing."

"Not exactly." She had the worst urge to reach out and touch one of those nicked-up hands of his, to offer the comfort of physical touch, but restrained herself. She didn't know this guy well enough, didn't know what she might be wading into, or how he would react. Nor did she have any equivalent in her own life from which to speak. The closest she could come was the loss of her parents. Nothing to compare to what this man had been through. Nothing to give her even a small window on his world. She felt so inadequate.

"It's like this," he said at last. "I was in command. That made me responsible. It was my job to ensure the mission was completed, but it was also my job to bring my men home safely."

That took her aback. "How could you guarantee any such thing in a war situation? At least I'm assuming it approximated one. People get hurt and killed even when you do your best."

"That may be true, but that's not the way it feels. Or the way it's viewed. Those men had to put complete trust in me, and I blew it. It wasn't the first time, given the situations we went into, but thank God it'll be the last."

"God," she whispered. Then, "What do you do? Brand all that in your head and heart forever? Take responsibility for things that probably weren't under your control?"

"Sometimes there's no good answer, but it doesn't make me any less responsible, okay?"

"I don't know how you can stand it."

His black eyes seemed to burn. "We all take that responsibility for each other. But being in command ultimately placed it on my shoulders. It's how we work, how we think and how we survive."

She couldn't imagine it. She reached for the only comparison she could think of. "I understand survivor guilt, but this seems much worse."

She had his attention again. "Survivor guilt? What happened?"

"Three years ago. My mom and dad decided to take a vacation. Dad had this little Cessna twin-engine four-seater plane. Anyway, they spent months planning a trip around the country and I was supposed to join them for part of it over my spring break. I was going to fly to Minneapolis to meet them and come back a week later."

"But?"

She sighed and turned her coffee cup around in her hands. She'd never talked to anyone about this. The last time she had tried had been a disaster. Her boyfriend hadn't wanted to hear it, then had turned on her only a few weeks later. At the time she had been sure she deserved all the scorn he heaped on her. "I had to postpone it. I told them I'd meet up with them in Sioux Falls. Somewhere between Minneapolis and Sioux Falls they crashed."

"You feel guilty about that?"

"Hell, yeah. They think my dad had a stroke or something. My mom didn't know a thing about flying. But I did. If I'd been there…" She didn't bother to finish the sentence. "I haven't flown since." She rose and went to refresh her coffee, bringing the pot over to the table and doing the same for him.

"You might not have had time to do anything," he said.

"I could give you the same argument if I knew more about what you were doing. Tell me something."

"If I can."

"How many times did you and your men go out knowing some of you, any of you, might not come back?"

"Every time. We made the likelihood as remote as possible."

She spread her hands. "What more can anyone do? You said you'd lost men before. Is this time different?"

"Only that it's recent. Only that it was an ugly phone call. Only that I wasn't there."

"Sometimes people just need to blame someone," she said quietly. "It helps, for a little while. But that man knew what he was getting into, and I'm sure his family did, too." Not that any of this was helping. "Sorry, I'll shut up. It is what it is, and me running on like some kind of Pollyanna isn't going to help a damn thing."

He surprised her by smiling faintly. "The effort is appreciated."

"But useless. That much I know from experience."

After a minute, he sighed and leaned back from the table. "Actually, I didn't come over here because of that. These are things I just have to deal with. I'm surprised I even brought it up."

"What good is a friend if you can't talk about whatever comes up?"

"Are we friends?"

The air suddenly felt pregnant, though with what, she couldn't say. It was as if it was waiting for something. And in that pause she felt again her attraction to him, an almost overwhelming need to rise and round the table and climb into his lap. Or stand behind him and rub his shoulders just so she could feel the contours of the muscle beneath. None of which had anything to do with friendship.

Dang, and she thought she'd put that away during his

absence this week. Apparently not. His gaze had focused in on her again, boring into her in a way that suggested he was no more immune to her than she to him.

Dangerous. Fighting back instincts proved difficult, but not impossible. She drew a deep breath, remembered his question and said, "I hope we're becoming friends."

He changed the subject so quickly that she wondered if she'd imagined the moments that had just passed. Maybe she was projecting her own feelings on him. How the hell would she know?

"I wanted to thank you again for suggesting Nate meet me. He's been introducing me around."

"Good. I hoped he would."

"Mostly to people who have backgrounds like mine."

At that she had to laugh. "That's Nate. That's why I thought of him. I was sure the first people he'd have you meet were people who could understand without asking the questions you can't answer. I couldn't do that, obviously."

"Obviously," he agreed. "But he did introduce me to one nut job. Fred Loftis. A guy with a giant grudge against Jake Madison."

"He's a nut, all right. I'm not exactly sure why he's got it in for Jake except his daughter came home a few weeks ago and moved in with him. They're getting married, which you would expect to settle any problems Fred has, but no. I hear he's been ranting about people living in sin."

"Living in sin is part of the fun of life." Briefly, those dark eyes seemed to twinkle.

Allison felt her cheeks heat a bit. "Maybe. Anyway, for Loftis I gather just about anything that doesn't hurt is sin. You should have seen how he dressed his daugh-

ter when she was in school. It should have been a crime.
A lot of people picked on her."

"But not you?"

"I was a couple years behind her, so I never got involved with that. I only caught up enough to know what
was happening when I got to high school. Before that, I
was oblivious and we seldom crossed paths. Well, even
in high school we didn't cross paths, but I heard things."

"It's hard for me to imagine not crossing paths in a
town this size."

"It's hard not to once you've grown up." It's one of
the things she loved most about Conard—the rooting
of a close-knit community, something she desperately
needed after the loss of her parents. "Kids are pretty
well age segregated, though, and into different things
at different stages."

"I guess so."

She bit her lip. "So are you thinking Loftis planted
that poison? Did you come back to that?"

"Not really. He may be an ass, but I think he knows
better than that. I think Nate introduced him to me so
I'd cross him off my mental list."

"You told Nate about your suspicion?"

"Just mentioned it. I got quite the lecture on how dangerous it is in these parts to mess with a man's livestock."

Allison laughed quietly. "It is. Not that we have a
whole lot of trouble with that. Most people raised around
here get the message early in life."

"It sounds like it."

"What makes you think Loftis knows better, apart
from what we all understand around here?"

He sipped coffee and leaned forward. "How's this?
The guy's a bully. I've met plenty like him. Lots of blus-

ter, but he only picks on people smaller or weaker than him. A rancher who is also chief of police would definitely be off his list. He'll rant about it, but he won't do a damn thing."

She nodded. "That's my read, too. He's got a cowed congregation, and pretty generally avoids everyone else. It makes me wish we had another pharmacy in town, though. I'd like to be able to patronize someone else."

"So he's it?" Jerrod just shook his head. "And getting to the real reason for my visit…"

"Yes?"

"Are you collecting more samples tomorrow? If so, I'd like to help."

She'd been seriously thinking about telling him to get lost the way he had all week, but his revelation about his buddy's death… Well, he'd come to her with something he probably hadn't shared with anyone else around here. And he'd listened to her talk about her parents. She felt closer to him again, and figured that right now he needed something to do more than ever. "Yeah, I need to take comparison samples. In case they find toxin in the ones I took last week, it would be nice to know how fast it's breaking down. Plus I want to get up on the side of the mountain a little. We've got an additional worry."

"What's that?"

"The bait animal they found was a raccoon, and it was loaded with poison. It wouldn't be biting any livestock collars unless it was rabid, and it wasn't. So it must have eaten some contaminated carrion. That means there's at least one more dead animal out there, maybe more. I've got to look around."

"But no reports from hunters?"

"Not yet. Although if you want the truth, after the

warning we put out, they're probably staying miles clear of the area. Game animals are mostly grazers, but given what happened to those cows…" She shrugged. "Would you want to risk bringing tainted meat home to the family?"

He didn't bother with the obvious answer. Always a man of few words, it seemed.

"But you're still worried about it," she said finally.

"I'm worried about *you*."

The statement warmed her, but it also zinged straight to her groin, causing an almost painful clenching inside her. How did he do that? A simple statement of concern and she was reacting sexually. Any casual acquaintance might be concerned about her but she wouldn't react this way.

"Why?" The word came out a little more ragged than she would have liked, but at least she got it out. She began to think he might be even more dangerous to her than the poison she was tracking. He had no roots here, no reason to remain that she could see. In a day or two or a few weeks, he might just vanish as stealthily as he'd appeared. And even if he didn't, what did she really know about him? He didn't talk much; she'd only spent a few hours with him. He could turn out to be an awful person, and if she was foolish enough to get involved, she might become wreckage in his trail, as she had become wreckage in her ex-boyfriend's trail.

She just wished her body would listen to her brain.

"Why?" he repeated. "Because you're out there tracking a poison that you tell me is so deadly it has to be used only in certain ways with special authorization. You say the chance of tracing it back to its origins is nigh impossible, but what if the guy behind this doesn't know that? What if he thinks you're trying to do exactly that?"

"I haven't been making a secret of what I'm trying to do," she argued.

"Maybe not. But that doesn't mean you've told people *everything* you're trying to do. Somebody did something wrong and they know it. They know a rancher lost two cows, which is probably very expensive, and maybe that what they did with that poison isn't legal. Some guy could be looking at ruin if you figure out who it was."

She shook her head. "If it'll make you feel better, I'll make sure the whole damn world knows I won't be able to figure out who did it."

"It might help. I'm not saying there's a real threat, not yet. But there is your car window getting smashed."

"That had to be some stupid prank. You know eighteen-year-olds." Her mind was trying to be rational about this, but she could feel her emotions fighting it. She didn't want to believe this was possible. Not here.

Damn, he was bringing his ugly world with him. Maybe she should usher him to the door right now.

"It probably was a prank," he agreed. "But what if it wasn't? What if somebody wanted to get those samples out of the back of your car in case you had something that could be traced? What if he didn't succeed only because he got interrupted. Heard someone coming?"

She looked down, feeling every emotion rebel, but even as she tried to find a way to tell him he was wrong, her thoughts began to run over all the reasons he might be right.

Someone using that poison might not understand how it spread. Few people did, mainly because those who used it had it safely contained in collars. That didn't mean, however, that there weren't leftover stocks of the stuff sitting in a barn or two somewhere. On hand just in case. Despite it having been outlawed. It's not like anyone had gone around to collect all the stuff. She seemed to remember from her reading that at the time it had been outlawed, folks had been told to bury it.

Well, how many people had decided it was easier to leave the cans sitting on a shelf than dig a deep hole to put them in? There could be dozens of stockpiles out there, forgotten until someone came across them and had a use for them.

But what kind of use? To start with, you needed bait soaked in it so some animal would eat it. You couldn't just sprinkle it on the ground. Odorless and tasteless, it wouldn't have attracted any animal.

So it couldn't happen accidentally, unless some coyote had bitten a collar containing the stuff. And no one would blame a rancher for using a legal collar to protect against coyotes. At least not other ranchers, although environmentalists would create an uproar.

"What are you thinking?" Jerrod asked.

"I'm trying to figure the odds that a coyote bit a collar and got sufficiently poisoned to kill a raccoon. It's not beyond the realm of possibility."

"No." His eyes were boring into her again. She wished she didn't feel as if they bored right to her womanhood. She shifted uneasily.

"You're thinking something else," he said after a moment.

She was, and not entirely about bait and poison. She shifted again and corralled her thoughts. Before she could speak, he did.

"How would you use this poison if you didn't have a collar?"

"Mix it in water, soak a big piece of meat in it and put the meat out where you wanted to kill something. Hoping, of course, that you got your target animal. Lots of things eat meat." She paused. "Like wolves."

"You've got wolves?"

"A couple of packs up in the mountains. They came down here from Yellowstone a while back. They're off the endangered list now, though, so if somebody had a wolf problem, he could get a hunting license. Or, if they're bothering his stock, he could just shoot them." She paused again. "Well…there's an exception to that, too. In order to maintain a minimal number of breeding pairs, wholesale slaughter still isn't allowed. Even so…"

She trailed off again, thinking. Or trying to. Amazing how difficult that could get around Jerrod. "Okay, if you know anything about wolves, you know it isn't hard to wipe out a pack. You can break one up by killing a couple of them. You can break up a pack by burying its den. They've even used rubber bullets, hoping to teach them to stay away from certain places. At one time or another pretty much everything has been tried to appease the ranchers. They have a worse problem up north around the Yellowstone boundaries in Montana. You know what's interesting to me?"

"What?"

"Wolves have tight-knit family groups. Those packs have the kinds of connections to each other we don't think of animals as having. Yet despite all that social cohesion and interdependence, a wolf pack is easy to destroy. Once you do that, most of them will die."

"I didn't realize that."

"That's the point I was coming to." Fascinated now, she rose and got more coffee. "If you have a wolf problem, you don't have to kill them all. All you have to do is destroy the pack structure. The rubber bullet thing I told you about? It didn't teach the wolves to stay away, it broke up the pack. It's amazingly easy to do."

"So why poison?"

"Because like you, maybe somebody doesn't know that. We have an ongoing fight around here, believe it or not. Some ranchers want them all exterminated. Others think they're good for the environment—and studies would bear that out. But when losing one cow or a couple of ewes could be the difference between making it or going bust, even one wolf looks like a serious threat."

"So you're thinking somebody went after the wolves in the mountains?"

"Maybe. It would explain a lot. But it's just a theory."

He surprised her with a smile that actually leavened his face. It was breathtaking, she realized, to see this man look as if he'd left his shadows behind, even if only for a few minutes.

"I like it when you get excited about something," he said. "You light up like a Christmas tree."

Now her cheeks *really* heated. "Thank you," she said, her voice muffled. She wasn't used to compliments of that kind.

His smile remained, surprising her. "Well, if you're going into the mountains, you're definitely not going alone. Tomorrow?"

"I guess so, after I get some more samples from the Madison ranch."

"What exactly would we be looking for?"

She shook her head. "The bait would be eaten by now.

The question is by what and how many. So I guess we'll be looking for dead animals that have probably already been gnawed over pretty well. It won't be pretty."

The shadow returned to his face. "I've seen worse. What time should we leave?"

"Early. Say six. It'll be light by the time we reach Jake's place."

"Good enough. And this time I'm bringing coffee."

She laughed as she rose to walk him to the door, even as she felt disappointment that he was leaving too soon.

He turned just before he left. She was following too closely and he bumped into her. He might as well have been a live wire. Heat and sparks sizzled through her, and she caught her breath.

He caught *her*. She must have been tipping, she thought hazily, but didn't give a damn. He could have steadied her by grabbing her elbow or something, but he didn't. Instead, one of his powerful arms wrapped around her and the next thing she knew she was pressed to his chest.

Still trying to catch her breath, she tilted her head and looked directly at his scarred face. Directly into his black-as-night eyes. But somewhere in those dark depths she could have sworn she saw hot, burning coals.

"Damn," he whispered.

Before she truly registered the word, he bowed his head and kissed her. In an instant she went from feeling as if a high-tension wire sparked inside her to melting. She'd never reacted to a kiss that way before, with an amazing softening, as if everything inside her simply let go.

She went nearly limp in his embrace, which he took as an invitation because his other arm wrapped around her, holding her tight. He made her feel safe, she realized dimly. Incredibly safe.

And his kiss. His mouth astonished her by how supple it felt when he looked so hard. He didn't crush her lips against her teeth or demand entry, but instead simply moved his warm lips against hers, caressing, offering, promising a surprising gentleness.

The weakening in her grew even as the movement of his mouth over hers elicited a deep throbbing within her. She wanted him, and she knew beyond any shadow of a doubt that she had never felt this degree of longing for any man.

But that was a mystery to ponder later. Right then all she wanted to do was enjoy this new experience of feeling utterly safe, utterly cherished, by a man who looked like a lethal weapon. The contrast enchanted her, holding her in thrall.

Her breasts grew exquisitely sensitive, begging for a touch. Her center grew heavy until she wondered if she could bear her own weight.

Then, before she could even absorb all he had created in her with the simplest, lightest of kisses, he lifted his head; his arms loosened their hold.

"Tell me I shouldn't have done that," he murmured.

"I can't," she answered on a mere breath of air. She didn't want to open her eyes, didn't want this to end.

"Oh, hell," he said.

"Hell?" She opened her eyes to find him smiling.

"I'm in trouble now," he said without explanation. Then he stepped back, releasing her with evident reluctance.

"Tomorrow at six. I'll be out front."

She stepped out after him, watching him trot back

toward his place. It was then she noticed the crews putting up Christmas decorations on the light poles. They'd probably decided that the way this winter had started, the earlier the better.

Rubbing her arms against the chill, she hurried back inside, wondering how magic had just come out of nowhere and touched her.

Because his kiss had been sheer magic.

Chapter 5

Jerrod was sure that kissing that woman numbered among his greatest acts of idiocy. If he'd wanted her before, he wanted her worse now, and now he couldn't pretend to himself that she didn't reciprocate. Waiting for 6:00 a.m. seemed like an eternity, which didn't surprise him. He'd had plenty of eternal waits at the start of a mission when the clock seemed almost to move not at all. He was used to it.

But he wasn't used to it happening because of a woman. Reason told him to clear out of this town before he got involved with her. It wouldn't be good for her, not when he had so much to sort out about himself, and at this point he couldn't make any promises more than a day or two down the road. Nor was he fond of flings. He'd had his share, and figured in the end they left the most important things unsatisfied.

But while hitting the road again might be wise or even necessary, he was worried about her. She was planning to go into the woods and look for additional dead animals. If someone was worried that he could be found out, he might be watching and might try something.

Hell, she wasn't even following the most basic of security rules—to vary her schedule. Where would you find Allison McMann on Saturday? Out taking samples from a toxic mess. Then there was her school schedule, cast in stone, although it probably put her pretty much beyond reach because it was unlikely she was alone much on campus.

The thing with her car window bugged him, too. He supposed the folks around here knew better than he what fit in the normal category, but whether they thought it was some kind of hazing incident, or simply vandalism, he couldn't rest easy about it. Coming as it did right after she collected those samples, he found it a whole lot easier to think someone had been trying to steal them from her car.

And yes, he knew how eighteen-year-olds could do stupid things on impulse with little rhyme or reason. Half the time if you asked them why they'd done it, they wouldn't be able to provide an answer.

Nor had Nate Tate calmed him down any. It sounded like the Wild West out here. Screw with a man's livestock and get killed?

That sounded more like a motivation to him than a reassurance, and Allison had walked right into the middle of a potentially deadly situation. At least by his lights, and he was as aware as anyone that his lights might be too tightly focused from all his years in covert ops.

He still couldn't ignore it. So he had to hang around

until this was past, until she wasn't collecting any more samples or hunting any more dead animals. Until a poisoner would feel that he was safe from discovery.

He remembered, too, that he had felt they were being watched out on the Madison ranch, and then again here in town. The latter could just have been someone on this street looking out the window, but the former? Allison herself thought the hunters were avoiding the area now, so who would have been there?

That bugged the hell out of him.

He glanced at the clock and checked the time. Ten more minutes. So he let his eyes close and considered the shape of the situation. If someone had asked him to explain what he meant by that, he doubted he could have explained.

A combination of things would come together inside him, from highly honed senses to experience. It happened outside rational thought, at a more visceral level. But even as he tried to get the shape of what he was sensing here, he knew something wasn't right. Either he lacked an important piece of information, or he was misleading himself somehow.

Neither one would have surprised him at this point. At some level beyond conscious reach, he sensed something very wrong. Or that something teetered on the brink of going wrong. It might not even have anything to do with Allison or her samples and the poison. Anything was possible.

Turning the pieces around inside himself, he waited for them to fall into place like tumblers in a lock, but they stubbornly refused.

Great. Something was bugging him, he trusted that

feeling implicitly, but as yet the only direction he had for it was Allison.

So Allison it would be. He'd keep an eye on her until this was over.

He could think of plenty of worse things to do with his time.

But few as dangerous to his soul as this one. A grim smile came to his mouth as he tugged on his outerwear and picked up two big thermoses of coffee. He patted his sides to check that his weapons were still firmly in place.

He possessed a card that allowed him to carry concealed weapons anywhere. They hadn't taken that from him yet, and might never. Given his skills, he was well aware that he could be reactivated in an emergency. A knife in one belt holster, a 9 mm in the other.

He had all he needed in that regard. But he had to admit, trying to turn into a civilian when he knew that if something blew up he might be called back on an instant's notice didn't make the transition any easier.

To hell with it, he thought. It would never happen. In the meantime, he had to protect Allison without becoming an emotional threat to her himself.

Allison had just started loading the back of her vehicle when Jerrod appeared. "You didn't get a snowmobile suit," she remarked in what she hoped was a teasing tone. She also hoped that he'd put her instant blush down to the cold this morning, and not to last night.

"It'd just get in the way," he said enigmatically, then trotted up to the porch to pick up the last case and bring it to her.

"Thanks." She slammed the back hatch, and once

again faced the taped-up window. "Can I admit that every time I look at that window I get a burn on?"

"You can."

With surprise, she saw that his eyes almost danced. Talk about lightening up. He sure had in some ways. "I'll be glad when the new window is in. Then I won't keep feeling the urge to shake some young idiot."

"I can't blame you for that. There's something maddening about being treated this way and not being able to confront the miscreant. Leaves things all bottled up."

"Like you?" she asked.

Instantly, she wished the words unsaid. His mood immediately darkened, the last vestige of a smile vanished.

"Like me," he said shortly.

Good job, Allison, she thought unhappily as they climbed into her car.

"Sorry," she said as they settled into the front seats. She'd left the car running while she loaded it, so it was warmed up and ready to go. "That came out wrong."

"No, that came out honestly. And you're right."

She didn't say another word as she backed out and turned to drive through town toward the county road that led toward the Madison ranch. She'd really put her foot in her mouth, and after that kiss they'd shared last night it seemed mean of her. Even if it was true, it was still mean. As near as she could tell from what little he had shared with her, he had plenty of reasons not to say much.

The heater started to blast, and she reached up to unzip the front of her suit. His jacket was only partly zipped; he wasn't dressed as heavily as she, so she didn't turn down the heat. Instead, she listened to the hum of the engine and the blowing air inside the car, and a silence that seemed too long and heavy.

"I received a medical release from duty," he said eventually. "Shrapnel lodged near my spine. So that rules out the kind of heavy physical training and activity I used to do because they don't want it to move."

"They can't get it out?"

"Too dangerous, they said. I don't know. They seem to avoid surgery around the spine on principle. If I ever experience tingling or numbness, that will change, but right now everything's in a good equilibrium."

"That's good to know."

"So far," he agreed. Another long silence, then, "Anyway, they still want me for other things. I can't talk about them. They'd be less of a physical problem, and I have skills they can use. I could go back to work in the Alphabet Soup world tomorrow if I wanted."

"Alphabet Soup?"

"Places that have initials, some of them in lieu of names."

"Oh." Right off the top of her head, she thought of a few and wondered about the others.

"Or if something were to happen where I'd be useful, I could be reactivated immediately."

"They can do that?" The notion shocked her.

"Of course they can. They *released* me from active duty. What they didn't give me was a final discharge. I'm on something that some call ready reserve."

"Oh, wow. I didn't know about that."

"Well, it's not exactly the same as regular reserves. I don't have to show up one weekend a month or anything, but I'm inactive right now. Like I said, that could change. If it doesn't change in a few years, I'll be considered too rusty and out-of-date to be useful, and I'll get my discharge."

She turned that around in her head. "You must have a hell of a skill set."

"Some of which will be useful even after I get a discharge. But right now I'm betwixt and between, as they say."

"So you really don't know what tomorrow holds."

"No. I don't. I'm required to keep myself in shape, so I've been doing a lot of running and calisthenics, but other than that, I really don't know what could happen. I've had some job offers I don't want. But if they activate me, I've got to go in a couple of days. Sooner if the situation warrants."

She nodded. "But if you can run and do calisthenics... Jerrod, isn't that a threat to your back?"

"No, that's okay. No more heavy lifting, though, and a few other things that need caution. Really, I'm doing fine."

"Except they've managed to prevent you from finding a perch to settle on." She couldn't imagine it. Well, she could, and she figured she would find it extremely irritating to live that way.

"In a way, I suppose that's true. In another, it isn't all that different from the way I've been living all along."

"But surely now you should feel like you can settle into a new life? Haven't you already given enough?"

He didn't answer, leaving her to think that must have been a stupid question.

After a couple of more miles had passed, he finally said, "I'm not likely to be reactivated. It would have to be something really bad for them to call on me. So yes, I'm trying to settle into some kind of life. So far I don't seem to have gotten the hang of it."

"With something like that in the back of your mind? It certainly wouldn't help, but what do I know?"

She heard him shift beside her, and glanced his way. He was looking straight at her.

"Sorry," she said. "I don't know what I'm talking about."

"You know more than you seem to think. Yes, it's at the back of my mind. I don't expect it to happen unless there's a huge crisis. But then I didn't expect to wind up like this, either, so I didn't have a plan in place. My fault. And it's been surprisingly difficult to come up with one. When you do the kind of job I did, you don't look beyond the next mission. You can't afford to. I'm a great tactician. Give me a goal and I'll know how to go for it. But setting the goal? I haven't had to do that in a long time. You'll have to give me an F, Professor."

"I don't think so. Most of us aren't quick to adapt when our entire lives get upended unexpectedly. There's this thing called grief, you know. However it shows itself, when we go through a total change like you are, we grieve, and grieving tends to paralyze us for a while."

"You think I'm grieving?"

"More than you probably imagine."

She didn't dare look at him now, for fear she had offended him beyond hope. The tough guy—and she was sure he was a tough guy from what he'd told her so far—probably couldn't imagine that he might be mourning his old life and the changes that had happened so suddenly. It probably sounded weak to him, a guy who was apparently used to dealing with difficulties she could only guess at.

"That's a different way to look at it," he said a while later. "I've grieved when my buddies got wounded or killed, but I never thought of this as something to grieve about."

"Why wouldn't it be? In an instant everything changed, from what you can do to the way you lived. Even your expectation for at least a few more years went down the tubes. Grief isn't limited to losing someone we care about."

"Even so, after six months you'd think I'd be getting past it."

"Getting past it might be easier if you weren't on— what did you call it?"

"Ready reserve."

"Ready reserve," she repeated, cementing it in her mind. "So here you are, knowing you could be called back at any minute. That's got to make it hard to settle. And I'd almost bet some part of you is hoping to be called back. You'd be busy again, have purpose again. Apparently you were wedded to your old life or you wouldn't have done it for so long."

"You might be right."

No *might* about it, she thought. This guy would love nothing better than to be reactivated, to feel that adrenaline rush again, to do the things that had been so important to him. Whatever his duties had been, she was sure he'd felt he was serving his country in important ways, and now that was gone.

Oh, yeah, he'd like to get that call.

Which made her feel inexplicably glum. One kiss wasn't enough to tie her in emotional knots, surely? She was too mature for that. Or not. She sighed quietly and turned into the Madison ranch.

Here today, gone tomorrow, she warned herself. Keep a safe distance. She'd been through one painful breakup and didn't ever want to repeat it.

They weren't greeted by Jake this time, although she'd let him know she was coming. Instead, his fiancée, Nora, stepped out, hugging her jacket close.

"Jake just said to go back in," she called. "He's working in town this morning. Coffee and cookies here afterward if you want."

Allison waved and called her thanks through the window she'd rolled down a few inches. "I hope I can find the place again," she remarked, trying to remember exactly where Jake had taken her. Being led hadn't helped.

"I can get us there."

She glanced at Jerrod. "Great sense of direction, huh?"

"One of my skills," he answered. "Once I've been somewhere, I can get there again."

"I hope some of it rubs off on me."

He laughed, letting her know the heavy stuff was behind them. "Directionally challenged?"

"Well, I know how to find the mountains, and from the mountains I can find the road. In between there's a lot of room."

He laughed again, making the day seem a whole lot brighter. "Just keep going. I'll let you know when to make a course correction."

During the week, dry snow and wind had combined to pretty much rearrange the landscape. She couldn't even see tire tracks from their passage last time.

But with Jerrod's guidance, they arrived at the fences she remembered. He hopped out to open and close them. Then, without a single misstep, they were staring at the roped-off area again. Some of the caution tape had snapped and fluttered in the breeze.

"I guess I'd better replace that," she remarked. "We still don't have toxicity results."

"I can do that."

Of that she had not the least doubt, and it freed her up to get started. This time she needed fewer samples since they were a comparison. What she really wanted to do was find a place to cross that stream and see if there were dead animals on the mountainside. It had been a couple of weeks now, though, so she didn't have high hopes. The carrion eaters would have scattered the remains. But if the toxin was still effective, some animals might have died only recently.

She hoped like hell she didn't find that.

"Are you prepared?" he asked when she finished up.

"For what?"

"Hiking in the mountains."

She looked at him from beneath her brows. "I grew up here, mister. I can hike with the best." She pulled a hiker's backpack out of the rear seat of her car.

"Food, survival blankets, matches, the works. Enough for two. We learn early out here." Then she handed him a radio. "And this, too."

He nodded approval, and insisted on shouldering the backpack. She didn't argue, figuring he knew what his back could handle. She could haul its forty pounds, and often did in the summer, but that didn't mean she was too proud to accept his help. That left her with her corer and sample case, but he relieved her of the heavier case, as well.

Damn, he made this a breeze.

But she noted that once they'd found a place to cross the stream, he paused. Slowly, he scanned the area ahead and to either side of them, almost as if he expected to see something.

Probably something he was trained to do, she decided.

But the instant they stepped into the woods, she saw a man transformed. Unlike most of the people she hiked with, he didn't scuff over the ground, and he became quieter than the world around him. There was little snow under the trees, but he disturbed neither leaf nor needle that she could tell. She glanced back over her own shoulder and saw that she had left a trail already, but nothing marked Jerrod's passage.

He lifted his feet, she noted, and planted them quite deliberately. But more than that, he seemed to flow rather than walk. Not even the backpack made its usual noises as it shifted because it didn't shift at all on his frame.

"How do you do that?" she asked.

"What?"

"You're not leaving a trail. You're so quiet. I've never carried that backpack anywhere that it didn't make some noise."

"Practice."

Little enough of an answer, but probably the best one he could provide. His parka didn't even rustle. She wondered what kind of fabric it was, or if it was the way he was moving. Regardless, she almost winced at the amount of noise she made with every step. The legs of her snowmobile suit rubbed together loudly. And even as she tried to lighten her step, she could still hear it.

But what did it matter? she asked herself. He was trained to move silently. She was just out here hunting for dead animals.

"What area do you want to search?" he asked.

"Now, that's the question. It's been two weeks since the cattle died. By now anything that was poisoned back then has probably disappeared. Depending on whether it poisoned other animals…" She shook her head. "I've got to check, but I don't have a whole lot of hope. The animals can travel for hours before they even get sick."

He surprised her by squatting and picking up a dried twig. "Okay, let's make a plan."

She squatted, too, grateful that the woods were breaking the wind. It seemed warmer under the pines, even though there was less sunlight.

"We might have to come out here several times," he remarked. "We're not going to be able to cover a very big swath on foot in one day. So we need to break it up. We can either follow a circular pattern, starting at the farthest point and moving inward, or we can start here and circle out. Or we can make a grid search." He lightly drew arcs that expanded outward. Then next to it, he drew a grid.

She thought about it as she stared at his rough drawing. Reality was beginning to settle in. "It's already getting toward noon, isn't it?"

"Not quite. I figure about eleven, maybe a little past. But that still only leaves us four hours before we'll wish we were on open ground. These woods will darken up fast."

He was right. "Maybe I should come here in the morning first thing."

"If you want. But since we're here, we might as well look around. My recommendation would be to stay close to the ranch today. If you want to spread out farther, it'd be better to have a whole day for it."

He *was* good at tactics, and she felt a little stupid for not having thought of all this herself. Just march into the woods and look around for dead animals? It had sounded okay until she really thought about the task.

"I went off half-cocked," she remarked.

"No, you're just not used to thinking in these terms." He flashed a small smile. "That's what you have me for."

"So suggest away."

He straightened and motioned her to do the same. "Now take one step away."

She did, then watched in amazement. Squatting had caused their feet to twist and move the pine needles around, leaving a clear mark. In moments, using that twig and his gloved hand, the marks vanished as if they'd never been.

"Is that really necessary?" she asked. For the first time she truly accepted that he believed there might be danger in what she was doing. For all she'd been dismissing the possibility that someone might think she was a threat, his actions seemed to bring it home. There *could* be someone out there stupid enough to think he could be traced by the poison. After all, he'd been stupid enough to use it.

All of a sudden, the woods didn't feel anywhere near as friendly.

"Better safe than sorry," he answered. But she didn't like the way he straightened and listened. As if he expected to hear something.

"Someone or something is watching us," he said quietly. "Do you feel it?"

Actually, she did, but she wasn't sure that the feeling hadn't been caused by him mentioning it. But then she realized she'd been uneasy for a while.

"Let's go," she whispered. "Now."

He nodded and turned with her, leading the way back down slope.

"And sometime," she added quietly, "you're going to have to teach me how to walk like that, without leaving tracks."

"It's just a matter of not scuffing. On this kind of surface, it's easy. On dirt or mud, it's a different story."

So she picked her feet up and tried. That wasn't easy, either.

But as they got closer to the stream and the ranch, her uneasiness began to dissipate.

Maybe he'd caused it all. That was an unwelcome thought.

Up on the mountain a man sat, rifle now slung over his shoulder. Annoyance barely began to cover what he was feeling. He had thought this would be easy, but those two were never far apart for long out here. While he had the advantage of knowing where his target would be, at least on weekends, he didn't have the advantage of taking just his target.

Not with two of them. And now they had a radio, making it all the more difficult. He'd seen the woman carrying it. If he decided to take them both out, he'd have one chance and he'd have to be quick or he wouldn't have time to cover things up and get out of here. Yeah, the cops were generally far away, but if they got reports of someone shot, they'd be all over this place with their helicopter.

Not as easy as he'd first thought. Not that he'd be stopped. No way.

And now they were leaving, but he had no idea why. His opportunity was walking away with them. He'd hoped the next hours would open things up, but apparently not today.

He counseled himself to patience, but since he'd made up his mind that he needed to do this, he just wanted to get it done.

Cussing under his breath, he climbed the slope again, sticking to rocks as much as possible so as not to leave even a minimal trail. He'd get his chance. He was sure of it.

But bashing that woman's windshield should have scared her off. It had been meant to warn her off snooping around.

He bared his teeth to the wind as he climbed. Some people, he thought, were either too stupid or too stubborn for their own good. He had to find a way to take advantage of that, to encourage these two to separate.

He only wanted one of them. Only one of them would be justified. Being justified mattered to him.

He was so busy trying to figure his way around this complication that he barely noticed how quiet the woods were, except for the wind. He didn't even notice the remains of the wolf he'd killed a few hundred yards below the cave he'd taken over. Already the carrion eaters were reducing it to nothing.

That wolf didn't matter. His target did.

A target that he thought of as an object, not a person. He'd learned that trick a long time ago. Only after he completed his task would he allow himself to savor what he achieved. Only then.

Right now it was just a target to be removed.

Still uneasy, Jerrod walked with Allison back to her car. After he opened her door for her then closed it, he stood looking back at the mountains. Someone was up there, he was sure. It might just be a hunter who hadn't gotten the warning. Or somebody who liked winter hikes.

He wasn't buying it. They'd been watched, and he tried to think of ways to get back here without Allison to check it out. Nothing occurred to him. Given his concern that someone might want to stop her investigation, he didn't know if he should leave her alone even in town.

He walked around the rear of the car and took in once again the shattered and taped rear window. Message? He feared it might be, one that had missed entirely, at least as far as Allison was concerned.

But if it was a message, it hadn't missed *him*. Since she was back out here today, she'd certainly sent a clear signal that she wasn't quitting. That could ratchet up any threat to her considerably.

He slid in beside her finally and closed his own door.

"What were you looking at?" she asked.

"Just scanning the mountains for general terrain. We'll map out a search pattern tonight." Unless he could think of a way to persuade her not to pursue this any further. Somehow he doubted he would succeed. She brushed away any suggestion that this might be dangerous with all the ease of someone who had never lived in a truly dangerous world.

She might be right, too. He could well be overreacting, but he couldn't bet on that.

As the car warmed up, he started to smell Allison's shampoo, something laced with coconut. The woman smelled good enough to eat. In fact, he'd like to lick and taste every inch of her. Spend hours in her bed learning every inch of her. Sweep them both away on the red haze of urgent need.

Damn, he needed to wrap concertina wire around some of his own thoughts before he got stupid enough to act on them. What could he offer her, anyway? Until he got himself sorted out, he had no business messing with a woman, or worse, messing in her life.

When they pulled up to the ranch house, he felt an instinctive desire to just keep going. He figured having lunch here was apt to remind him just how rough around the edges he'd become over the years. This wasn't like going to a bar with his buddies.

Ah, suck it up, he thought. It was his own fault he'd grown short on social graces over the years. He just hadn't made the effort. Too damn hard to talk to the women who haunted the bars because they were starry-eyed about guys in uniform, and no need to talk to the ones who just wanted a roll in the hay. Yeah, he'd been invited to dinner and barbecues by his buddies and their families when they were stateside, but he'd been in the company of men who understood the rough edges, and their wives who had learned to smooth them over a bit.

This was different.

He also might be making entirely too much of it. He ought to be able to handle an hour or so of small talk. It wasn't as if his brain was crippled. Not much, anyway.

Suspecting that he had become a coward for some reason, knowing damn well he'd faced harder things, he climbed out and accompanied Allison to the front door.

A pretty blonde opened it and invited him in. So this was Nora Loftis, daughter of the unlikable Fred Loftis, that Nate had introduced him to. Sympathy sparked in him. He couldn't imagine growing up under that man's thumb.

They moved directly to a large dining room with a long table that was already set for three.

"Fancy," Allison remarked.

Nora laughed. "The first time I came here to visit Jake we ate here, too. Rosa has very definite ideas about how visitors should be treated. I have to admit, though, that it felt odd to be sitting at such a large table with only one other person."

Rosa, dark haired and beaming, appeared carrying a tray. "The kitchen belongs to me," she said firmly.

"And you're not kidding, are you?" Nora said with a twinkle in her blue eyes.

"I am not," Rosa said firmly, as she placed large earthenware bowls of chili in front of them. A long loaf of crusty bread followed on a platter. "Plenty more if you want it."

Then she left them to eat.

"Jake's sorry he couldn't be here," Nora said. "He hoped he could make it but something came up. How's the sampling going?"

That made it easy at least for a while. Jerrod ate some of the best chili he'd ever had, delighting in both its taste and its heat, while Allison did most of the talking. He put in a word from time to time, just to be sociable, but this was her bailiwick.

Of course, it didn't last, though. Nora eventually turned to him. "You just moved here, didn't you?"

"A few weeks ago."

"Right about the time…" Nora trailed off, stared into the distance, then shook herself and returned her attention to Jerrod. "Are you planning to stay?"

"I don't know yet."

Her brow knit a little then smoothed over. "Well, this county has a lot to offer, depending on what you like. Hunting, fishing, hiking, Nordic skiing. It's great if you like the outdoors. Otherwise, maybe not so much."

Her smile looked amused, and he felt his own face stretching into a responsive one. "I'm outdoorsy, all right. As for the rest…" He shrugged.

"What did you do before?"

"Military," he said.

"Big change for you, then."

Just as he was beginning to wonder if he was about to get grilled, Nora turned the topic to her own work as an archivist at the library, and Allison's job teaching.

He found himself mostly watching Allison, the animation that livened her face. It occurred to him that he'd probably never get sick of watching the play of her thoughts and feelings over that pretty face.

Aw, cut it out, he told himself. He was sitting there with his jacket on and only partly unzipped, looking like he was ready for flight, because he was armed. He had a cell phone in his pocket that could ring at any moment with the news he was being reactivated. He figured Allison was right, too, that he was at least partially paralyzed by grief or something over the sudden change in his circumstances, and losing his entire reason for existing.

Drifting. He was drifting, and probably making a mountain out of a molehill over this whole poison thing because he didn't know any other way to think or act.

He had no right to inflict that on anyone.

The chili was great. He had a second bowl of it, and ate so much bread that Rosa brought another loaf for him to dig into. If he was being a pig, nobody seemed to think so, especially Rosa, who gave him an unmistakable look of approval as she brought him more to eat.

He complimented her on the wonderful meal and she smiled even more broadly. "I like a man who eats," she said.

"I'm certainly doing that."

By the time they left, he felt he'd walked through that potential minefield reasonably well. Maybe he hadn't forgotten as much as he thought. Or maybe reasonable manners once learned were never entirely forgotten.

Once they were headed back to the main road, Allison asked a surprising question. "I've always wanted to know something."

He tensed a little. "About what?"

"Do they really make you eat square meals in the academy?"

The question shook a laugh out of him. "Actually, yes, but only during plebe summer. It's just part of the discipline, although I've gotta say it makes eating extremely uncomfortable. Worse, though, was being quizzed throughout the meals. That went on all year."

"But what exactly is squaring?"

"Mainly it's simple once you learn it. You sit on the edge of your chair, perfectly straight, with your chin tucked in. Really tucked in. Then you have to keep your eyes straight ahead while bringing your fork or spoon straight up before then moving it horizontally to your mouth. You repeat the process in reverse, putting your hand in your lap until you're ready for another mouthful."

"So it's hazing?"

"I don't think I'd call it that, although I suppose you could. Mainly I think it's one of the many introductions to 'these are the rules, follow them no matter how stupid they seem.'" He paused. "For a few days it's absolute hell, but you get the hang of it. And considering how I've seen some people eat, it may be a good thing."

"You've got a point there." She laughed. "Okay, I always wondered about that. Don't ask me why, it just intrigued me since I first heard of it."

"Well, it doesn't last forever. You should see us hunkered around a fire in the middle of nowhere eating our rations. No manners at all."

"In that situation, they'd seem out of place. So you can have a square meal at my place tonight, in the other meaning of the term. If you don't mind stopping at the grocery with me. I want to pick up a few things and make something nice. I've been eating out of jars, cans and packages all week because I didn't cook last weekend."

"Meaning?"

"I usually prepare food once a week and freeze it. I didn't do it last week and I need to today if I can. Okay about the store?"

"Sure," he said. "And if you want to cook for the coming week, I'll help. I can take orders."

"That might be fun."

It also might be stupid, but he realized he was seeking every possible excuse not to let her out of his sight. Whether the urge rose from concern about her or from his own desire for her, he didn't know.

Wise or foolish, there it was.

The grocery store didn't take very long. Allison had a pretty good idea what she wanted and needed and didn't get sidetracked or linger over things. She rapidly filled the cart he pushed for her.

Exactly the kind of shopper no retailer liked, she thought with amusement as she stood in the checkout line.

However, she was not as amused about spending the rest of the day cooking with Jerrod. It somehow struck her as an intimacy she wasn't prepared to share, although she couldn't figure out why.

Yes, they had to plan tomorrow better if she really intended to look for dead animals up on the mountainside. Most likely a fool's errand, given the amount of territory up there and the likelihood that any dead animals would be quickly eaten and their remains scattered. Equally foolish given how far some of these animals would be able to travel before they sickened.

But she still felt compelled to look. If she found any freshly dead animals, then they might have a serious, ongoing problem. It could mean that the poison was still at work or that it had been used again.

The instant she had that thought, an icy uneasiness trickled through her. *If that poison had been used again.* All of a sudden she wondered if Jerrod's concern about her safety might be justified. If someone was still using the stuff, her poking around could well get her into trouble.

It could be linked to the smashed tailgate window. That might really have been a warning, not a stupid prank.

The uneasiness followed her all the way into the house, while she put away the groceries Jerrod carried in for her, while she changed into something comfortable and warm. By the time she got back to the kitchen, Jerrod had started a pot of coffee.

"What if someone is still using that poison?" she said as soon as she saw him.

He leaned back against the counter, folding his arms. For the first time, she noticed he was armed with both knife and pistol. "My God," she whispered.

He looked down, then looked at her. "I wasn't going out there without protection. Want me to ditch this stuff?"

"Ditch it where?"

"I can put it by the front door with my jacket, or take it home."

She met his inky gaze almost reluctantly. He really did come from a different world. Well, not totally. Plenty of people hereabouts had guns, and some wore them. But somehow this felt different. Maybe because she hardly knew this man and he was in her house?

Nor did most people around here carry in town. There were guns aplenty, mostly reserved for being out in the countryside hunting or on the ranch. Guns were part of life. Why this reaction?

Because there was only one reason he would have carried those weapons today. And it explained why he'd eaten lunch with his parka still on.

"I'll go home," he said.

"No." The word was out almost before she knew it was coming. "I'm just surprised." That was certainly true. "I don't have any guns. Well, except for the shotgun in the attic. It was my dad's."

"A moral objection?"

"No. This is gun country. I'd have to object to most of my neighbors if I felt that way. I'm just not used to seeing weapons inside my house."

"Then I'll get rid of them."

"It's okay. Really. This is you, right?"

Something in his eyes narrowed. "Yeah," he said, his voice rough. "This is me. This is me on high alert. I don't need to be on alert in your kitchen."

"I hope not."

Without another word, he unbuckled his belt and removed both holsters from it. The sound of leather slipping against denim, the sight of him tugging at his belt, caused a sensual shiver in her despite the situation. She repressed it swiftly.

"I'll put them with my jacket."

She wondered why he hadn't done that while she was changing. Maybe because he was so used to being armed he hadn't thought about it? But the idea that he'd felt it necessary to accompany her to the ranch like that...

She sank onto a chair, the house not quite silent. The coffeepot made its familiar noises, but there was a less familiar noise now, a man in her little entry hall ditching weapons.

She felt as if she'd just run head-on into the brick wall of a very different reality. That was crazy. There were guns all over this county, so why was she reacting this way?

Because it was Jerrod? Because he had just given her a truly honest glimpse of the life he had led before his wounding? Because she was sure that unlike most of her neighbors, he wasn't armed to deal with varmints? No, he was armed to deal with people.

She nearly shuddered.

"Maybe I should just go home."

She looked up. He was standing in the doorway of the kitchen now, his face like chiseled stone. Her reaction had stung him, as if she were rejecting *him*.

"No, stay," she said quietly. "Please. I was just surprised. Nothing more."

He pulled out the other chair, swung it around and straddled it. "I suppose I should apologize, but I forgot I was armed. I'm used to it. I don't think about it often."

She nodded. "And I'm acting like a foolish civilian. I get it."

"I don't think you're foolish at all. This is me, like you

said. You're not used to the things I'm used to. We just had a culture clash."

The sense of shock was easing, and her heart was slowing down again. She managed a faint smile. "Well, if you don't disappear in a couple of days, I suppose there'll be more of them. It's just that I don't know you very well. I probably never will."

He frowned faintly. "Maybe not. I don't seem to be in a position to promise much of anything right now."

"Because you could be reactivated?"

"Partly. But mostly because I haven't figured out what I'm going to do yet. I'm still adjusting."

"I get it." She did, too, and the understanding didn't make her happy. Jerrod was beginning to knit into her life in a way that made her reluctant to think of him going. And it wasn't just because he could ignite her desires so easily. Something else was getting to her. His extreme protectiveness of a woman he hardly knew? Maybe. It had been a long time since anyone had made her feel protected, and it was only now that she realized how much she wanted that feeling, even if she didn't need it.

Crazy thoughts, she told herself. "I'm struggling here," she said finally. Might as well just have it out in the open.

"How so?"

"I sit here pondering you when I have almost nothing to go on. Then I ponder why you evoke the feelings you do in me when there's little basis for them. You're making me crazy."

His facade cracked a bit and she thought she caught a glimpse of humor, just a quick one. "I'm crazy making, I suppose."

"So it seems. Anyway, for all intents and purposes,

you're a stranger to me. That should make it easy, right? Wrong. I'm entirely too wrapped up in you."

He leaned forward against the back of the chair and put his hands on the table. Spread out like that, she could see the signs of a life lived the hard way. The assortment of dings and scars were almost an encyclopedia.

"Didn't you wear gloves in the field?" she asked suddenly.

"Of course." He looked down at his hands. "But not quite often enough."

"Apparently," she said drily.

"I wear them because they're necessary, not because I like them. I hate not having the sensitivity of my fingertips."

Oh, hell, she thought. That had been a simple statement of fact, but it struck her as sensuous beyond belief. The thought of sensitive fingertips touching her kindled the fire that never quite went out when he was around, and that all too often leaped to a blaze even when he wasn't. She ached to make love to this dangerous stranger, and perhaps that was the craziest thing of all.

She dragged her gaze from his hands and forced herself to stand to get a couple of mugs and the coffeepot.

"Like now," he said.

"What?" She turned, met his eyes, and almost dropped the mugs and pot. How could black eyes burn that way?

"You have a fascinating face," he said quietly. "Nearly everything you think shows on it."

"Oh, God." She wanted to sink, to fall into a hole beneath her feet. To hide. "Don't strip me."

"I'm not stripping you. I just enjoy your expressions. Don't ever play poker."

"Wouldn't dream of it." She cleared her voice and managed to sit again and pour coffee.

"You want me," he said.

"Is this where I go bury my head somewhere or throw you out?"

He laughed. Man, she envied how comfortable he was with this. She just wanted to sink. "No. Because I want you, too. The thing is, neither of us is sure that would be right, so we're just going to hang fire."

"What's that expression mean?"

"It comes from explosives. It's when a fuse appears to burn out, or an electronic trigger doesn't work immediately."

"But it's still dangerous?"

"Let's just say I wouldn't approach a brick of explosive that had been triggered but didn't go off. I'd wait a good long while."

She nodded and managed to steal a look at him. Seeking safer ground she asked, "I guess you know a lot about explosives?"

"Enough. I know a lot of things that mostly won't be useful now. But my training runs deep, Allison. I don't go into any potentially dangerous situation unprepared. That's why the gun and knife."

She considered his words. "I guess you could be pretty lethal without them, though."

"If necessary. It's not preferred."

"I don't imagine it would be. Look, I'm sorry, I was just…shocked. Unprepared. That's all. I wasn't being critical of you. I was trying to deal with something unexpected, and I guess I did a lousy job of it."

"It's okay. But what you said about maybe someone

is still using that poison? I've been wondering about that all along. One use seems kind of strange."

"One use would be enough, depending on what you're after. But I feel kind of foolish for not having thought of it sooner. What if this guy is still putting out bait? What if he's after something where one application might not be enough?"

"Like a wolf pack?"

"That would be one. Especially if you don't understand wolves enough to know how easy it is to break up a pack. Regardless, when I think about repeated uses of that stuff, I stop feeling like you're being hypercautious."

"A nice way of saying you've been wondering if I've been exaggerating the possible danger to you."

"Well, yes," she admitted, feeling her cheeks warm again.

"You have a beautiful blush," he remarked, then moved on quickly. "You say this guy can't be found by tracking the poison. Maybe not, and maybe he doesn't know that. Or maybe he's still using it and now that you're going out there again, and into the mountains, he might be even more worried. I've found that people who are willing to break the law about one thing don't generally worry too much about it when it comes to other things."

"Like murder? Are you suggesting someone would kill me over this?"

"I don't know. It might satisfy them just to put you out of commission. Or maybe they wouldn't come after you at all. I don't read minds. But on the off chance, I just want us to be careful."

She couldn't argue with that. It was hard, though, to think about poison when a little tape was running in the back of her mind, the sound of his voice as he'd said he wanted her, too.

They were hanging fire? She wondered if she'd be able to stand it.

But he continued as if he hadn't just probably read her dancing thoughts on her face. Sheesh. Like an open book. She hadn't heard that in years. Or maybe he was just unusually good at reading faces.

"So what do you want to do first?" he asked. "Cook or make our plan for tomorrow?"

Chapter 6

With a huge pot of marinara sauce simmering on the stove and a big chicken casserole in the oven, they sat at the table with a laminated topographic map Allison had borrowed from the geology department.

It covered a much larger area, making it more difficult to focus in on the small area they'd be searching. Jerrod, Allison noticed, didn't seem to have any trouble making sense of it, though. It was as if he had reading maps in his blood. More of his training and experience, she supposed.

"What I'm going to suggest," he said after studying it for a few minutes, "is that you use a grid pattern."

"Why?"

"Partly because it'll work better on this terrain, and partly because I want to fan out and circle around you."

"Protection?"

"Again, partly. But also I'll see the areas you're not likely to. Does that radio of yours have GPS on it?"

"The sheriff said it does."

"Good. I've got my own GPS gear."

"Will it work in the mountains?"

He arched a brow at her. "What do you take me for?"

The way he said it elicited a laugh from her. "Okay, okay."

"Tell me one thing, though."

"What's that?"

"Why'd they pick a chemist to do this? You said you can't even test the samples in your lab. Why not somebody else?"

"Because I understand exactly what I'm dealing with and how to take precautions. Plus I'm linked in with the state lab through the college, and I once took a class in hazardous material handling."

"Just wondering."

"Why? You think they should have sent in a whole team, armed to the teeth?"

Now it was his turn to laugh. "No. Not yet, anyway. I think we're dealing with a single offender."

"And you could handle four or five by yourself?"

She'd meant the question to be light, but the answer he gave her was anything but.

"If I need to."

He tossed that off as if he were utterly confident of his abilities. Allison supposed he had enough experience to know. Returning to the map, he checked coordinates and began to draw lines with an erasable marker. They were far from straight.

"You won't be able to follow a beeline, given the terrain. But this is pretty close to what you should be able to do, if the map is accurate. Stay away from ravines, though, and watch out for loose rocks." He paused and looked up. "Sorry, you probably already know that."

"Yes."

The grid he was drawing was already implanting itself in her brain. Not that it would do her a whole lot of good, she thought with some humor, being directionally impaired as she was, which she'd proved earlier today.

"The GPS will keep you on track," he said as if he read her mind. "And I won't ever be farther away from you than a shout, okay?"

"Okay." That *did* make her feel a little more secure. Yes, she liked hiking, but she generally stuck to marked trails. Now she was proposing to head out with a GPS and map? Oh, boy. What was she thinking?

But she thought of the devastation this toxin could cause, and how important it was to know, insofar as she could find out, if there were other poisoned animals. Right now they might not pose much of a risk, but if the snow started to melt, contaminated water would run down the slopes into the stream below. A lot of ranchers depended on that stream.

She was rapidly losing interest in the map and the plans for tomorrow, though. Almost as if a magnet drew her attention, she once again grew increasingly aware of the man who sat across the table from her.

While he was absorbed in his task, making his own mental map she was certain, she indulged the luxury of just looking at him.

Her eyes traced the contours of his sturdy shoulders, the strength in his arms as he moved. The chiseled lines of his face that could look so cold or so incredibly warm.

That mouth, which had kissed her like she'd never imagined possible.

Was it so wrong to want more? If she was willing to take the risk, to toss caution to the wind and enjoy a brief affair, was that so awful?

It was so easy to remember how his arms had felt around her, how his mouth had felt on hers and to extrapolate from there to being free to run her hands over him, to feel his hands running over her. So easy to imagine sharing intimacy with him.

Of course, it might not measure up to her imaginings. Her one serious relationship had taught her that. Not only had she found lovemaking to be rather boring after the initial burst of excitement, but the guy had wounded her deeply by saying she was a lousy lover.

Was she? She had no idea. One person hardly provided an accurate gauge. As one of her girlfriends had said when she was crying about it, "Don't listen to him. How are you supposed to become a good lover if you don't have a good teacher?"

Good question. But remembering that comment still had the power to make her hesitate and hold back. She looked down, feeling a sting in her cheeks, a sting of humiliation. Did she really want to take such a risk with Jerrod? What if he felt the same way?

"Allison?"

She didn't want to look up. If he could read her face as easily as he said, she'd probably reveal this whole embarrassing story with one look. Or at least enough of it to complete her humiliation.

A chair scraped and the next thing she knew he was squatting beside her. "No," she said quickly, hoping he'd back off. Her thoughts had wandered down trails they shouldn't have followed, and she just wanted him to back off so they could get back to business. Business was the only safe place to go.

But he didn't listen. With a strength that surprised her, he lifted her right out of her chair, knocking it over in the process.

"Jerrod!"

"Shh," he said.

He carried her so easily, one arm behind her shoulders, one beneath her knees. Confused, delighted, hopeful and afraid, one clear thought nevertheless burst through. "Your back!"

"It's fine," he answered. Moments later they were in her living room. He set her on her feet, but before she could figure out which way to run, he settled on the sofa and pulled her down so that she straddled his lap. His hands gripped her waist, making it clear she was going nowhere.

Oh, God, how had things become so intimate so quickly? She could feel his heat between her legs and was sure he could feel hers, too. In an instant she was open to him, layers of clothing notwithstanding.

She had to reach forward to prop herself on his shoulders, to resist that last little bit of contact because alarms rang deafeningly in her brain. This could get out of hand so fast. So very fast.

"Jerrod," she said, but didn't know what she wanted to say. *Yes? No? What are you doing?*

"You should have seen your face," he said. "Whatever was bothering you was bad, wasn't it?"

Being close to him like this seemed to be sucking all the air from the room. Her heart was skipping beats, and between her legs, awareness of his heat, his closeness, was turning into a steady, aching throb.

"You wanna talk about it?"

She managed to shake her head.

"Okay." He released her waist and lifted her arms so that she started to fall toward him. The next thing she knew, his arms wrapped tightly around her and held her hard against his chest. Her chin rested against his shoulder, and her nose nearly touched his neck. How was it possible that he could smell so good?

But his scents, a male muskiness tempered by the time they'd spent outdoors, and even with the cooking they'd been doing, enticed her. It took all her willpower not to just burrow in, but she couldn't help drawing those aromas deep within her.

He hugged her, and she needed it. And while it was an unusual hug, she decided it was probably better for his back than standing slightly bent to hold her. Whatever, it felt so damn good she never wanted it to end.

Everything else slipped away as warmth, heat, even an internal light seemed to fill her. Little by little, her arms inched up and wound around his neck, holding him as he held her.

Even as need pulsed within her, she felt a contradictory relaxation seeping through her. Muscles she hadn't realized were tight let go, until she felt more like a puddle than a body. He made her let go just with the power of his embrace, and only in the letting go did she realize how much tension she had been carrying within her.

He didn't say anything, just held her close. He made no moves, although she had a ratcheting desire for more, even though part of her remained frightened.

Better not to know, she told herself, and gave in to the

relaxation, the simmering heat, the feelings that might have been.

Right now seemed perfect. Why ruin it?

Jerrod couldn't remember the last time he'd held a woman this way, to provide comfort, to take nothing. Surprised, he realized that he enjoyed it. He got some inkling of why so many of his buddies had married, even though they could be home so rarely and for such short periods. Maybe the only reason that he'd missed that train was because he had insisted on maintaining his emotional distance.

Right now he wasn't, and he liked it. Something inside him began to unwind from the corkscrew it had been in for so long. Dangerous? Probably. But he was damned if he was going to give it up right now.

Not when she leaned so trustingly against him, not with her arms around his neck. He wouldn't give that up until he had to.

He didn't even mind the stiffening of his staff, the throbbing need that demanded to be satisfied. It seemed part and parcel of this experience, this rarer-than-diamonds experience of just holding a woman to offer comfort.

God, who would have thought a simple hug could be so important? Or that he was so hungry for one?

Certainly not him. All that camaraderie and companionship he was used to sharing with his men that had filled his life for so long had apparently been lacking something essential: hugs. Real hugs. The kind he could only get from someone like Allison.

For the past six months, he'd been pretty much solitary. A hermit within his own mind. Grieving, maybe, the way Allison had suggested. But now, he didn't feel alone at all.

Seldom had he wanted something to go on forever, but he wanted this experience to never end.

After a bit, he dared to rub her back gently, intending only to comfort. A soft sound escaped her and she relaxed against him even more. It was a gift so great he made up his mind to never do anything that might betray the trust she was placing in him.

It was so different from the trust his men had placed in him, trust in his skills and knowledge, in his tactical sense. A trust he had often felt he hadn't really deserved, even though he'd had to earn every bit of it.

This was pretty much unearned. It came from a woman who had little reason to trust him, and it was independent of anything he might do. It wasn't earned, it was freely given.

He swelled inside with an amazing sense of worth. That he had a purpose beyond doing, a purpose that came from simply being. It was enough for her that he was here, that he hugged her, held her. Nothing depended on him except these moments of comfort, freely offered and freely accepted.

It damn near turned his world upside down. He'd spent his entire adult life being judged by what he did, not by who he was. Now that he felt like next to nothing at all, she was showing him that something else mattered, too.

An internal earthquake rocked him, and he knew to his very core that he had been changed forever by this embrace. He couldn't imagine what it might mean, or where it might lead.

Nor did he get time to even start thinking about it.

The oven timer began to beep from the kitchen.

* * *

"Damn," said Allison.

"Damn?"

"If I don't get that casserole out of the oven soon, it won't be very edible. Right now I'd cheerfully let it burn, but that would be a criminal waste."

Having been in places where hunger was an ever-present companion, he appreciated her concern, but he was awfully reluctant to let her go. Still, with a sigh, she pushed herself upright and twisted off his lap, reminding him just how badly his body wanted her right now.

Down, boy, he warned himself with genuine amusement. He'd cut his own throat before he risked the trust she had just shown him. He waited a few minutes before following her into the kitchen. The casserole rested on a hot pad, and she was stirring the spaghetti sauce gently.

"Smells good," he said as if they hadn't just shared an intimacy that would forever linger in his memory.

"It does, doesn't it?" she said pleasantly. "I may use some of this for our dinner tonight. Or I could make us something different. I'll see."

Our dinner? He liked the sound of that. He only wished he could learn what had made her hang her head like that. Allison didn't seem like the head-hanging type. Brisk, confident, usually cheerful and certainly competent. But something had brought her low in a way that had troubled him greatly.

But he couldn't just come out and ask. She'd been quite clear she didn't want to talk.

Nor could he blame her. There was plenty he didn't talk about, either, because of the restrictions that hemmed him in or because he simply didn't want to share them. Things better kept locked in his mind and heart. They might fester there, but that was the price of the life he had chosen.

In a moment of brutal self-honesty, it struck him that he might be the cork in the lines of communication here. He'd told her little enough about himself, all of it superficial. That couldn't possibly encourage her to share anything really personal about herself.

But that cork had been part of his nature so long, he wondered if he could get rid of it. With so much of what he did classified, it was sometimes hard for him to remember that not *all* of it was off-limits. Easier not to talk at all.

Yeah, that would inspire someone to share confidences.

When she didn't seem to need any help, he poured them both cups of coffee and carried them to the table. She joined him a few minutes later. The laminated map with his markings still lay between them.

Back to business, he thought, and that was directly where she headed, rebuilding a barrier. It was a barrier, he realized, that he might have to find a way to dismantle himself. If he really wanted to. If it would be good for her. Hell if he knew.

"I wish I knew when we'd get the results on last week's samples," she said.

"Me, too."

"I mean, if the toxin is dissipating, and we don't find any of it in the woods on the mountainside, then this incident will probably be closed. We'll have to conclude that something must have gone wrong."

"Such as?"

"Well, someone could have buried the toxin, and weathering could have exposed it. Although I'd expect a much bigger mess than a dead raccoon and two cows. Or some coyote could have bitten a collar and the raccoon ate the meat."

"Wouldn't you know who around here is using these collars?"

"Not necessarily, although I guess the sheriff is asking around."

"Okay." He waited as she looked down again.

"This isn't working," she said finally.

"What isn't?"

"I'm going in pointless circles, covering the same ground repeatedly. We either find signs of the toxin spreading or we don't. We finish looking tomorrow. There's just so far one person can look."

"Why do you think you're going in circles?"

"Because I am. I keep jawing about the same things over and over, as if it's going to release some wholly new ideas."

"It did today. You thought that someone might still be using the poison."

"But I'm not sure where that gets us, honestly. And you'd already thought of that, anyway."

"It crossed my mind."

"You should have said so." She rested her chin in her hand and sighed. "I want to solve this. I want to be able to tell the ranchers their herds are safe. I'm not sure I'll ever be able to do that. We may be testing water for a while, and keeping an eye out for a long time. We'll probably never really know what happened. When some of these animals get poisoned, they can travel awfully long distances before they die. I heard of a case of a wolf a few years ago where she traveled maybe a hundred miles. How do you trace that back?"

"Hard to do."

"I'm looking for a needle in a haystack," she admitted. "I was all hot to trot because this is important, but beyond making sure how far that toxin is spread, I can't do a damn thing."

"That's important, though," he reassured her. "Very important. You've got a rancher who has a whole big section of his ranch off-limits. He's probably going to need to know if it's safe come spring."

"He will. But still." She drummed her fingers briefly, her chin still resting in her other hand. "I guess this stuff just appalls me beyond belief. I don't get why we manufacture such deadly things and then go 'Oops, we made a mistake.' And even after that, we bring it back in what we think is a safer form. There are toxins every bit as bad that have been created since, all in the name of getting rid of vermin. Too bad if we poison everything else in our rush toward bigger crop yields."

"People have to eat," he reminded her. "It may be easy to forget that, especially in this country, but I've seen rampant starvation. I'm not saying we don't need to find better ways, but I can sure understand how we get into this trouble."

"I suppose." She sat quietly for a little while, then jumped up. She went to stir her sauce again, but he sensed agitation in her. What was going on?

All of a sudden she asked, "Do you believe that some people are just lousy lovers?"

In an instant he felt his mouth grow dry and his palms grow damp. Shock hit him. The last time he had felt this way was when he had discovered he had walked right into a minefield without realizing it.

That question sounded like a minefield of major proportions. And he sensed a single-word answer wasn't going to suffice. She was worried about that? Why?

He hesitated, choosing each word with care as if he were disarming a bomb. "That depends," he said finally, then hated himself almost immediately. A waffle answer. He never would have tolerated it from one of his men, so why should he use it for escape? "I mean, I suppose someone could be a bad lover if they didn't care enough to try to be a good one."

Her back remained to him, but it suddenly looked so vulnerable. He closed his eyes and thought carefully. "A lazy lover could be a bad lover. One who isn't willing to put any effort into it. And that could very much be a two-way street."

"How so?" Now she faced him, but her eyes were tight. This mattered greatly to her, but he sure wished he knew how.

Picking his way through the minefield, he spoke slowly. "Well, say you have a guy who just wants to get himself off. He tells the woman what he wants. She does it. But what if he doesn't give her what she wants? What if he never asks her, or never listens if she says? What if she's inexperienced and just doesn't know? She'd lose interest pretty fast, I would think, and probably wind up writing grocery lists in her head while he satisfied himself. He might be content with that, or he might notice her lack of interest and blame her. I don't really know. I've never had a lousy lover."

Some of the tightness eased from around her eyes. "Never?"

"Not once. Like I said, it's a two-way street. You pleasure your partner, your partner pleasures you. You find ways to make each other content. You work at it a bit, like everything else in life."

She bit her lower lip and turned away. Had he blown it? He clenched his hands into fists, wishing he knew what was behind this, because he was sure he could be a lot more helpful with a little knowledge.

"But most of my relationships were empty."

At that she turned to look at him again. "Really?"

"Really." It was about time he loosened that cork a bit, he decided. "When you do what I did, you walk into a bar near a military base and it isn't long before women are all over you, you know? Some are hoping for the special guy to show up, but too many are looking for a notch in the bedpost. They get off on guys like me, on the feeling they're playing with fire."

She frowned and slowly came back to the table to sit. "How did that make you feel?"

"For a while it was fun," he said with brutal honesty. "Then I got tired of it. It wasn't that I was ready to settle down. I didn't feel that way at all. But I wanted something that would last longer than a few nights or weeks, depending on when I next shipped out. It never seemed to work out that way. There was never the kind of click that said 'this is the one.'"

"I'm sorry."

"I'm not." He gave her a half smile. "Imagine what she'd be feeling right now with me so messed up and unsure of what I want out of life."

"Maybe she'd be right alongside you, trying to help as much as she could."

"Maybe. But I watched a lot of marriages go down in flames because guys were gone so much. And I saw others burn up when the guy was home all the time. The wife wasn't used to having him underfoot and interfering. Which is not to say a lot of the guys don't have good marriages, but while we were active, more ended than endured. And the ones that endured… Well, a lot of them didn't work so well when the man retired. A lot of guys felt like a fifth wheel in their own homes. Some handled it better than others."

"I imagine."

"Regardless, I always felt it was wiser to stay single. I figured the day would come when I'd be ready to settle down and wouldn't be gone all the time. The right wife for the right stage in my life."

"That actually sounds sensible."

"Does it?" He studied her and realized she no longer avoided looking at him. Apparently he had navigated the minefield well enough. But she'd also clued him in to something very important: someone had once told her she was a lousy lover. Apparently the scar cut deep and hadn't gone away. In fact, she had probably never tried again.

That pissed him off, but getting pissed wasn't going to fix a damn thing.

"This settling-down thing," she said slowly.

"Yeah?" He tensed again, wondering whether a bullet was headed his way.

"You never really wanted to do it?"

"Not like some. It wasn't a goal. It was just something that I figured would happen eventually, or not. So far it hasn't. What about you?"

"I don't think about it much, either. Oh, maybe in a vague way sometimes. But my mother once said something to me that I took to heart. She said you can fall in love a lot of times. But for it to work, it has to be the right person at the right time."

He watched her sherry-brown eyes lift again to him, and they almost looked tentative, as if she wasn't sure how he'd react. Damn, what had he done to have her acting like a cat on a hot stove? She hadn't been tentative around him before. "I'd agree with that."

Then she smiled, that breathtaking smile that he never saw enough of. Nor did he think it would ever be possible to get tired of it.

Deciding that now might be a really good time to end this conversation, he rose. "I'm getting antsy. I'm used to a whole lot more physical activity. If you don't mind, I'm going to go for a quick run before dinner. I'll be back soon."

He didn't miss the change in her expression, but he ignored it. So she didn't want him to go, even for a little while. Okay, he got it. He didn't really want to go, either. But he needed to run a bit, and they might as well both get used to him being gone. It was only a matter of time.

Which, he supposed, using her mother's maxim, meant she might be the right person, but this was definitely the wrong time.

Wondering if Jerrod had taken flight from her, or if he'd been honest about needing the exercise, Allison returned to her cooking. The chicken casserole needed to cool more before heading for the freezer. The marinara was coming along nicely, but that was meant to be used however she wished for a few weeks. She wouldn't have made such a big pot otherwise.

That left tonight. She decided on a whim to make chicken marsala, and defrosting a couple of additional chicken breasts for Jerrod would be no problem. He might not come back, of course, but all that would mean was that she'd have leftovers tomorrow.

It sounded so simple, but something about it hit her hard and she found herself gripping the edge of the counter and squeezing her eyes closed against the huge wave of disappointment that ripped through her.

Oh, no, she thought. No, no, no. She hardly knew the man. She'd met him, really, just over a week ago, and most of the past week he'd kept clear of her. How could she possibly give a damn whether he showed up for dinner tonight?

He was planning to help her on her wild goose chase tomorrow. She'd see him again. But she would see him for all the wrong reasons, she realized. He'd be there to protect her, not because he wanted to actually be *with* her, and that was a whole different kettle of fish.

This was crazy. How many ways had he basically told her that he was a rolling stone, at least right now? How unsettled he still was, how much adjusting he still had to do. He didn't need to speak volumes. The little he'd actually said to her had painted a very clear picture.

She had been avoiding involvement ever since her breakup with Lance. She never wanted to experience that kind of rejection again. She'd been so unprepared for the savagery of it, the way he had attacked everything about her. Not just a simple "This isn't working, I think we should split," but a full-on frontal assault on everything about her that had shattered her self-image until it lay like shards of broken glass around her feet.

She had been in love. She had believed he was in love with her. Then that, following hard on the heels of the deaths of her parents, while she was still grieving and still full of guilt. He had turned on her, rather than supporting her, and had shredded her in the cruelest way possible, criticizing everything about her.

It had taken time to rebuild her confidence. She freely admitted to herself that most of that confidence revolved around her jobs and friends. When it came to men, she still had none at all.

Yet here she was, crazily attracted to a man who might well be capable of the same savagery that Lance had thrown at her. Who might be capable of cruelties she could scarcely imagine.

A man who made her feel open and vulnerable and surprisingly safe simply by holding her and kissing her once. She ought to take that as a huge warning, but instead, she'd welcomed it.

Dangerous, indeed. It ought to be as plain as day that this guy opened her in ways that could allow him to crush her. And she didn't know him well enough to be sure he wouldn't.

She had believed she had known Lance, and look how wrong she had been. She hadn't begun to know Jerrod, and wasn't sure it would ever be possible, even if he remained right next door for the next thirty years.

She needed to put the brakes on what was happening inside her, but she wasn't sure how. The feelings kept coming with a mind of their own, yielding to no reason, no logic. Thinking about a fling with this guy... Was she crazy?

If she could get this disappointed because he wanted to go out for a run, what made her think she could sleep with him for a few days or weeks and escape unscathed?

Equally bad, what if he was wrong and there really was such a thing as a lousy lover, and she was it? Did she want to find that out? It was bad enough telling herself it had just been one guy. What if it was two?

Damn, she wished she'd gone out for a run, too. Nerves fluttered in her stomach and made her feel jumpy all over, a feeling she wasn't accustomed to.

Ask him for dinner? Why? She could just say goodnight and see him in the morning.

But another thought wormed into her head, one she couldn't ignore. If she remained a coward and avoided men forever, she would never know if Lance was wrong, and she might miss something wonderful.

She also remembered what a friend had once said to her, a friend who was a psychologist. *Your subconscious is pretty smart. Let it roll.*

So maybe she was having all this emotional uproar over a guy who might vanish with the morning mist in a few days because that made it safer. Having an affair go bad in this town meant you'd be seeing that person everywhere forever, and how much worse to have one go sour with a colleague.

So maybe she was drawn to a rolling stone on purpose. She'd never have to see him again if it all went bad. Or if a few nights with him simply proved she was a lousy lover. She wouldn't spend the rest of her life looking at a reminder.

There were other, equally painful ways she could lose, but running away from the risk seemed like a cowardly thing to do. She'd been cowardly for too long now.

Opening her eyes, she let go of the counter and pulled two more chicken breasts out of the freezer. Chicken marsala for two, coming up. She hoped he liked it.

Jerrod ruminated as he ran. There was a time for thinking and a time for action, and the two rarely coincided all that much. Which was not to say he'd gone into trouble with his brain on hold, but that was not the time for deep thinking. Deep thinking came first, and after, but not during.

Right now was thinking time. He hadn't taken any irrevocable steps with Allison, but she'd just revealed a lot to him that made him feel like he needed to walk around her with caution. He didn't want to hurt her, he didn't want to trigger her mines and he wasn't sure that he was the right guy to step into all of this.

A fling might do her a world of good. Nothing about Allison suggested to him that she would be a lousy lover. Far from it. So a couple of nights might be enough to repair her self-image.

On the other hand… It was that other hand that worried him more than anything. Women, most especially inexperienced women, tended to get emotionally involved very quickly with a lover. Since he didn't know what, if anything, he had to offer in that department, he could wind up hurting her in another way.

But the fact that he was even thinking about this gave him a vague sense of amusement. Never before had he weighed the pros and cons before taking a woman to bed. The women in his past had all been as savvy about this game as any guy, ready to move on when the time came.

Allison was a whole new class to him. A woman who was as near a virgin as made no difference, he guessed. Although how could he be sure? She hadn't come right out and said anything. He might be putting it together all wrong.

But he doubted it.

He started cussing with every step as he ran. The day was waning rapidly, and he figured running around the streets of this small town after dark might be problematic. Switching course, he headed back to Allison's, still cussing with every exhalation.

A wise man would back off, keep a distance and when this whole poison thing was settled, skedaddle from her life, if not this town.

But maybe he wasn't a wise man. He kept remembering hugging her, being hugged by her, and how it had seemed to fill some gaping hole inside him. Hard to walk away from that.

As he was coming down Allison's street, all the streetlamps turned on, and with them the early Christmas decorations. It looked like a freaking winter wonderland.

But just as the thought crossed his mind, he felt those eyes on him again. That makes four, he thought grimly. Two when they were out taking samples and now two on her street.

Someone was watching Allison. He didn't like it. Forgetting all his other concerns, he increased his pace to a flat-out run, took her porch steps in one leap and slipped inside the front door, taking care to lock it behind him.

Sitting on the hall table, under a watch cap he hadn't worn, were his gun and knife. He wanted to put them on, but didn't want to rattle Allison needlessly.

They'd bothered her. They weren't part of her life. He guessed that meant his past would bother her, too, if he gave her more than an inkling of what he'd done.

Hell. Damned if he did and damned if he didn't.

But one thing was for absolute certain: no matter how difficult it might become to be around her without taking her to bed, he wasn't going to leave her alone until he was certain she was safe.

That much he knew he could do right.

* * *

A pot of water boiled on the stove, fogging windows and raising a cloud of steam. Allison stood at a frying pan, stirring something that smelled out-of-this-world good to him.

"Chicken marsala coming up," she said brightly enough, though her back remained to him. "You'll stay, won't you?"

Of course he'd stay. There was a watcher out there. The meal would be a fillip. "It smells good. How'd you make it so fast?"

"It's really not difficult, and you were out for a while."

He supposed he had been. He cleared the map from the table and carried it to the living room. "Want me to set the table?"

"Dishes are in the cabinet to the left of the sink."

Odd how some things never deserted you, like riding a bike. It had been a long time since he'd done more than grab a plate, knife and fork for himself, but he still remembered how to set it all up right. As he laid everything out, the smells grew more delicious.

"I serve this over egg noodles," she remarked. "Is that okay?"

"That chicken you're making smells so good I could probably eat it on cardboard. Egg noodles are fine."

She laughed, but it was a tight, small sound. He wished she would look at him. He stood there, feeling like a fifth wheel, staring at her back. He tried to rerun their conversation through his mind, wondering if he'd said or done something wrong. Damned if he could think of a thing. Which didn't mean anything, either.

He almost sighed, and he wasn't exactly the sighing type of person. He wished there was some flashing neon sign to guide him, but he was coming to realize that this woman was entirely outside his experience. Sour humor reminded him that he was similarly outside hers. That put them on even footing, and equally uncertain how to proceed.

Of course, everything could be stuffed into a mental box and they could both pretend they hadn't had an oddly intimate discussion earlier.

And it *was* odd. He hardly knew her, yet he'd talked about things he seldom discussed even with his buddies. He'd pulled the cork at least part of the way out of the bottle and opened up, only to wonder now if that had been unwise.

But he was not a man to hang back from a tough situation, nor one to avoid a dangerous one. Standing here like this, wondering, didn't suit his nature at all. His only concern was that he not inflict harm on her.

Well, how much harm could he do right now? Probably very little, so best to sort out a few things *before* he was in a position to hurt her.

Taking the bull by the horns, he went and took the woman by the shoulders. A flicker of amusement passed through his mind as the ridiculous comparison chased through his brain, but he moved until he stood right behind her. "Are you all right?"

"I'm fine."

He hated those words. They seldom meant what they said. She also failed to turn her head even a little bit toward him. The intensity with which she stared at the pan she was stirring could have been a red flag.

"What's going on, Allison?" he asked quietly. "Are you mad at me?"

Seconds ticked by in silence. "No. Not you. Me."

"Why should you be mad at yourself?"

"I don't want to discuss it."

A brick wall slammed into place. He could honor it, just shut up, eat dinner and then return to his house. He could keep an eye on her from there. Or he could just walk out now and…and what? Insult her after she had invited him to dinner? Well, that would certainly sever any tenuous ties between them, but it would also make it difficult to keep an eye on her tomorrow.

"Damn it," he said.

"What?"

At last she turned a little to glance at him. His hands remained on her shoulders, and he noted that she didn't try to escape his touch. What the hell was going on here?

"If you won't tell me why you're treating me to the back of your head, things are only going to get worse."

"What things?" she demanded.

He stepped back, giving her space, recognizing the signs of her irritation. Now he'd find out, and he probably wouldn't like it.

So be it.

She reached over for a bowl and dumped the egg noodles into the boiling water. After a stir, she set a timer. "What things?" she repeated.

"That's for you to say."

"There are no things," she said firmly. At last she faced him, back to the stove, her feet planted firmly. "There is nothing between us. You feel obligated to protect me from a remote threat, and I'm grateful for that. But beyond that, there's nothing but an acquaintance."

"Okay," he said. But even as he spoke, he realized it was far from okay. He'd opened up to her, telling her things about himself he didn't share with anyone. Was it the weapons? Was it his talk of sexual experience? "No," she said. Her face softened a bit. "No. It's not okay. You were kind this afternoon. That scares me."

Scared her? The words exploded in his head. This was so far from anything he had anticipated that shock rocketed through him. It was almost like being ambushed, and he'd been through a few of those. "What scares you?" he asked finally.

"What I'm doing."

Damn, could she be any more obscure? "The poison? What, exactly?"

She shook her head slightly. "I don't know how to tell you. I need to think, okay? Just sit down. The noodles are almost ready."

He didn't want to leave it there, but he didn't seem to have a choice right now. He took a chair at the table and decided that this was a time to wait.

She was scared because he'd been kind? What the hell kind of sense did that make?

Allison turned to take care of the noodles. The timer was ready to ding, so she switched it off, waited a few seconds then pulled out the colander and twisted it until almost all the water ran off. She dumped the noodles in a big ceramic bowl and reached for the chicken marsala. She always just mixed it together.

Focusing on the mundane tasks helped, but only briefly. She was about to put this dinner on the table and face the man who was full of questions for which she had no answers.

God. What was going on with her?

She placed the bowl on the table, pulled a tossed salad

out of the fridge and sat. "Help yourself," she said as pleasantly as she could.

He took a healthy portion, commenting again on how good it smelled. He even took a large plate of salad, which for some reason she had thought might not appeal to him.

He waited until she served herself, then started eating silently. Her fault, damn it. Her fault. He'd been nice to her and she had gotten scared? How could she possibly explain that?

The dinner may have been delicious, but she barely tasted it, and her appetite seemed to have died. Apparently he noticed the way she was picking at it because he said, "Would you be more comfortable if I just took off?"

His taking off would only worsen the problem, she realized. His going out for a run had started this unwelcome cascade of feelings that had led her to this point.

"It wouldn't help at all," she managed to say.

He returned to eating, his head down.

She studied him, and didn't like what she saw. This was the second time today she had sensed that he felt rejected by her. He was tough, he could handle it, but who was she to make anyone feel like that?

Somehow she had to find a way to let him know it wasn't him at all. Finally she put her fork down, telling herself not to be a coward and just spit it out.

"You're a rolling stone," she said.

He lifted his head, his dark eyes settling on her. "Right now, I guess. Didn't use to be in any meaningful sense. I mean, I gave fifteen years of my life to Uncle Sam. But right now, I can't disagree. I *am* at loose ends."

"Unless you get reactivated."

"True. It's not likely, but it could happen."

"Do you *want* it to happen?"

At that he put down his own fork, leaned back and gave her his full attention. "No."

"No?"

He shook his head. "Not even in an advisory capacity. You may be right that I'm grieving, but that doesn't mean I want to turn back the clock. I'd go if called, but I'd rather not be called, for a whole bunch of reasons."

He waited, but when she didn't speak again, he resumed eating. She picked up her own fork and took another mouthful of salad even as she tried to figure out how to explain the tangled skein inside her. She owed him *some* kind of explanation. She was grateful, though, that he didn't seem inclined to press her.

She put down her fork again. "Jerrod?"

He looked up from his plate.

"I'm sorry. I'm confused. It's just that…"

He waited.

"I like you," she said finally. "You already know I'm attracted to you. But you were kind to me. And that… Well… I'm not used to that kind of kindness anymore."

She saw his eyes widen a shade. "I didn't do anything special, Allison. I'm sure you must have friends."

"I do. But that's just it. They're not men I'm attracted to."

His hard, harsh face softened in the most incredible way. She wouldn't have thought he could look like that. "You were hurt, weren't you. Bad relationship?"

"It ended badly, that's for sure. And it's just so weird because, well, it was like I was crying out inside for some kind of reassurance. Some kind of kindness a friend couldn't give. I don't know how to explain it. Then you gave it to me, and I got scared."

"Why did it scare you?"

She couldn't blame him for wondering. "You know, emotions are a mess."

He smiled faintly. "Tell me about it."

"Fact of life. Messy, mixed up, hard to put into words. But basically, I guess, our conversation made me feel closer to you, and then I got scared because I'm not sure I want to take that risk again."

"And I'm a big risk." He didn't ask her. He stated it. "I get it. All I can say is I don't want to do a single thing to hurt you."

"I don't think you do." She sighed and pushed her plate to the side. She'd eat later if her insides managed to settle down. "No, it's me. I realized something. I suddenly understood just how much something has been lacking from my life, all because you offered it to me briefly. Pretty pathetic when a virtual stranger says or does something to make you aware of just what you're missing."

"I wouldn't call it pathetic at all." He'd cleaned his plate, seemed to contemplate seconds then pushed his place setting aside.

"Don't stop eating on my account. There's plenty."

"I may get more later."

There it was again. *Later*. As if he planned to be around. Well, he would, she supposed, at least through tomorrow.

"So tell me about the jerk who wrecked you," he said.

"I didn't think he was a jerk until our breakup. Blinded by love, I guess. And I *was* totally in love with him. Apparently foolishly in love."

"You know, I'm no expert, obviously, but I always thought love, if you were lucky enough to get it, ought to be cherished like diamonds."

"It doesn't always work that way." And now her throat was tightening. She tried to clear it. "I appreciate the sentiment. Anyway, it took two years, but I found out just how bad he was. If there was anything wrong with me that he could throw at me, he did. It was pretty savage."

"And all the worse, I warrant, because he knew you so well and you'd trusted him completely."

She nodded. Now her eyes burned and she lowered them, not wanting him to see the glisten of unshed tears. "Yeah," she said hoarsely. "All the worse. Then add to it that I'd just recently lost my parents. I was already a gaping wound."

"There's no excuse for that," he said flatly. "None."

She couldn't even answer. Of course it was inexcusable, but here she'd been sailing along thinking she'd put the worst of that behind her, albeit that she tended to avoid relationships with men, and all this had made her aware of how fresh the wounds still were.

Lance had cratered her in important ways. It was just that simple. Scary to discover just how deep that hole still remained after all this time.

Scary to realize just how vulnerable it had left her.

"This is getting to be a habit," Jerrod remarked. Before she knew what he meant, he once again scooped her up off her chair and carried her to the living room. She didn't even protest about his back. She was past protesting. She was afraid, but everything about him both exacerbated those fears and eased them. How crazy was that?

This time he held her across his lap, his strong arm supporting her back. Only then did she realize that a tear had escaped and run down her cheek.

"I'm sorry," she whispered thickly.

"No need. Looks like we're the walking wounded."

She managed a short nod, and just leaned into him, resting her cheek against his shoulder, grateful for his strength. She hated her own vulnerability, but could no longer hide from it. It had been lurking in the depths of her mind for years, but today it had leaped up to bite her.

He rested his other hand on her thigh, a comforting weight through the layer of fleece. She felt surrounded by his strength, something she never before had imagined she needed. Apparently she did.

"God," she whispered finally. "I feel like someone took a can opener and exposed my insides."

"Not me, I hope."

She shook her head against his shoulder. "It wasn't you, it was me. Something I needed to face, I guess. You can live in a fool's paradise just so long."

"So talk to me. I can at least listen."

"I don't know what to say. I honestly hadn't realized how gutted I still felt."

"Until I was kind. Or what you call kind."

"Exactly. I was bopping along, telling myself I wasn't really interested in a relationship, ignoring the whole thing, feeling that the right guy would either land in my lap or never show up. It wasn't a priority. And in a small town like this, you have to watch it. If a relationship goes south, you're going to be seeing that person for the rest of your days."

"Must be fun."

"At my age, yes. It's not high school anymore where all that is so fluid, people just move on. Another breakup like that and I'd never escape it. I can't imagine seeing Lance every day. I don't know how I'd deal with it."

"So this happened when you were away?"

"In grad school."

"Oh, the supreme age for male jerks."

At that, a shaky laugh escaped her. "Maybe so. Anyway, I've been ignoring it for a long time now. Locked it away. I don't know what possessed me to bring it up to you."

"I'm trying to remember how we got there. Strangely, I don't."

"What's strange about that?"

He tightened his arm around her shoulder briefly. "Because I usually have a tenacious memory for detail. But maybe that applies only to operational detail."

"Well, I don't remember exactly, either, but we got there. And opened my can of worms, which now I need to deal with."

"Maybe. Or maybe you can go back to the way you were. You seemed happy enough when I met you."

"Don't even go there," she said sharply. Her chest tightened even more. "You have nothing to do with the mess inside me."

He shifted a little but kept right on holding her. "Maybe not, but I sure as hell don't want to make it worse."

She pushed a little away from him and twisted so that she could look him in the face. "You're making me see something I needed to see. Knowing my own vulnerabilities is an asset."

"True. That's one of the things they trained into us. Accurate self-assessment. Otherwise you're a danger to yourself and your team. Know your weaknesses."

"Makes perfect sense to me. Now." After this she'd be aware, and less likely to be swayed by some guy just because he was kind to her. Safer. On surer ground, just because she'd faced the crater within her.

Although, thinking about it as she laid her head on his shoulder again, she wondered. Other men had been friendly and kind to her since Lance. What was it about Jerrod that had gotten past all her defenses? Had it just been a weak moment? Or did it have something to do with the fact that she was sexually attracted to him? Had that made her respond more intensely?

She didn't know. Stifling a sigh, she rested in his embrace, an embrace she needed, and wondered what it all meant.

"Jerrod?"

"Yeah?"

"Do you have any sisters?"

"No. Why?"

"Because you understand women so well."

At that, he barked a laugh. "I doubt it. I did have a mother who taught me to treat ladies with respect. I doubt she'd be awfully proud of some of the things I've done if she was still around."

"So you lost your parents, too?"

"Yeah. Dad had a fatal heart attack, and Mom... Well, I think she died of grief. Six months later while I was away on a mission."

"I'm so sorry." She tried to hug him back. He was right; they were both the walking wounded. There was a lot of food for thought in that. "I think," she said quietly, "that your mother would be extremely proud of you."

Outside in shadows up the street, a man watched the house, growing both cold and impatient. He knew better than to allow impatience to rule him, but that didn't mean he didn't feel it.

Those two were getting awfully close, which created complications. Spending too much time together. He only wanted one of them, but it was beginning to look as if he might have to take both of them.

It wouldn't be impossible. Far from it. But it would leave a bigger trail, even if he managed to get them in the woods. And while the guy could just disappear and everyone would probably think he had just moved on, the woman, not so much. Her roots burrowed throughout this community, which would give him at best twenty-four hours before she was missed. Maybe less.

But he planned to be long gone before anyone started looking, anyway. He hadn't expected this to get so messy, but he had a lot of experience with that. Little threw him off his stride or he wouldn't still be here.

He also knew who was responsible and who needed to pay, and while he didn't want collateral damage, he wasn't afraid of it. But damn, not even smashing the woman's car window had persuaded her to stay home.

Finally he headed to the seedy motel on the edge of town, deciding to take a night in relative comfort compared to the cave he'd been using. With the truck stop right across the street, one night there wouldn't draw any attention to him.

It was clear to him now that he no longer could get away with taking only his target. No, the situation had compounded. It was time to revise his plans.

Rather than feeling disappointed, though, he felt energized. On the hunt. All senses in high gear.

He could do this.

Chapter 7

Finally they had to move. Happy as Allison was to sit on Jerrod's lap, she figured he must be getting stiff and she certainly needed to stretch.

At her first attempt to pull away, he released her immediately. She swung to the side, put her feet down and stood, stretching widely. "Thank you," she said.

"I should thank you. I think I needed that hug at least as much as you did."

She turned, eyeing him. Given her initial impressions of him, given what he had said about the kind of work he had done in the military, the softer side of him amazed her. She liked it. She only hoped he wasn't play acting.

But then nothing about him suggested he was capable of that. Oh, maybe as part of his job, but she didn't get the feeling he'd treat ordinary people that way.

In fact, thinking over what he *had* told her, she concluded he was brutally honest about himself and with himself. He offered no apologies. He was what he was.

She wondered at the adjustments he must have made to come to such a self-acceptance. Clearly, she hadn't arrived there, as today proved.

After a moment, he, too, stood and rotated his torso a bit as if stretching his lower back.

"Pain?" she asked.

"It's not usually painful, but it can sure stiffen up."

"You should have said something."

He flashed one of those surprising smiles. "When I was having such a good time?"

She couldn't stop the blush that heated her cheeks and was quite sure he could see it. His smile changed to a grin, but he didn't say anything except, "Can I make some coffee?"

"Sounds good to me." She realized as he followed her back to the kitchen that something within her had settled. She no longer felt the fear and ache that had been plaguing her at dinner. She doubted the crater within her had healed that easily, but right then she felt relaxed, warm and very much okay.

Maybe that was the most dangerous thing of all, that his holding her could affect her so deeply. But she was damned if she cared right now. It was enough to feel better.

This time she sat while he made the coffee. "It's time to get serious," he said as soon as he'd finished measuring the coffee and water and had started the pot.

"About what?" She thought they'd been pretty serious for a while already.

"Someone is watching you."

In an instant, all her relaxation vanished. "How can you know that?"

He faced her. "If humans have one preternatural and inexplicable instinct, it's knowing when we're being watched. It's a feeling never to be ignored. I felt it when we were out last weekend, I felt it when we were in the woods today and I felt it again when I came back from my run."

A trickle of ice ran down her spine. She didn't doubt him because she had had the feeling, too, but had completely ignored it. Having it in town was meaningless. She had been too busy when they'd been out taking samples to notice anything but what she was focused on. But she didn't doubt him.

"Anyone could be watching here in town," she said. "People stand at their windows and look out."

"Agreed. But this is different, and I felt it when we were out collecting samples. Someone is watching you."

"Is that why you've been so certain I was wrong that nobody had anything to fear from me because I doubted I could trace the toxin?"

"Partly. The point here is not whether you can trace it but whether someone *thinks* you can. We've been over this. I don't think the damage to your car was just a prank."

She compressed her lips. "I know. I've been having trouble with that, too. It's a small campus. We've never had trouble with serious vandalism, and the whole idea of some kind of fraternity prank might be nice to believe, but I can't quite swallow it."

He nodded. "Regardless, get used to being joined to me at the hip. I'm sleeping on your couch until this is settled. And when we go out tomorrow, I'm going to sweep around you to see if I can find out who is so interested in what you're doing."

She stared at him. "You know, right at this instant I could almost hate you."

He lifted his brows. "Why?"

"Because I was feeling so damn good just a minute ago and you smashed it. Shattered it. Maybe you're used to this kind of thing, but I'm not."

"And here I thought I was moving us to a safer place."

"Safe? This?" She gaped at him.

"Safer than what's going on inside me." He closed the distance between them, bent over her until her head was fully tilted back then swooped in for a kiss that took her breath away. She was gasping when he released her mouth, and the desire she had tamped down had become a conflagration again.

"That," he said shortly. "The thing that has you scared and eager and worried if you'll be wounded again. Easier to talk about a criminal and his intentions, don't you think?"

She should have said yes. She should have been grateful that he'd tried to evade this. But his kiss had put paid to that. "No," she heard herself say as if from a distance. The thrumming in her body seemed to lift her to a new plane, instantly connecting her with her physical being so strongly that everything else vanished. Need swamped her.

He must have sensed it. Hell, he must have smelled desire all over her, but he backed up anyway and pulled mugs from the cupboard.

"You don't know me," he said. "For all you know, I could pack up and be gone on Monday."

"Will you?" Her heart skipped beats as her stomach sank.

"I don't know. Probably not, but that's been my mode of operation since I got out of rehab. Stay for a short while and move on."

"I thought you came here deliberately because of Seth Hardin."

"I suppose he was at the back of my mind, but most of the time I was drifting." He brought the coffee to the table, then started clearing the dinner dishes. For the first time she actually saw him wince, and felt instantly guilty for how long she had sat on his lap. "Anyway," he continued, "Hardin made this sound like the best place on earth. After a few weeks, especially the past week, I'd be reluctant to swear to that myself."

Maybe because the tension needed some sort of release, a laugh escaped Allison. The sound must have surprised him as much as it surprised her. "It is a fantastic place. It has its problems, but I came back here after grad school, which ought to tell you something. I could have taught anywhere, but I wanted to be here."

"So maybe I should give Conard City a chance?"

"Certainly don't judge it by this. You'd be surprised how many of our problems come from outside."

He stilled then. She had never seen anything quite like the way he became so motionless he might have been stone. After a moment, he said, "That's an interesting thought."

"What? That this trouble started because of someone who doesn't live here? I've been thinking that since all this started."

"Really? Why?" Once again that inky gaze lasered

in on her as he turned his back to the sink. He appeared to have incredible focus when he wanted it.

"Because I'm naive," she said. She watched his brows lift, and she shrugged. "It's true. I know almost everyone around here. I don't think any of our ranchers would do this. Yes, they grumble about the wolf packs up in the mountains, but so far as I know not a single cow or sheep has been lost to them in this county. Coyotes are a bigger problem, especially around birthing season, and then they keep close watch. So this seems like an extreme reaction. I'd bet it came from elsewhere."

"You could be right."

"I hope I'm right. But like I said, we'll never know. We'd have to catch this guy red-handed, either with the poison or with bait. Not gonna happen except by accident."

"Not very likely." Although he was thinking he might catch someone if he kept his eyes open tomorrow and swept the area while she hunted for more dead animals. While she was right about the fact that anyone might be watching here in town, when combined with being watched in the virtual middle of nowhere, his hackles raised. Someone was up to something, and it certainly seemed to involve Allison.

Although her remark about trouble coming from outside… That bothered him. She was thinking outside this county, but he thought farther than that. Could he have brought trouble on his own heels? He couldn't imagine any for a fact, but there was no way to be certain.

Looking across the table at her, he knew he'd never wanted a woman more. But the most important thing to him was protecting her. Lots of people didn't get that about men like him, because they often went on missions to kill. But the whole point of every single one of those missions was to make larger numbers of people safe. First and foremost, they were protectors.

He turned back to the dishes, ignoring the way his back muscles had begun to scream. The spasm would ease.

"Just sit down," she said. "I can clean up."

"You cooked. Only seems right that I wash."

How did you argue with that? she wondered, although she didn't really feel like disagreeing. Being around this guy was like taking an emotional roller-coaster ride, and she felt nearly worn out from the soul-searching she had done today.

But she noticed that his ordinarily fluid movements seemed stiffer, maybe a bit more cautious, as he scraped plates then rinsed them before loading them into the dishwasher.

"Jerrod? How bad is your back?"

"I told you. Some shrapnel. Usually not a problem."

"But it's a problem right now, isn't it?"

"On and off. I just have to deal with it."

"Then let me do the dishes."

He shook his head. "I need to loosen the muscles. It'll pass. Moving is good."

So she let him be and wondered what kind of mire she was sliding into here. He frightened her, but he made something inside her feel satisfied. He might leave at any moment, which would probably be safer, but she also knew she was getting to the point where she'd miss him like hell if he went.

Where did that leave her? Half in and half out of some kind of undefined relationship? Because she sure as hell didn't know him well enough to love him. But she also knew she wanted him. Maybe she could go for the sex and escape the rest?

How would she know? At her age, she ought to be familiar with her own emotional makeup, but if there was one thing she was learning it was that she didn't know herself at all. She'd had one big relationship in her life. How could she judge if she was capable of spending a couple of nights with a guy without getting more involved?

She tore her gaze from him and stared into her mug of coffee. This was all getting too complicated. A little over a week ago, she hadn't known this man at all. She'd settled into a nice life of teaching, having a good time with friends and had even been excited about playing a small role in trying to find out how much land had been contaminated.

She supposed it was a mark of how dully content her life had become that she could get excited about going out to take samples of soil. But she had believed that was the way she wanted it.

Now she wondered, and it was all the fault of a stranger she had invited into her life. And if she was to be honest about it, she was attracted to the aura of danger around him. Not that he had done anything to make her fear for her safety. Far from it. But she sensed he was a man capable of things beyond her imagining, and that he had been as dangerous as the danger he had lived with so long.

That struck her as an immature thing to be drawn to, but there it was. Jerrod Marquette was the most attractive man to have crossed her path in years, and she couldn't exactly explain why he drew her. She ought to be attracted to ordinary, stable guys, not some rolling stone from parts unknown who was probably headed back to parts unknown soon.

Except that she remembered her thoughts earlier in the day, about how this might be her mind's way of trying to get her to deal with her fears since Lance. The brain could apparently be a tricky thing.

Jerrod finished the dishes without saying any more, but as he dried his hands he asked her if she had any ibuprofen.

"That bad?" she asked as she jumped up to get the bottle from the back of the kitchen cabinet.

"Bad would be hunting for a doc to give me something stronger. It's not like that. Moving helped some."

"You shouldn't have held me for so long."

"Like I wanted to stop?"

And there it was again. The air seemed to thicken instantly and her insides grew molten. "Sheesh, Jerrod!"

A laugh escaped him, one of the few she had heard from him.

"I'm a pain, I know."

"You were the one who said you wanted to discuss safer things and then you come out with that?"

His grin remained. "It was just a hug."

She put her head in her hands, as if abandoning hope, but secret delight filled her. She ought to be concerned that he could flip her switch so easily, but in truth she was enjoying it. She guessed she had been starved for excitement all the while seeking the calmest, most uncomplicated life possible.

This was turning into a day of amazing revelations.

"I'll behave," he promised, but there was a tremor of humor in his voice.

"Oh, don't," she replied, raising her head. "Please. You're keeping me on my toes."

"Or on the brink of despair."

Finally she had to laugh, even as she smoldered inside. It struck her that he had been tiptoeing around her in a lot of ways, and that maybe she'd only gotten to see a small part of him. She welcomed this lighter side of him.

"On the brink of something, for sure," she answered.

"Well, pick your brink and decide if we're going to avoid it or not."

A giggle escaped her. "Right."

"I'm not kidding," he retorted, but it was clear he struggled to wipe the smile from his face. He sat across from her, wincing a bit, then lifted his own mug of coffee. "You have a wonderful laugh and a truly great smile. I like them."

He might as well have lit the fuse on a string of firecrackers. She felt each little popping explosion deep inside, pushing her hunger for him up another notch. Just as she figured she was going to tip over the brink and right into his arms, he sighed and started twisting his torso.

Pain, she reminded herself. He might make light of it, but he was still in pain. Now would not be a good time for either of them. "Does it go away quickly?"

"Usually. It's being a little stubborn tonight. Maybe I shouldn't have taken that run earlier. It was cold, and I stayed on pavement. I prefer to run on softer ground."

"Have you been doing a lot of that?"

"There's a lot of wide-open space out there. I've been enjoying it. Running, walking, taking it all in. In a way it's a new experience for me."

"What is?"

"Being able to go out like that without wondering

what was behind every rock and tree. No threat. I enjoyed the freedom."

More food for thought. They had led very different
lives, and she tried to envision being immersed in a world
where threat was almost always imminent. "I can't imagine the adjustments you're making."

"Some are harder than others," he admitted.

Maybe, she thought, he was seeing a threat to her only
because he was accustomed to viewing things that way.
Maybe he couldn't entirely let go of being on high alert
for an attacker. That thought had crossed her mind before, but knowing him better now, she couldn't quite believe he was manufacturing all of this out of some highly
developed sense of paranoia.

Mainly because he was right. Someone had smashed
the rear window of her car. Someone had used an illicit
poison and might not realize it likely couldn't be traced
to him. Someone might indeed think they had something
to fear, and smashing her window might have been an
attempt to scare her off.

Maybe she should scare more easily, but that wasn't
the world she came from. Not at all. She might have more
to learn from Jerrod than she realized.

"How serious do you think this threat is?"

"Probably minimal unless you happen to get close to
something. But since we wouldn't know what's close, we
might not know when we're getting into trouble."

"What a thought."

"It's one I'm used to." He shrugged a little and she
saw the hitch in his movement.

"More ibuprofen?" she asked. "My doc said it's okay
to take four at a time if I need to."

"Standard prescription dose. I'm okay. It'll get to work

in a minute." He paused. "Allison, I'm honestly not trying to frighten you. And I'm sure you must think I'm as
near a nut as makes no difference."

"I don't think that at all!" In an instant, flashover occurred. She went from the deep-seated ache he caused
in her to anger. "I think you're an experienced soldier.
I gather the stuff you did was like special ops, SEALs,
whatever. In an agency that nobody knows about, which
I guess means your missions were even tougher. But I
do *not* think you're a nut. God, I hate this."

"Hate what?"

"We've been bouncing all over the emotional map
today. I think I hurt you at least twice...."

"No way," he interrupted.

"Hush. My reaction to your weapons. That couldn't
have felt good. And then I said something a little while
ago and I saw your reaction. Or felt it. Regardless, up
and down, back and forth and now you're calling yourself a nut?"

"It must seem that way."

"Well, it doesn't. There's some adjusting going on
here for both of us. All I know is, I'm worn out. Back
and forth, up or down, who knows? I'm questioning myself, my feelings, my thoughts.... How about a break?"

"Sure," he answered. "What kind of break?"

"Well, that's the problem, isn't it? I'm starting to feel
like one of the six hundred riding into the valley of death
in that poem about the Light Brigade."

His jaw dropped a little. Clearly, she had astonished
him.

"You know," she said, "cannon to the front of them,
cannon to the left... However it goes. Danger everywhere."

"Oh, man. I didn't want to make you feel that way."

"Of course you didn't. And it's not you. At least not all you. Unfortunately, that's how I'm feeling and I need a break."

He hesitated. "So what kind of break do you want? Cards? TV? Just find a chair and read a book?"

Escape wouldn't be enough, she realized. She needed to deal with something. Act. Take care, somehow, of at least one of the things that was plaguing her.

"I don't know," she said. "It's the middle of the night, and I need action. But there's none to take right now." Well, there was one thing, a voice inside her whispered. One question she could get answered, one she could put to rest. Unless it cratered her even more.

But that was out of the question. His back was hurting. Damn, the frustration inside her had begun to reach a boiling point.

Then it struck her how badly she was overreacting. What had really happened? She'd learned something about herself, painful to be sure, but necessary. She'd faced an internal terror that she had needed to face. Ordinarily she coped well with things, so why was she having trouble coping today?

The reason sat across from her. She could deal with it all except for wanting him so badly the ache nearly overwhelmed her. Even the possible threat he sensed pursuing her wasn't troubling her as much as being near him.

Skewed priorities, she tried to tell herself, but knew they weren't skewed at all. She needed to take one final step to heal that hole inside herself, and what better time than when the man she wanted was here and, if he was correct, she might be facing a very real danger. One that had him concerned enough to not want to leave her alone.

A week ago he couldn't even say hi to her. Now he was planted in her house like a knight-errant ready to go into battle carrying her scarf. Worse, he might be right to be concerned.

What if I never have another chance to find out?

Jerrod watched the emotions play over her face, for once finding her nearly unreadable. He could tell she was troubled, and he hated to think he'd made her life harder, but he couldn't ignore the parameters of the situation.

He had instincts honed from long years in the worst situations imaginable. That he still lived and breathed owed to those instincts, owed to trusting them. They were telling him that something was seriously wrong, that some kind of noose might be closing in. That some threat was stalking her.

It barely rippled across his thoughts that he might be the one at risk because he had come to a place where he knew no one, and few enough even knew he was here. Nor did he have any reason to think anyone wanted *him*.

But it was possible. Anything was possible. He closed his eyes, feeling for the shape of the problem, little as he knew. Letting gut instincts add themselves to knowledge. No, any way he looked at it, Allison seemed to be at highest risk here, and he honestly didn't know enough to gauge just how bad that risk might be.

So, until proved otherwise, he had to assume the worst case. Wisdom from long experience advised him that it seldom paid to assume anything else. Best to be prepared for the worst.

When he opened his eyes, he saw Allison looking at him. Something in her expression… He could almost feel the aching need in her, one answered immediately by his own body.

It would be wrong, so wrong, that he knew he couldn't live with himself. He had nothing to offer, nothing to promise. Every cell in his body might be hammering for satisfaction. With every breath she drew he couldn't help noticing the rise of her breasts. When she moved, his gaze wanted to fix on her rounded hips. And when she smiled…

She hadn't done a single deliberately provocative thing, which ought to warn him off, yet everything about her seemed to provoke his most primal needs. When had that last happened to him, if ever?

He was a man accustomed to women wanting him, women who knew how to offer themselves, how to flirt, how to get his attention and rev his motor. This woman wasn't at all like that. She practically broadcast her own innocence, even though it was plain to him that she wanted him, too.

But wanting wasn't enough this time. He'd had to break a lot of rules in his life in order to accomplish his missions, but he still had a few bright lines he hadn't crossed, and he wasn't about to start crossing them now.

The air between them was almost pregnant with need, and yet she didn't seem to know how to protect herself. How to take charge of what was trying to happen between them. So he had to do it, somehow, and he wasn't much more experienced at that than she.

How did you put a halt to something like this without hurting a woman? She had already admitted how exposed and vulnerable she felt, and while she didn't blame him for that, it remained he had managed to stir all of this up for her. So how the hell did you unstir a pot without just stirring it more?

He never should have kissed her either time. The memory of her mouth against his created longings deeper than thought. Hell, those two kisses had almost seemed to touch his soul.

Spending all afternoon and evening alone with her, talking with her, holding her… In one day he'd gotten a taste of the kind of life he'd never really known, at least not since leaving for the academy over fifteen years ago. It was not a life he had pined for, either. At least he thought he hadn't.

But now… Hell. Using his back as an excuse, he rose. "I've got to move." Pacing helped calm him. It always had. Even in the most dangerous of situations, as long as he was marching, calm accompanied him. It didn't mean he wasn't fully alert, but it was more useful to be calm. Always.

Her kitchen was big enough, so he didn't leave the room, although he could have expanded his path. Somehow he felt that might be the wrong thing to do at this juncture, and he always listened to such feelings.

"So," he said. The short circle he was marching granted him a bit of detachment with more on the way.

"Yes? So?"

"So," he said again. "I'm trying to figure out how to tell you more about me."

"It's none of my business, Jerrod."

He halted and looked straight at her—maybe not the wisest move. Emotions flickered in her brown eyes, the endless play of minute changes on her face, all of it seemed to be broadcasting her uncertainty, her desires, her fears. If he was mixed up, she beat him by a mile right then. It would be a smart thing to keep in mind.

"Yeah, it's your business," he said. "I'm planting myself in the middle of your life. I'm scaring you, probably in more than one way and… Well, you need to know something about me. It only seems right. You've trusted me in some pretty important ways. Now you get to decide if that trust is misplaced."

"But…"

He just shook his head and resumed his pacing. "I can't give you details. Classified. I can't even tell you what countries I've been to. Classified. Or how many languages I speak. Classified. Covert really means covert. I can tell you that you might have come across the results of some of my work in the papers, but I can't tell you any more than that. I can tell you that you can count the number of people who actually know what I did, apart from my team members, on your fingers and toes, and many of those in the know don't even know who I am."

"The invisible man," she murmured.

"Damn near. For my protection. For theirs. I had a public role for general consumption that had nothing to do with what I really did."

"So you could be at risk?" Her voice sounded thin.

"It's possible, but not likely. I was deeply buried. Very deeply buried. I can tell you that I infiltrated solo on a number of occasions because it would have been dangerous to place additional operatives."

He glanced at her and saw she looked horrified. Some part of him took savage satisfaction in that. Maybe she'd toss him out on his butt and he could protect her from afar. That would certainly protect her from *him*.

"Anyway," he went on, still pacing, "I did a lot of

things you're better off not knowing about. You'll sleep better not understanding some of the dangers we've faced over the years, or how they were handled."

"What you said about preserving innocence."

"Exactly. It's important. But I'm a dangerous man when I need to be."

"I'd already guessed that," she murmured. "Why are you telling me this?"

"Because I owe it to you. Because you need to know who and what you're dealing with. I spent a lot of years doing things that will never appear on a résumé. Things that don't qualify me for a normal job."

She appeared almost sad as she gazed at him. "How do you feel about that?" she asked.

He pulled the chair back, spun it around and straddled it, stretching his back by leaning forward as far as he could. "How do I feel about it? Why?"

"Because I want to know."

He paused only a moment before hitting her with the hard truth. "I'm proud of what I did. It needed doing and I did it. Period."

"Good."

He arched a brow. "Good?"

"I'm glad you're proud of what you did. Is that so hard to understand? I may be a country girl, but I'm not totally innocent. It would be nice if we lived in a world where no one had to do what you did, but we don't. I get it."

If he'd been hoping she'd send him packing, clearly that hope was gone. He stared at her, thinking she probably couldn't guess the smallest part of the missions he had been sent on, then realized that while she might not have clear images of them, she at least seemed to sense they had often been ugly. Not always, but often.

Then he spoke a thought aloud, one he'd never given voice to before. "I wonder how much intentions make up for dirty hands." The thought that sometimes came to him in the middle of the night, the question he would never be able to answer.

She flew from her chair and came around the table, leaning against his back and hugging him around his shoulders. "Oh, Jerrod," she whispered. "Don't ask yourself that."

"I do sometimes. Inevitably. The problem is I'm not fit to be my own judge and jury. I did what I had to do. I trusted that I wasn't being misused, and that's the end of it."

"You saved lives," she said almost insistently.

"I know I did. Most of the time, anyway."

The heat mushroomed in him again. Her embrace felt like a balm in some inexplicable way, but it also ignited the very fire he'd been trying to extinguish with his honesty.

He could feel the firm mounds of her breasts against his back like burning coals. The warmth of her arms wrapped around him made him crave her skin against his. God, he was beginning to walk around in a permanent state of arousal, all because of one woman and her enchanting, intriguing nature and smile.

He squeezed his eyes shut and fought for the self-control that was so deeply ingrained in him that he couldn't believe he was in danger of losing it.

"So," he said, trying to lighten the moment before it turned into a nuclear explosion of need, "you still want to hang with me?"

"Why wouldn't I?"

But she seemed to get the message. Her arms began

to loosen and he felt her warmth against his back begin to withdraw.

Funny, but that withdrawal seemed to push him over the tipping point.

Ignoring his back, he twisted and rose at the same time, swinging his leg over the chair and catching her around the waist so they stood face-to-face.

"I'm dangerous," he reminded her.

A fleeting second passed before he saw a smile begin to dawn on her face. "I know."

That was apparently working on her like an aphrodisiac. "What am I going to do with you?"

"I can think of a few things."

It was the first coquetry he'd seen in her, and it fascinated him. Was this the pre-Lance Allison peeking out? "I'm sure you can. And I can think of a hundred more. Every single one of them delicious."

He wrapped her tightly in his arms then, pulling her up against his body, leaving her absolutely no doubt about how much he wanted her. Her eyes widened, then her lids drooped almost sleepily. She was his for the taking, but for once in his life he felt no triumph at a conquest.

Now he definitely had to protect her from himself. Maybe from her own self, as well.

Bending, he kissed her gently, and felt her worm immediately closer as her arms wrapped around him. She had made up her mind. But he hadn't.

Battling every urge that demanded he do otherwise, he lifted his head. Holding her with just one arm now, he found her breast through her sweatshirt and rubbed his hand over it gently. It was every bit as full and firm as he had thought. A soft sound of pleasure escaped her. Everything inside him demanded he press on, except for one sane voice that reminded him how vulnerable she was.

"I'm sorry," he murmured. "Not tonight. I just can't tonight."

He dropped his hand from her breast and waited for her eyes to flutter open. "Your back?" she whispered.

He nodded once, then kissed her again before letting her go. It was one of the hardest things he had ever done.

"I'm sorry," he said again.

She surprised him. Rather than take umbrage, she reached out to cup his cheek, running her finger over the scar there. "Knife?" she asked.

"Yeah."

"Let me get you a heating pad. It might help. Then I'm going to bed." Her smile was crooked. "This day has worn me out."

It had worn him out, too, he realized. An emotional lifetime had passed in just a few hours.

Chapter 8

Long before dawn, the hunter returned to his mountain aerie. He would be ready if they came again, and he'd thought of a way to separate them. Taking down two was not in his plan, and he was sure he could fix that.

Humming, he drove into the mountains and began his hike. Parking a few miles away from his base was the most minimal of precautions, and he'd taken more careful ones than that. When he left, no one would even be able to guess that he'd spent so much time in that cave.

When he left, he was going to feel ever so much better, too. So he continued to hum as he hiked.

Allison woke in the morning feeling like hell. For all she'd been worn out the night before, she hadn't found sleep easily. All the things she had learned about herself insisted on roiling around in her mind, and desire for

Jerrod wasn't very far away. She'd engaged in an internal battle, and every time she'd thought sleep was right around the corner, an adrenaline rush would hit her with anxiety as a thought surfaced, or a feeling drove her mind in the wrong direction.

Then, too, her dreams had been plagued. Not by fear, but by passion. She'd awakened so many times in a state of aching arousal that even as she sat up in the morning she felt astonished. Jerrod caused her to have the most unabashedly erotic dreams.

The shame of it was, she thought with sardonic self-amusement, that all that arousal hadn't been enough to assuage her. It had just ratcheted everything up until she wondered if her own body was going to turn into her worst enemy.

He had kissed her, she told herself. He had held her a few times. Then he had backed away, and she wasn't at all sure he had done so because he was in pain.

He might say he wanted her, but she was beginning to wonder. She'd all but offered herself on a silver platter last night, and then he had retreated.

So maybe there was something wrong with her?

She heard him in the kitchen. Impossible not to notice when she had lived alone so long. She hoped the couch hadn't been hard on his back. She headed for the bathroom, wearing her fleece robe, and could tell by the humidity that he'd showered this morning.

It was the only way she could tell. He had cleaned up so well after himself that she wondered if the room sparkled more than usual. Fresh towels even hung neatly on the rack. Well, she thought, there was something to be said for military training.

By the time she dressed and headed for the kitchen,

good smells filled the air. Apparently he'd found the stash of bacon she kept in the freezer. The aroma made her mouth water and she figured she'd work off the excess fat in a little while by hiking around a cold mountainside.

"Good morning," he said. He stood at the stove, cooking the bacon. The carton of eggs waited nearby.

"Good morning." The late-winter dawn wasn't yet lighting the world, making the moment seem somehow out of time. He looked so good in his jeans and an untucked flannel shirt. She wouldn't have minded waking to that sight every morning. "Can I help?"

"Toast would be great. Carbs for the hike."

"So lots of it? How many slices do you want?"

"I'm a man of big appetites." He astonished her with a wink, then returned to the bacon.

"How's your back?" she asked as she pulled the toaster out and set it on the counter. There was a fresh loaf of rye bread in the breadbox that she suspected wouldn't survive this meal.

"Much better."

"Good. I was worried about the couch."

"I was fine. You have a comfortable floor."

Aghast, she turned to him. "Not the floor!"

"When my back hurts, a board would be welcome. The floor was great, and the blankets were warm. I slept like a baby."

She wished she could say the same. Stifling a sigh, she popped two slices of bread into the toaster and pressed the button. "So we're walking the grid today?"

"As much as we can or need to. I'm going to be scouting around, like I said. If this creep is watching, I'll pick up his sign. I wonder if he realizes that taking an interest like this is the surest way to get himself caught."

"He probably wasn't counting on you."

A chuckle escaped him. "Probably not."

She switched her attention from him to the toaster. Back and forth like a Ping-Pong ball. Unfortunately, she couldn't ignore the toaster. It had been burning her toast from time to time.

"Jerrod?"

"Hmm?"

"Seriously now, just how much danger do you think I'm in?"

She waited while he forked bacon onto a plate covered with a paper towel then started putting more in the pan.

"You know I can't say for sure."

"I know."

"You want a threat estimate?"

"Is that what you call it?"

"Yeah. Okay, here it is. A week ago, after you explained how hard it would be to track this guy, I was only mildly worried. I actually got a little less so after your car was bashed."

That surprised her. "Why?"

"Because I figured he just wanted to scare you off. Scaring people off suggests someone who doesn't want to do anything really bad."

She nodded and popped up the toast. It was ready. In went two more pieces, then she reached for the butter dish and a knife. "What's changed?"

"You keep going back. That probably changes it for him, too. Maybe you're close to finding something he can't hide."

"Oh, I find that hard to believe. It would be easy to remove the poison from the area."

"But not from the animals. What would happen if you found an entire wolf pack poisoned?"

"An investigation," she said drily. "Pretty much like the one I'm doing now. People in these parts are more worried about livestock than what happens to wolves. We have a few who'd erupt over it but I'm not sure it would get anywhere near as much attention as Jake Madison losing two cows, frankly."

"Interesting." He absorbed the information, and though she could see only the side of his face, she could tell that he was adding that into whatever calculations he was doing on his "threat assessment."

"Does that change your mind?" she asked finally.

"About the threat? No."

"Try explaining to me, please."

"It's hard to explain. Sorry. It's an accumulation of things. My training, my experience. At some point it boils down to the gut. The feel I'm getting from a situation. I can't always put it into words."

"But you trust your gut feelings?"

"I'm still alive."

That was a pretty stark statement. As she made more toast, she decided that given her own lack of experience in this kind of thing, she'd be safer trusting his gut than ignoring it. If he happened to be wrong, no harm would be done.

"I'll be honest," he said. "I can't predict. But I'm getting a bad feeling. It's almost like it's in the air."

"Because you felt watched?"

"Not just that. Something else is bugging me. I'd gladly tell you if I could. Maybe it's just that this character isn't going away. He really, really ought to just crawl back into his hole, don't you think?"

"It would be smart."

"But he's not. Something is working on him, and he can't let this go. That's enough right there. But it's more and I wish I could put my finger on it for you."

"How in the world do you evaluate something this vague? I'm a scientist. I want my numbers. I want stuff to be orderly. I want proof or disproof."

"You want facts, and I'm sorry I can't give them to you. But events have shapes."

"Shapes?"

He spread one hand as if he didn't have the words, then began flipping the bacon in the pan. "Shapes," he repeated. "Hard to describe. It's almost like I see vectors."

"Vectors, I get."

"I'm sure you do." He flashed a smile her way. "But it's not just lines of force. It's a feeling about how they might go together, adding up to what I call the shape of a situation. It's fluid. It changes as I get new information, but right now I'm not liking the shape of this at all. So today while you're taking samples and looking for dead critters, I'm going to do a wider sweep, looking for signs of whoever is so interested in you. That'll be more information to add to my assessment. I promise you one thing, though. I won't be more than a shout away from you at any time. I'll be moving around you constantly."

"A one-man encirclement?" she tried to say lightly.

"Pretty much." But he was dead serious. "It's possible, Allison. Remember, we're up against somebody who can't move any faster than I can. He's no ghost. He's a human. As such he'll leave signs and probably make noise no matter how quiet he thinks he is."

"Unless he's like you?"

Jerrod didn't answer. She once again saw that stillness come over him, as if some thought arrested him, but before she could really be certain, he finished the last of the bacon and was cracking eggs into the pan.

"Just one egg for me," she said quickly.

"Don't be ridiculous. We've got a hard hike and a lot of cold ahead of us. Load up on carbs and fat. You'll be glad you did."

Forty-five minutes later, they were ready to leave. Jerrod ran next door and came back with a lightweight backpack. Her own was ready for short mountain hikes. She pulled out a box of energy bars and split them with him.

This time when he donned his pistol and knife, she didn't look away. In fact, she almost wished she were armed herself. Her thoughts strayed to the shotgun that had been her dad's, tucked away in the attic, then dismissed it. It hadn't been touched or cleaned in so long it was probably next to useless. Not that she wanted to shoot anything. Her dad had loved hunting in the fall, but she'd never developed a taste for it.

Jerrod filled his own pack with water bottles. "I'll keep you supplied," he said.

Good enough for her. What a strange morning, to awaken with unsatisfied desires having plagued her all night into a world that seemed to come right out of a movie.

Well, her life had been askew almost since the moment she'd spoken to this man for the first time. She was getting a glimpse of his world, probably a very minor and mild one, but it was utterly different from her own.

No wonder he was having a problem making the transition to her world. It was almost like watching opposing forces collide.

Certainly she felt as if her entire world had upended,

and as if everything she had once found so familiar had taken on an unfamiliar appearance. As if she had taken one step to the side of reality and was seeing an almost identical but parallel universe. She wondered if her world would ever feel the same again.

Jerrod once again followed her in his own truck. He seemed determined that they have two vehicles, although from her perspective it seemed wasteful. He must have a reason, though. He didn't seem like a man who did much without a reason.

Except possibly kissing her. Given the way he had withdrawn last night, she wondered why he had kissed her in the first place. As she jolted over roads beginning to roughen with the early-winter cycle of freeze and thaw, she touched her lips and wondered if she had failed at even something as small as a kiss. Or maybe a kiss was a big deal, and she'd gotten an F.

Yeah, *his* kiss was a big deal, she thought almost sadly. His kiss had set her on fire like a torch, even though it had been gentle and undemanding. None of the fancy stuff that Lance had found so essential. Nope. Just the gentlest of kisses from a surprisingly warm and soft mouth.

Maybe her problem was that she needed gentleness as much as she needed kindness. Many more of these discoveries and she was going to start feeling like an open wound.

Oh, cut it out, she told herself sternly. If the man didn't want her, he didn't want her. That didn't really say anything about her at all. He hardly knew her. Maybe she wasn't his type. Maybe he got turned on by buxom blondes.

The image that popped into her head then dispelled

her fleeting sadness and made her giggle. She envisioned the worst caricature of a bad dye job and an overdone breast augmentation, as if from a comedic movie. Somehow she doubted Jerrod's taste ran to that extreme.

She took them by a different route as the sun lifted above rosy clouds to the east. Since they were going to stay on the mountain, it seemed pointless to cross the river again at the Madison place.

She had an inkling of what Jerrod had meant by the shape of a situation. Thinking about how the two poisoned cows had turned up on the Madison ranch, and how the apparent bait had been nearby, she was getting a shape in her own mind, one she wouldn't be able to complete without knowing if that toxin was stronger somewhere else.

But she couldn't imagine why anyone in this county would attack Jake Madison. He was generally very well liked, and between growing up here and having been a cop for the past decade, he knew just about everyone in the county. She couldn't think of a reason anyone would want to hurt him like this. And face it, the loss of two of his cows was a hurt. He wasn't working two jobs because he was in tall clover.

While she didn't try to stay plugged in to the local gossip, a lot of it came her way regardless. She knew Jake's fiancée's father, Fred Loftis, was a nasty man, and he'd made no secret of the fact that he felt shamed by his daughter living with Jake. But Jake and Nora were engaged. Everyone knew it and kind of shrugged off Loftis's complaints.

Given that she'd long thought of Fred Loftis as a disturbingly ugly man, she supposed it was possible he'd placed the poison. But that went right out the window considering that Jerrod was sure someone was watching them. Her. Loftis wouldn't have time for that. He had a business to run and a church to rule. So that shape just plain didn't fit what was going on now.

She wondered what Jerrod would say to her shaping of the events, but given that it was so hazy and incomplete, she brushed aside any thought of telling him.

They crossed a narrow wooden bridge over the creek, then drove down a snowy but still passable road on its far side. She had to drive slowly to avoid skidding, but for once in her life she was strangely reluctant to arrive.

She realized she had grown afraid of whatever was troubling Jerrod. Given what he had told her, she was sure he was a man very clued in to reality, not one to go off into fantasyland. As he said, he was still alive.

Glancing into her rearview mirror, she saw once again the shattered glass and the duct tape holding it together. At the time it had seemed easy to blame it on some weird student prank or hazing, maybe because that fit better with what she expected from the world. And maybe that wasn't very realistic.

Bad enough that for the first time in her life she didn't want to take a walk in the woods.

They pulled into a lightly wooded area where they could turn around, and parked. It was near enough to the area she wanted to check out, and she feared they might not find another place to turn around on this wagon track. She supposed hunters and hikers used it from time to time, but this was state land, and clearly this road didn't get a lot of attention.

Jerrod joined her beside her car and helped her settle her backpack. Then she pulled out her small sample-gathering kit, slung the strap over her shoulder and gave him the brightest smile she could manage.

"I'm ready."

He smiled back, but she noticed his gaze was already on the march, scanning constantly, skimming over her and returning to the woods around.

"We're about a half mile from where you wanted to start your search," he said. "Still up for it?"

"Absolutely. It's essential to find out if this toxin is anywhere else other than the Madison ranch. If it isn't, I guess that would answer some questions, too."

"I'd think so." They started walking along the road. In the distance, across the river, she could barely make out the small dot of Jake Madison's barn. At least that was what she thought it was. He owned a big spread. From this distance she might be looking at some outbuilding she had never seen before.

As they walked, she paused occasionally to take a sample from the stream side of the road. God, she hoped they all came back negative. This poison was so insidious, it was terrifying to think of it being loose in the environment.

In an instant, everything that had become muddled in the past twenty-four hours snapped into clear focus. She had a mission, an important one, and everything else could wait.

The morning sun was low enough to cast light beneath the firs and shower the patchy snow of the hillside with gold. Here and there stands of deciduous trees stood looking like depressed skeletons, waving only an occasional flag of their autumn color. Beauty and quiet filled the morning.

But something evil might lurk here underfoot. Or in

the woods, given what Jerrod suspected. She was reminded of it when they parted ways: she to begin pacing her grid and taking samples, he to scout around her.

He walked away as if they were merely casual acquaintances, turning to call back, "See you in a few hours."

But she knew that wasn't true. He wasn't going to be that far from her. He had promised. A show for someone watching, maybe?

The back of her neck prickled, and frantic butterflies erupted in her stomach. Never before had she seen these woods as treacherous.

Now she did.

Jerrod turned into the woods, and soon they closed behind him. He paused, getting a feel for the air, tasting it and smelling it for human scents. He'd learned long ago that people left scents behind them, and while he was no bloodhound, it was possible to detect, however faintly, the odors of sweat or an aftershave if you trained yourself to pay attention.

He was listening, too, for any sounds that didn't fit with the forest.

Nothing. He scanned the area, saw no movement that mattered then began a silent stalking in the woods. A few yards up he picked up Allison's scents. Good, she was close.

He scanned the ground with every step he took, picking up signs. He could tell where animals had passed easily enough. They left small paw and hoofprints and didn't care if they disturbed needles or leaves.

He did. He kept to the pine needles and avoided the leaves as much as he could, taking care not to even twist his feet as he moved. The ground was loamy, but when he glanced back he could see that his footprints were rapidly disappearing as the loam rebounded. If a man wanted to track him, he'd have to get close first.

Good.

He swept back and forth, looking for the dead animals that had Allison so concerned but also keeping an eye out for signs of human passage. As he went, he occasionally paused to arrange sticks or leaves in a way that would tell him if someone had passed by.

After a bit, the ground grew firmer, less resilient. Any tracks here would last awhile.

There was almost a natural path to follow, he noticed. Maybe a game trail. It wanted to pull him along, and it would have been easy to stick to it, but he was doing a sweep, which meant he stepped off the trail, stepped over underbrush and looked elsewhere.

Someone had been up here. He knew it as sure as he breathed. They'd been watched twice. It might be meaningless, but he refused to bet Allison's life on that, especially when she had said hunters had been told to stay away because of the toxin.

He couldn't imagine the kind of mind that would want to unleash something like that on the environment, so it was probably someone who had no idea of how far that poison could spread and how. He knew now, though. How could he not, when Allison had told him? It had probably been the talk of the town since the cows died, too, between everyone knowing Madison and the warnings to the hunters.

His mind kept wandering to Allison and he had to keep yanking it back. He needed his full attention on the task at hand, but his thoughts kept drifting to the way she had felt in his arms. Curvy, soft, yielding. Like a woman should, he thought, although it was hard to tell in her preferred clothing. That was another thing that got to him—the way she dressed. It seemed more like a defense.

He'd felt her curves pressed against him; he had a mental image of what lay beneath that baggy fleece, and figured a confident woman would flaunt it at least a bit.

She hid, and now he knew why. That ex of hers had ransacked her good. Damaged her deeply. He'd have loved to give the guy a piece of his mind, but such wishes were useless.

All he knew was that a beautiful woman was avoiding half of life because some man had gutted her. Over the past day or so, he'd watched her face up to how deeply she had been wounded, but he doubted she knew the parameters herself, even now.

But he could see them, maybe because he was on the outside. She wanted him, and last night she'd been on the edge of taking the leap when he had stopped her. His back had been an excuse because the simple truth was that as much as he wanted her himself, he didn't want to add to the stack of wounds she already had.

What the hell could he promise a woman right now? He'd been a gypsy for the past six months, his life had given him a mountain of unmarketable skills unless he wanted to turn into a mercenary and while he was probably getting ready to put down a root or two, inside, part of him would always be rootless. His home had been an organization, not a place.

But Allison called to him with every breath she took. Watching the thoughts and feelings flit over her face fascinated him. He hoped she never lost that openness.

Pay attention! The alert in his head dragged him back

from the precipice of thinking about making love to Allison. Imagining removing her clothes, imagining her initial shyness until she realized how desirable she was. Imagining that she would soon lose her shyness and want to be a full participant.

Pay attention!

Everything drained from his brain except the woods around him. Had he smelled something? Heard something?

He froze, waiting, extending his senses. Again a whiff of Allison on the air. But was there something else?

Nothing else came to him. As far as his nose and eyes could tell, the two of them were alone out here. But at some level he didn't quite believe it.

He was off the game trail, just beside it. He took another cautious step, careful not to crush undergrowth in a way that would leave a trail. One step.

Then he saw it and his blood chilled.

Moments later he heard a gunshot.

Allison had been picking her way up the mountainside, making no particular attempt to be quiet, focusing as much as she could on the tedious task of taking the occasional sample and wondering if she was wasting her time. Probably. Given the way things went, the toxin would continue to dissipate; she'd be out here again eventually to make sure it was completely gone, and that would be the end of it.

No excitement, really. Not for her, other than that she was glad to help her neighbors by finding where it was safe for them to allow their livestock to roam. She hoped she'd get some results from the state lab tomorrow. If everything came up clean except a small spot around where the cows had died, then...

Then what? she asked herself. Would that mean Jake Madison had been deliberately targeted or that he was just the unfortunate victim of something that had been done far away from here?

Given that the so-called bait had turned out to be a raccoon, she was definitely concerned that there was something else contaminated, probably up here. But what if she found nothing? And even if she did, by some stroke of luck, would even that tell them where the poison chain had begun? Of course not. She stifled a sigh. She liked answers and solutions, but doubted she was going to get any this time.

None of this really made sense. It didn't even make sense that Jake's dogs hadn't done the doggie thing and dined on the dead raccoon. They were fine, but there should have been no reason for them not to eat the carrion. Had they seen something that had made them wary? Wary enough to drive the other cattle away and ignore the free dinner? She wished dogs could talk. She tipped her head back, looking up the mountainside, thinking that if they found anything on this slope they were going to need a whole team out here to identify the contaminated area. All one person could do was take occasional samples that wouldn't delineate the entire problem.

She unhooked her radio from her belt and pushed the GPS button. Immediately, it gave her location on the grid they had worked out last night. Time to turn right and start down again.

Last night. Just wow, she thought with a secret smile. She'd have liked it better if Jerrod hadn't backed away, but she'd known he was in pain. She probably should have been more cautious herself. Not because of him, but because she was so emotionally worn out from yesterday's discoveries about herself. She hadn't guessed how tiring facing a little self-knowledge could be. Of course, it wasn't understanding herself better that had tired her, it was the emotional storm that had swept through her.

Funny, but she felt better today. More comfortable inside herself. Almost as if a spring breeze had blown through and swept away some cobwebs.

She still had to be careful of Jerrod, though. The guy had nothing to hold him here, and she suspected that his leaving eventually might be painful if she became too intensely involved. Making love with him, tempting as it was, might simply result in ripping the scab off a wound she had only just realized hadn't healed yet.

On the other hand, he might just wipe all that crap away.

She could have laughed at herself. Out here in the woods, away from Jerrod, it was so easy to be sensible. As her disturbed night had proved, though, and after practically offering herself to him, she knew full well at least part of her didn't want to be sensible. No, she wanted to jump in with both feet, enjoy the kind of lovemaking she had once imagined and…

Her mind drew up short. The lovemaking she had once imagined? What kind of litmus test was that? Little in her life had lived up to her imagination. Lovemaking probably wouldn't, either. But from what Jerrod had said, she gathered it might be better than what she had known with Lance.

His words about selfish lovers echoed inside her. Had Lance been selfish? Looking back, painful though it was, she thought it was entirely possible. He hadn't spent much time on her or on lovemaking after the first seduction when she'd gotten high as a kite only to crash with disappointment when it was over.

And what had Lance done when she'd been left high and dry? He'd said, "You're a virgin. You'll get it."

She'd never really gotten it, she supposed, and he hadn't seemed to care all that much. She shut up about it when he finally said, "What's wrong with you? Are you frigid?"

Maybe there *was* something deeply wrong with her. Maybe she was a fool to believe what Jerrod had said. Well, there was only one way to find out, and she wasn't sure she should take the risk. On the other hand, avoiding it was getting her nowhere.

Honesty compelled her to admit to herself she wouldn't even be considering this if Jerrod hadn't managed to arouse her so much. The attraction was one thing. She could deal with that. But those kisses? Needs long tamped down now raged freely in her.

So what was she going to do about it?

She twisted to take another sample container out of her shoulder bag. As she did so, a shard of wood hit her in the cheek. Turning her head swiftly, she saw the groove in the tree trunk beside her, then heard the gun report.

She froze. "Hey!" she shouted. Damn it, she was wearing an orange vest over her coat and an orange hat. How much more did she need to do to prove she wasn't wild game?

An instant later, something crashed into her back and pushed her down on the ground.

"Don't move," she heard Jerrod mutter in her ear.

"It's just a hunter," she started to say, but his hand clapped over her mouth.

Anger surged in her but before she could struggle, he whispered, "I need to listen."

So she nodded into his hand and let herself relax. Well, as much as she could when a bullet had just grazed a tree not six inches from her head.

After what seemed an eternity, he began to lever himself off her. "Don't move," he said so quietly she almost didn't hear him.

Slowly he rose up. Twisting her head a bit, she could see him straighten beside the tree and look at the graze mark. Apparently it told him something because he squatted beside her.

"It came from upslope," he said, keeping his voice low. "Did you notice much time between the tree being struck and the report?"

"A little."

He stared out into the woods. "There's a good sightline here. Can you estimate how long?"

"Long enough that I snapped my head around and looked at the tree. It wasn't long. I was just starting to realize what happened when I heard the report. A second or two at most. It seemed like I barely shouted before you jumped me." She hesitated. "It was probably a stray bullet. It *is* hunting season. It might have come from anywhere."

He didn't answer, but she got the feeling he was working out another shape in his head, and it didn't involve some magical stray bullet.

"I've got to get you out of here," he said finally. "I'm not going to leave you here indefinitely while I try to track this guy down."

"I appreciate that." Her own tartness surprised her. Reaction to the scare? Hell, she hadn't had time to get scared. No, that was beginning now, as her heart accelerated and began to pound uncomfortably. Her mouth turned dry. "Can I get up now?"

"Wait." He was still talking quietly, so she clenched her hands into fists and forced herself to be still and silent, no easy thing to do when her heart was now pounding so hard she felt as if she couldn't catch her breath. The event had begun to hit her.

"I don't hear anyone approaching. The breeze is downhill, so I'd smell him, too, or at least his weapon. How good is your sheriff?" he asked finally.

"Good. Former DEA."

"Can you call him on your radio?"

"He set it up and told me to push the yellow button if I wanted help."

"Call him. And tell whoever you talk to that they may be entering a crime scene. I'm going to scout a little."

Oh, God. In an instant, her fear seemed to redouble. Every time she told herself that it had to be a stray bullet from a hunter, she couldn't help remembering how close it had come. Nor should any hunters be in the area, although it was possible the rangers had missed warning a few.

Of course, it was possible. She tried to shake herself out of her terror as she pushed the yellow button. Even as she did so, Jerrod somehow managed to disappear into the undergrowth and patchy snow. She felt agonizingly alone then.

Scout? Scout what, exactly? A few minutes ago she'd been ready to dress down the idiot who had shot her way but now she was afraid to lift her head.

A voice familiar to her answered. It was Velma the dispatcher, so iconic around here after all these years that no one would dream of asking her to retire. As clearly as she could manage, she explained what had happened.

"You stay put, I have your coordinates," Velma said. "It might be twenty minutes."

She wondered if she could stand waiting that long, or even if she would be able to move if she tried to. Fight or flight, they said about the adrenaline response. She didn't remember anything about paralysis.

All of a sudden her orange vest and cap seemed like a target. She wondered if she should try to strip them. She wondered if she should move at all. She wondered when Jerrod would come back. She wondered if she could possibly get any colder than she felt right then.

Her cheek lay on pine needles and began to itch. Moving slowly, she brought one hand up beneath it and rested on it. The guy must have heard her talking, had to know she was still okay, so why did she have to lie here? Because Jerrod didn't think that was any stray bullet.

Because he'd been looking at sightlines, and she didn't have to sit up to realize there weren't a whole lot of directions a bullet could have come from without impacting a tree before it got here, unless the shooter was awfully close.

She understood why he had asked about the lag time between the strike on the tree and the report. It could give him valuable information about how far away the shooter was. She remembered enough physics to understand.

At least her brain was still working. In fact, it was racing in time to her hammering heart. As the seconds dragged by like an eternity that had come to a full stop, she wished she could do the math in her head to occupy herself. But she didn't know the muzzle velocity of the gun that had been fired; she didn't know exactly how long had passed between the strike on the tree and the report. Without both those pieces of information, math would be useless.

So much for science. With the right information she could have known just how far away the shooter was.

Where was Jerrod? She knew he had the training to handle this kind of situation, but that didn't mean she wouldn't worry.

Her mind refused to stop processing. He knew how to handle a situation like this, she did not and she'd better just lie here like dead meat and wait this out.

Just as she thought every nerve in her body might snap from the tension, she saw him ease out of the undergrowth, keeping low. When he reached her, he hunkered down.

"He's gone," he said.

"If you're so sure of that, why are you keeping low and why am I still lying down?"

"Because I don't know what he's armed with. He's gone from where he shot at you, though." He held out his gloved hand and showed her a casing.

"What does that tell you?"

"Little enough. What do people usually use for hunting around here?"

"I don't know. Shotguns. Rifles. The sheriff would know better than I, since I've never been hunting."

"Well, this was a rifle."

"Maybe you shouldn't have taken the shell."

"I have a reason for taking it. I can show the sheriff exactly where I found it. From what I can tell, the guy hightailed it as soon as he shot. He left a mess of tracks where I found this."

"So maybe it was just a hunter." Adrenaline apparently lasted just so long. Her heart had nearly returned to a normal rhythm, and saliva moistened her mouth again. "Can I sit up?"

He leaned back against the tree, pulled his knees up and spread them. "Have a seat." He gave her a gentle tug as she started to rise, and the next thing she knew she was sitting between his legs, almost as if he was sheltering her with his own body. She wished she could feel his heat as she leaned back against his chest. God, she was cold.

"Are you okay?" he asked.

"Well, after my brush with death, I feel like this hat and vest are targets."

"Which makes this all the more curious." He left it at that. She didn't need him to spell it out. Her heart skittered nervously. Apparently she was far from finished with her reaction to this.

"Did he have a sightline?" she asked.

"Clear and straight."

That hit her like a solid punch in the gut. Her mind froze before the force of understanding. Someone had just tried to kill her.

She almost seemed to float out of herself then, as if she had detached from her body. This was unreal. Totally and completely unreal. As if it was a scene in a movie, she wanted to watch all this from the outside.

She managed to move lips that were stiff and unglue her tongue from the roof of her mouth long enough to say, "He's a lousy shot, then."

"Or not."

What in the world did he mean by that? Did she even want to know? She held the question back for later because she heard people coming up the slope at last. It sounded like several of them.

Gage Dalton and two deputies. Never in her life would she have imagined that she'd be this glad to see those men.

While Jerrod didn't appreciate becoming the instant focus of Gage Dalton's suspicions, he *did* appreciate that Dalton was a man who wouldn't be misled by appearances and wanted to know everything. It was the right way to go.

So he turned over his ID card, the one the military had given him when he separated. Dalton studied it, then looked at him. "Ready reserve?"

"Yes."

"I don't run into that very often." He looked Jerrod over. "Mind if I keep this card until I can check you out?"

"Help yourself."

Dalton questioned Allison first about events, the right way to go when the other witness was a stranger. One of the deputies wrote down everything, while the other stood like a guard, watching. Mostly keeping an eye on him.

Gage nodded when Allison finished outlining events then faced Jerrod again. "So you picked up the shell? Why didn't you leave it?"

"Because I don't know this guy's motives. I found something I need to show you, and I didn't want him to risk changing his mind and coming back for this. Then again…" Shoving his gloved hand into his pocket, Jerrod pulled it out and offered it.

One of the deputies snapped open a plastic bag and he dropped it in. Gage held it up, looking at it. "A normal hunting load, depending on what fired it." He passed it back to the deputy. "Show me where you found this."

"Sheriff," one of the young deputies hastened to say, "I'll do the climbing."

"Like hell," Gage answered. "You take Allison back down and get her warmed up. She looks blue."

Jerrod paused a moment, dropping a kiss on Allison's forehead. Her sherry-brown eyes tried to smile at him, but failed. "It'll be okay."

She nodded, then went with the deputy.

"Damn kids," Gage muttered as he walked upslope beside Jerrod, hitching with each step.

"What?" Jerrod asked.

"I may limp, but I'm not decrepit yet. I got a boy nearly as old as he is. Hell, I got more years limping than he's been alive."

Jerrod couldn't help but laugh quietly. "What happened?"

"Car bomb." That statement clearly closed off that line of inquiry. "Okay. You were sweeping around the area?"

"I was trying to. Looking for dead animals. Allison was concerned about whether there were any more."

Dalton nodded. "But you were doing more than that, weren't you?"

Jerrod hesitated.

"Come clean with me, man, and we'll get along a whole lot better."

Jerrod respected that, too. He was beginning to like Dalton. "Okay. I was a covert operative. That's all I can say about that."

"Which explains the ready reserve. So what do you think is going on?"

"Someone's been watching her. Or maybe me. At this point I can't tell anymore. Let's just say I was sure it was her. I was concerned about her safety after her rear window was bashed in. Hell, I was concerned before that. She keeps telling me it's impossible to trace this poison back to its source, but what if the guy who used it doesn't know that?"

Dalton nodded and paused for a moment. His face tightened a bit, then he blew a long breath and resumed the trek upward. "Yeah, the perp might not know that. So you were worried."

"Right. But that was it. Concerned. I came out here today to do two things—keep an eye on her and look for this watcher, whoever he is. At first I think she thought I was a little nuts about this, but then she had a thought, one I'd already had."

"Which was?"

"What if this guy is still using the poison out here? What if he was in a position to be caught red-handed? That might really put her at risk."

Gage halted and looked straight at him. "Why didn't you come to me with this?"

"A feeling? Because that's all I really had. A feeling that something isn't right, that someone is watching her out here and in town. I could have ignored the feeling in town, but not out here. But what would you have said to me?"

"That I had a feeling like that once, and to my everlasting sorrow I ignored it. But you couldn't have known that." Gage looked up. "How much farther?"

"Not much. Maybe fifteen yards."

"Good, because while I won't admit it to my deputies, climbing is a freaking pain in the back and leg for me. My wife keeps telling me I'm too stubborn for my own good."

"Stubbornness is all that keeps us going sometimes."

"No kidding."

At last they reached the point where the ground was disturbed, as if someone had taken off fast.

Gage spoke. "You didn't walk on that?"

"Hell, no." Jerrod pointed. "The shell was over here. I figure it ejected three or four feet."

"That's pretty powerful." Gage turned around and looked back down the hill. "I can see Dave from here. This was no accidental shot."

"No."

Gage looked around, rubbing his chin, then scratching at his burn-scarred cheek. "Okay. What strikes you about this, Mr. Covert Ops? Let's see if we agree."

"It looks as though someone inexperienced made a mistake and hightailed it as fast as he could."

"Looks?" Gage apparently latched on to his choice of words. A smart man.

"Looks," Jerrod repeated. "And it's just too damn convenient."

"What about the shell? You said you were afraid he'd come back for it."

"We don't know for sure what the guy is up to. But when I saw this, my mind began to run in another direction. I found something else earlier and I wanted to compare the casings."

"Casings?" Gage emphasized the plural. It was a moment before he spoke again. "It's scary, but I believe we're thinking alike. Run it by me."

"You looked downslope and you could see your deputy. Allison was wearing her orange vest and cap. There was no way on earth she could be mistaken for a deer or whatever else is in season. Ergo, he shot at her on purpose, but wanted to make it look like a mistake. So he messed the area up and left behind a casing. Very amateurish on the surface."

Gage nodded slowly. "But you know better."

"Let's just say I've set up a scene or two in my time just like this. It usually works."

"Yeah, it would. He wasn't counting on me, though."

"Meaning?"

"I believe you."

"I found something that may seal it. You up to a little more hiking?"

"Just tell me it's downhill." Gage paused. "And I don't think he's after Allison. We need to have a talk, you and me."

Chapter 9

Gage straightened after looking at what Jerrod had found earlier. He keyed his radio. "Velma, I'm going to need the team out here pronto."

After he got an affirmative, he looked at Jerrod. "You know, by showing me all this, you've made yourself look more suspicious."

Jerrod shrugged. "I don't care."

"Why? Because your military buddies will pull you out of jail?"

"Only if they need me, and that's not likely. No, I want to be sure Allison is safe. I want to get this guy. That's all."

After a moment Dalton nodded. "Get Allison home. God knows why, but I trust you."

Jerrod smiled faintly. "Because you know I've put

myself in the middle. Anything happens to her, I'm on the firing line."

"I may stop by later. Where will I find you?"

"At Allison's. I'm not going to leave her alone, not until we're sure she isn't the target."

"How likely is that?"

"Slim," Jerrod answered. "But as long as there's a remote chance…"

Dalton nodded. "Don't be surprised if a deputy or city cop knocks at random times until I check you out. You'll know you're clear when I send your ID back. Or when I stop by."

It went against Jerrod's grain to just turn this over, especially since he was getting a sense of the kind of opponent they were up against. He didn't see that he had much choice at the moment, though. The cops were going to clear all the evidence that they could find, and he'd only get in the way. Or maybe mess things up if he went haring off on his own. He got it, but didn't like it.

He'd be back out here, though. He had a score to settle, and he figured this guy was far from done.

Down by the river, he found Allison sitting in her SUV with the heat blasting. She didn't look happy, and he could only imagine the hell she had been going through, stuck here without knowing what was happening.

She rolled down her window as he approached, and the heat hit him in the face, just now making him aware how cold he had gotten.

"We can go home now."

"But what…"

He interrupted. "I'll tell you all about it. First let's get back and get some food. I need to warm up, too."

She nodded and rolled her window up again. The deputy who had been watching over her stepped out of the way and waved as they turned around and headed back.

She did need a meal, Allison thought. The power bars weren't doing it for her. In fact, they both could probably use one of Maude's steak sandwiches, a heap of fries and all the cholesterol they could pack in after this morning.

It bothered her that Gage had seemed so suspicious of Jerrod, and she wondered, inevitably, if she should be suspicious, too. What did she really know about him after all? But now it was Jerrod who was taking her home, not a deputy, and anyway, over the past couple of weeks, she had come to trust him herself. Was she afraid to trust her own instincts?

Maybe she should be, but when it came to Jerrod, her mind was made up. He drove behind her all the way back to town, like a watchdog, she thought. After this morning, she guessed she needed one. When she turned onto the side street and pulled in at Maude's, he pulled in right beside her. He was at her door before she could get out.

"You want to eat here?" he asked.

"I want to get home. Takeout, unless you object."

"If you know what you want, I'll get it."

"Thanks."

The cold and adrenaline had left her feeling tired, a very different kind of tired from yesterday. This would pass as soon as she had calories coursing through her blood and didn't have to shiver anymore.

Jerrod emerged from Maude's with a large paper bag. He acknowledged her with a nod, then slid into his truck. Moments later he was following her down the streets to her home. He pulled into his own driveway as usual, but arrived at her side, carrying the bag in one hand, as she fumbled with the key to her front door. Her hands wouldn't stop shaking.

"Damn it," she swore, not caring how petulant she sounded. "Enough already."

He took the key from her hand. "It's okay," he said as he unlocked the door and pushed it open for her. "It's been a rough day."

"No joke," she muttered. From wherever she had been earlier, she was now teetering on the brink of utter frustration and very real anger. She unzipped her snowmobile suit, cussed at the vest when it tried to tangle her up, and plopped on a living room chair to pull her boots off and the legs of the suit. She tossed her outerwear, left the suit in a heap and headed for the kitchen.

She wanted coffee *now*.

She had managed to remain rational and reasonable through being shot at, through questioning, through waiting, through the whole trip home, but now she was within the safety of her own walls, and the cauldron of emotions refused to be contained any longer.

Her hands still shook, whether from delayed shock or the fury that bubbled through her veins, she didn't know. She didn't care, either. She almost snapped at Jerrod when she rattled the coffeepot so hard against the water tap that he stepped in and took it from her.

"Sit," he said quietly. "Start eating. I'll deal with this."

"I can do it my damn self!"

"I know you can. But right now you don't have to. Eat."

She almost snarled, but did as she was told. The objective voice in the back of her brain tried to tell her to cool it, but she didn't want to cool it. Some idiot had shot at her and could have killed her. The image of that gash in the tree so close to her head kept popping up in her mind's eye like a crazy jack-in-the-box.

Oh, it was coming home now. No doubt. She sat at the table, looking at her trembling hands, feeling her stomach sink repeatedly. What had happened out there? Better yet, *why* had it happened? Even some crazed poisoner who was still using the toxin must realize how easy it would be to evade her in the woods. For God's sake, all she was doing was taking samples. It wasn't exactly going to work like following breadcrumbs home.

Jerrod put out two plates and utensils. He pulled boxes from the bag and began to open them. Steak sandwiches, a mountain of fries, a big salad.

"Hansel and Gretel would never have gotten home, you know."

"What?" Jerrod paused. She was almost hysterical enough to laugh at his frown of perplexity.

"Breadcrumbs," she said. "I was thinking of a trail of breadcrumbs. It's not like the poisoner is leaving one."

"Which, I take it, led you to Hansel and Gretel."

"Bingo. They'd never have made it home because the birds would have erased their trail."

"Ah. Probably." He put a half sandwich on her plate and pushed the salad her way. She scooped some onto her plate, relieved to see that her hands had grown steadier. "I wish I could be cool like you. I bet you don't get all crazy when you get shot at."

"Only because it's happened so often. You're doing just fine."

Only because it's happened so often. What a statement. If she weren't already such a mess, she might have felt more than mild astonishment that anyone could say that. "No, I'm not doing fine."

He left it alone, pouring coffee for both of them, then sitting across from her to eat. She knew she needed food, but her appetite seemed to have vanished along with her whole sense of personal safety. Shattered. Poof. Some-one had tried to kill her.

The anger surged again, strengthening her, and she bit into her sandwich. She had to keep her energy up and start dealing with all of this. "Somebody shot at me," she said, stating the obvious maybe because she needed to hear it out loud. "Tried to kill me. Why, for God's sake?"

"I don't think he wanted to kill you."

Her head snapped up. "You're joking. He shot at me."

"If you had stood where he stood… Well, if you'd used guns much in your life, you'd realize that a rea-sonably good marksman couldn't have missed you. It wouldn't even take a pro target shooter. No, he was aim-ing for that tree."

"You can't guarantee that."

"I think I can."

She stared at him in disbelief, as the cauldron began to bubble inside her again. "I'm supposed to believe that?"

"At the distance from where he shot, if he'd wanted you, he would have had you. You were a much bigger target. Even if you had moved, he'd still have gotten you. Frankly, it's damn near impossible to dodge a bul-let aimed at center mass. He aimed high. Your eye level. He missed on purpose."

"You can't possibly know that." She watched his face tighten and darken.

"Yes. I can."

She chewed on that mentally and gave up on her sand-wich. It was sticking in her throat. She reached for coffee to wash it down. "Maybe," she said quietly, "you'd better

explain so this innocent, naive civilian can understand."
She hated the petulant tone of her voice.

"Even hunters don't go for headshots," he said. "It's
too easy to miss your target. You go for the shoulder. Bigger target. If you want to shoot a person, you go for the
biggest part, too. The part that you can't miss. That was
a scare shot. And believe it or not, your sheriff agrees
with me."

Her insides twisted, trying to readjust. "So this guy
risked killing me to scare me off?"

"He's better than that. He wants you scared off, but
he had absolutely no intention of killing you or even
wounding you."

"Then why? Why, Jerrod? There are other ways to
scare me."

"Bashing in your car's window didn't work."

"Oh, man." She grabbed her fork and speared some
salad. Maybe that would go down. "I don't like the world
you live in."

His face darkened even more. "Sorry. I didn't mean
to bring it to your doorstep."

That got through to her, past her anger, her fear, her
frustration. Past the whole damn episode. "I didn't mean
that the way it sounded."

"Yes, you did. And it's all right."

"No, it's not. It's just that… I don't think you brought
this to my door, anyway. Don't blame yourself for that."

"I may have to."

She looked at him, feeling as if the world were slipping from beneath her feet. Everything in her seemed
to sag. "Please explain. I need to understand as much
as I can."

"Eat first," he said firmly. "We both need some energy. Then we'll talk as much as you want."

He was adamant, too. Not until she had eaten enough to satisfy him would he stop prompting her to take more. He finished his own meal as if he was ravenous. Then he carried coffee for them into the living room. She sat on the wooden rocking chair with its cheery pillows, refusing to get close to him, even as close as the far end of the couch.

Her world had been rocked this morning and she needed to deal with it. Even in the midst of all this, her growing cravings for him kept trying to take over. Diversion, she told herself. All that heated honey that kept wanting to run through her entire body, the need to throw herself into his arms, was merely a way to avoid thinking about what had happened this morning.

That would be exactly the wrong thing to do. She knew it, so she battled the urge to hide in sex with him, which might only wind up to be as shattering as what had happened this morning, and forced herself to attend to the ugly realities.

"Talk," she demanded.

He nodded, cradling his mug in both hands on his lap. "This morning, just before the shot, I found something to one side of a game trail. A gun had been fired into the ground."

"Why would anyone do that?"

"To get a spent shell casing. You've probably seen enough on TV to know how guns can be identified by the lands and grooves they leave on a shell."

She nodded. "Of course."

"Now just suppose you wanted to leave a false trail

behind. Say, one that couldn't be traced to you. You'd fire a disposable weapon a few times, pick up a few shells and salt them in your sniper's nest."

"Back up here. Sniper's nest?"

"The place he shot from. Anyway, I found a place where a gun had been fired directly into the ground. It left some powder on the snow and a rather big hole behind. Explosive gases from the muzzle. Unmistakable. I'm sure Gage has pulled out the bullet or bullets by now. Regardless, our guy now has a casing or two he can sprinkle where he wants to mislead. Evidence will never link him and his personal weapon to the nest."

"Okay." She got that. She also got that as the storm inside her settled, she was feeling the attraction to him stronger than ever. Wasn't it too late for adrenaline to be doing this to her? Probably. But the simple fact was, she was beginning to wish she was on the couch after all. Where she could feel his heat, smell his scents.

At least she could fill her eyes with him. That chiseled, often unrevealing face of his had become dear to her in some odd way. She could have spent hours staring at him as if he was a work by Michelangelo, scar notwithstanding.

Focus, she scolded herself. "So what else?"

"His nest was a mess. It looked exactly as if someone had taken a shot by mistake and then hightailed it. Well, almost exactly."

"What was wrong with it?"

He shrugged. "It's hard to imitate a panic you aren't feeling. Plus, he knew what he was shooting at. Plus, when he left, he took off on flat rocks. His egress was planned, and from what I saw around that hole he shot in the ground, he's good at covering his tracks. I doubt the sheriff will find any sign of him anywhere else."

"And from this you can conclude that he just wanted to scare me away."

He nodded.

"So he's afraid I might find something important."

"Not exactly. Neither the sheriff nor I think you're the target. Not now."

At that, she put her coffee down and jumped up. "You've got to be kidding. I get shot at, but I'm not the target?"

"It's entirely possible."

"What the hell good would that do?"

At that moment the doorbell rang. She started toward it, but Jerrod got there first. "Stand back," he said.

So she wasn't the target but he was still concerned for her? What the hell else could be going on?

It was Gage Dalton. He stepped inside and Allison kicked into automatic, offering him coffee.

"I'd love some. I wish this cold spell would give us a break."

Before she reached the kitchen, she heard Gage say, "Here's your ID, Major Marquette. Your boss says you're one helluva hero."

"Depends on who's talking," Jerrod answered. The two men laughed with easy understanding.

They could *laugh?* The rabbit hole seemed to be getting deeper by the minute. She had the totally selfish sense that after what she had been through today, the entire world ought to be upset along with her. She knew it was ridiculous, but so what?

She brought Gage his coffee. He'd taken the rocker,

so she sat on the couch. Jerrod sat at the other end, as if he felt her need for space.

But did she really want that space between them? Was it possible to be any more mixed up than she was now? Probably, but she didn't want to find out.

"Great coffee," Gage said after he sipped some. He'd unzipped his winter jacket, removed his gloves, but the tan Stetson still sat on his head. She realized there was no place to put it, and wondered if she should offer to take it from him.

And when had her brain turned into a flea circus? Her thoughts kept darting all over the place. His hat? What did his hat matter?

"We were all over that mountainside," Gage said. "The guy's gone. We did find the carcass of a wolf. Pretty bad condition, but we bagged it for necropsy."

Allison's heart sank again. "Not the wolves," she said quietly.

"We don't know the cause of death," Gage said gently. "It might have been natural, so don't get upset yet. The good news is that we didn't find any other dead animals."

"That is good," she agreed. So maybe the wolf hadn't been poisoned.

Gage shifted his attention to Jerrod. "We also found absolutely no sign that any human has been on that mountain recently except for Allison. Her path was easy to follow. Yours wasn't. Neither was his. And I've got a couple of very good trackers working for me. They have your kind of training."

Which meant what? Allison looked at Jerrod.

"I couldn't find his track, either, and I was sure as hell looking. When I couldn't find any sign of him where he'd shot into the ground, I figured he was no ordinary joe."

"Definitely not. And there's no reason whatsoever that someone like that should be interested in Allison. That leaves you."

"I know."

Allison looked from one man to the other. "This isn't meshing," she said. "Why would anybody shoot at me if they wanted Jerrod? He was out there today, too. By himself. He could have been taken out then."

"Except that I'm not easy to get to. Except that maybe he didn't want anyone around when he came for me. He might not want to kill anyone else. Certainly if Allison disappeared out there, the hue and cry would go up rapidly, maybe too rapidly."

"If you disappeared out there when you were alone," Gage said, "it might be a while before anyone noticed. And by the time we did, I doubt we'd find much of you."

"No better way to dispose of a body than on open ground in the woods," Jerrod agreed. "No evidence to cause a problem."

"My God." Allison felt stunned. Did people really talk about things like this so casually?

"Sorry," Gage said. "Just dealing with realities. So here's the way I see it. There is a remote chance that someone just wants to scare Allison away for fear she might be able to trace that poison. We know that's next to impossible, given how the animals travel before they sicken. But he might not know that, so I'm not completely ready to rule out that someone doesn't want her poking around and taking samples."

Allison set her cup on the end table and gave up all pretense of trying to look relaxed. Her hands clenched into fists. "Remote."

"I think so. I'd take it entirely off the table except I'm not ready to rule out anything yet."

Jerrod nodded. "But let's look at exactly what we *do* know."

"Lay it out," Gage said, rocking back a little and stretching as if to ease his back.

"Whoever is out there has some serious military training. Special ops kind of training. Today couldn't have made that any more clear. That could be almost anybody, and it doesn't give us a motive. It just *is*."

Gage nodded and drank more coffee.

"However, after what happened today," Jerrod continued, "I'm beginning to wonder if I didn't bring this trouble on Allison by becoming too concerned about her safety."

"It does seem more like your kind of trouble."

Allison looked between them again. "What are you talking about?"

"I may be the prey in this game, not you."

"But…" The word passed her lips with nothing to follow it. The world seemed to be taking a spin in a whole new direction.

Jerrod just shook his head. "Gage is right. This is my kind of trouble. It probably followed me here. I have no idea what or who, but that doesn't matter. What matters is that the best way I can make you safe right now is to stay away from you. Gage and the local police can keep an eye on you, but I need to stay away until I find this creep. It's just that simple."

The thought that rose in her then didn't have anything to do with relief, or anything else that had happened that day. No, it was a bitter thought, enough to sour her mouth.

He was leaving. Gone. Heading for the hills, just as she'd feared. Except as briefly as they'd known each other, she could already feel the part of her that would leave with him. It was like a piece of her heart ripping out of her, and the tearing hurt like hell.

She didn't say another word, hardly heard the two men talk for a little while longer. She ought to be grateful that a lunatic wasn't trying to kill her, but she wasn't. Instead, she sat there feeling as if that bullet today had pierced her heart.

How the hell was she going to survive this? She would, of course, but the impending pain was already settling over her. God, how had she come to care so much in such a short time?

A while later, Jerrod saw Gage out, then returned to the living room. When he stood in front of her, she finally looked up, feeling the hollowness in her own eyes.

"You're leaving," she said finally.

"Only for a while. Only to make you safe."

"Right." Sarcasm and maybe a little bitterness dripped from the single word. "Well, I can't say I didn't know you were a rolling stone."

He squatted then. When he reached for her hands, she pulled them back.

"Allison…"

"No. You can't be sure that shot wasn't intended for me. So what am I supposed to do? Stay locked in my house until some indefinite future date?"

"We decided…"

"That's the thing. You all decided. I don't remember being consulted on much from the very beginning. You started off worried about me, for reasons that didn't make real sense to me, and now it's about you? What am I supposed to believe?"

"It's confusing, I know."

"Then start explaining," she snapped. "Really explaining."

"It's my fault. I saw the shape of this thing but I didn't see it right."

"And that's supposed to reassure me? What if you've got the shape all wrong right now?"

"I learned a lot today. The shape is right now. Someone is after *me*."

"How can you know that?" The deadness was beginning to slip away, and every bit of the pain, anger and fear began to surface again. "You can't know that. Not for sure. So why are you leaving?"

"Because I put you at risk, and I'm not going to keep doing that. Do you know how that makes me feel, to realize I screwed up so bad that I have endangered you? I guess I was getting too used to being a civilian."

"Or not used to it enough. So what now? You skip town and we see what happens? Lovely."

"I'm not skipping town. I'm going hunting."

Understanding hit her like a sledgehammer. "You can't! That's dangerous!"

"It's what I'm trained for. Whoever he's after, he's going to be sorry he tangled with me."

At that, she pushed up from the couch, slipped away from him and began to pace. "So easy to say. Tough macho man, going to hunt a killer. What if you get killed?"

"I won't. But if I do, well, at least you'll know you're safe."

"Damn it, I'm not worth that!"

"People I've never met are worth that."

The statement drew her up short, and her anger fizzled, leaving her feeling sad, so sad. Her eyes burned as if she wanted to cry. "Jerrod, please. Please. I don't get any of this. He shot at me, not you. Why? Why should that mean he's after you?"

"Because he has now precipitated exactly what he wanted."

"Which is?"

"He knows I'll come hunting for him. He wants me alone out there."

"But no one's going to overlook it if you disappear now. Not the cops, not me."

"He doesn't know what the cops concluded about what they saw out there. For all he knows, I'm their prime suspect."

"How could that possibly be?"

"I was out there with you. For all intents and purposes, I was alone with you. I could have staged that shot, messed up the nest then come running to your rescue. And yes, I'm capable of doing exactly that."

Lead now settled in her stomach. "But the sheriff didn't believe that."

"It crossed his mind, trust me. I watched him reach the decisions. He may still wonder, but now he's got me in the picture, he knows I'm right on the line, so to speak, and won't try anything."

"So that's all he has to count on?"

"That and he checked with my former, um, bosses. He probably knows more about me now than you do."

She looked down, wishing she didn't feel as if her world was teetering. The whirl of thoughts and emotions in her head were almost enough to make her feel dizzy.

"Allison?"

She looked up into those dark, dark eyes, and realized how much she trusted him. Truly trusted him. "Okay. So this guy shot at me to draw you out. To make you come hunt him."

"And, if he's assuming the sheriff has his eye on me, he'll also assume that if I disappear everyone will think I skipped town to avoid trouble."

"I don't like this."

"I don't, either. I can't imagine why this is happening, although I guess I need to sort through my memory and try to figure out who I ticked off enough to want me dead at this late date. Most, I would assume, would be foreign nationals. I even think there's a contract on me from one mission, although all they have is a lousy drawing of my face." His hand touched his cheek. "Prescar."

"I wish I thought you were kidding."

He didn't answer.

She didn't know what to say, either. Right or wrong, she could read his face and tell he was absolutely determined. "Does Gage know you're going hunting?"

"Yes. My instructions are to take the guy alive if humanly possible. Meanwhile, he's staking you out."

"Why doesn't he do the hunting?"

"Because his men climbed all over the mountain today, Allison. No trace of the guy. Like a ghost, except he was there. So they need bait. I'm it. If this guy wants me, he'll come for me."

"And I'm the secondary bait."

"I guess, although I don't think you're the bait at all. It's just that none of us wants to take the risk."

"So you're going to take all the risks?"

Again, no answer. The turmoil inside her seemed to

have no end. For two days now she'd felt as if everything she thought she knew and believed had been tossed into a paper shredder and then blown around in a hurricane wind. How it would all reassemble, she hadn't any idea, but right now, right now...

"Do you have to leave now?" she asked finally.

"Not right now. If he's watching, he'll think the surveillance is on me."

"So sure?"

"If I was him attempting to do what he's attempting, that would be the logical conclusion. They didn't lock me up, but I'm being watched. I've been watched by cops ever since we got back today, from his perspective. So for now I want him to think I'm contained. It'll work for me when I slip out."

"And then you're gone."

"The key is getting out of here without him noticing. Thank goodness for Gage. He's going to make it look like this place is buttoned down good."

"That isn't what I asked."

"I know."

She watched his face change from the intense, hard-as-diamonds look that must be his operational face to something a lot softer and more human. Almost gentle. Surprising, given what she knew about him now. But then he'd always been gentle with her.

"I'm not good for you," he said. "You know that. I don't know where I'm going, whether I'm ready to settle. I have nothing to offer you right now."

"Yes, you do." Then she walked straight into his arms. As soon as she connected to his body, they wrapped around her, instinctively, perhaps, but they wrapped around her.

She wound hers around his narrow waist.

"Allison, it's been an upsetting day for you."

"Quit making excuses. Leave your world behind long enough to come into mine. If I never see you again, there's one thing I want to know. Now. Before it's too late."

His arms tightened. She heard him draw a deep breath. She could feel him hardening against her. He wanted her, too, and that had become the most priceless feeling in the world to her. All she had done was walk into his arms. A flutter of fear rippled through her, then vanished.

The power of passion amazed her. It swept away the entire day, the mire of emotions, the confusion, the fear, all of it. It focused her in that moment, and that moment alone. Everything else vanished.

Desire, long building, and equally long denied and suppressed, surged like a tiger escaping a cage. He hadn't even kissed her, hadn't done anything but hold her, yet her entire body seemed to be pulsing in time with the ache between her legs. Every cell cried out for his touch.

If this was all there would be, then so be it. She needed to know if his promise that she wasn't a lousy lover could be kept. She needed to know if he could take her to the places her body had been yearning for almost since she first set eyes on him. The places he had hinted at with just a few kisses and a few gentle touches.

This was the time, perhaps her only chance, with a man as dangerous as a sharp sword, as gentle with her as if she was a kitten, a man who had been through his share of women and probably had enough experience to make up for her lack.

A man she wanted as she had wanted no other. She tipped her head up, seeking his kiss, and met his dark gaze.

"Be sure," he murmured and closed his eyes briefly. "Please, just be very sure. Because I'm not going to be able to stop myself again."

Music to her ears, especially after last night.

"I'm sure. I've never been surer of anything."

Chapter 10

"I want to make slow love to you," he murmured, lifting his hand to brush her hair back from her face, to caress her cheek. "I want to take hours and hours exploring you."

The desire that almost never stopped simmering in her around Jerrod turned instantly into an arrow that pierced her very center. Internal muscles tightened, nearly cramping with the need those words unleashed. She had never heard any man say such sexy words to her. Hours and hours? Make slow love?

Oh, yesss…. Everything in her responded so strongly she felt as if a switch had flipped.

Nervousness about her own inexperience vanished completely. There was no room left in her for such thoughts. Every bit of her pounded in erotic rhythm: now, now, now.

Beyond thinking of anything else, it never crossed her mind to worry about his back as he lifted her and carried her down on the couch so that she straddled him once again. His hands gripped her hips, drawing her hard against the arousal she could feel, even through his jeans. A sense of heady power filled her to know that she could draw such a reaction from him, and she watched as he closed his eyes, and a muffled groan escaped him.

"You've been driving me crazy since I set eyes on you."

She was amazed he could say so much, however hoarsely. For her all the air seemed to have left the room, her ragged breaths audible in the quiet.

He pressed her hard to him once more, then lifted his hands to cup her cheeks and draw her close for a kiss. "Feel what you do to me," he whispered, then clamped his mouth to hers.

This was no gentle kiss such as he had given her before. He dived straight into the depths of her mouth, as if he wanted to burrow into her there, too; as if he wanted to possess and claim her.

The movements of his tongue found sensitive nerves she had never really noticed before. Nerves that excited her in the most amazing way, seeming to start a cascade that followed passion's arrow straight through her. Her hands gripped his shoulders, digging in hard, hanging on for dear life as she embarked on what promised to be the most amazing journey of her life.

Almost as if he felt the throbbing within her, he began to plunge his tongue in and out in time with it. Her hips responded, rocking against him, but he made no move to still her. He kept on kissing her until she felt her world narrow to his tongue and the pressure between her legs.

His hands left her face, stroking slowly down her sides, causing her to catch her breath. Through the layers of fleece, she felt them as if there was no barrier at all. Big hands, so sure, up her sides, then around to her back, then to her front once again. She almost held her breath, tipping her head back from his kiss, making a silent offering of herself.

He accepted, closing both his hands over her breasts, squeezing them at first gently, then harder. A moan escaped her as she learned something new about herself. No touch had ever before seemed to paint her with fire.

But she needed more, so much more. As if realizing it, he stopped squeezing her breasts, her aching breasts, and began to brush his palms lightly over her nipples. Even through the fabric, the sensation was sharp, exquisite, like hot wires ran from those engorging buds to her very center, causing her to clamp her legs against his, forcing the most primal of responses as she tried to get closer to his staff.

She needed him. She needed him in a way she had never needed before. She wanted to claw at his clothes, to get them out of the way, but perched as she was it was almost impossible.

"Jerrod…"

"Just for now," he whispered. "Just ride me."

Ride him? She doubted anyone had ever said anything so erotic to her. The images that filled her head were wild, crazy. As if she was astride a horse, she clamped her legs tighter, aggravating the ache deep within her until she managed to wiggle just a bit closer. At once he rose up to meet her. No pressure had ever felt so good.

He slipped his hands up under her shirt, finding the

naked skin of her midriff. Light caresses added to her torment, building the fires within her.

A groan was ripped from her. An instant later, his hands slid behind her, pressing her hips even more tightly to him. Thunder seemed to roar in her ears, her heart racing so hard now it deafened her.

Pressing, releasing, pressing…

She felt strung on a wire, held helpless by her own hungers, fearing she might never get the answer, afraid she might miss…

Then, with one wrenching spasm, she tipped off the tightrope. Who moaned she couldn't have said. Spasms of completion threatened to rip her apart. Jerrod gave one more jerk, one that added to her satisfaction.

She felt as if she were spinning away into the heart of an explosion.

Jerrod held her close to his chest, feeling the shudders pass through her and gradually ebb. He stroked her back soothingly, sprinkled kisses where he could, and waited.

God, he hoped he wasn't making a mistake. But even that concern couldn't dim what had just happened. He needed to tell Allison that she was a firecracker, whether she knew it or not. She'd well and truly lit his fire. Not since he was a teen had a woman gotten this kind of re-action out of him so easily.

He'd been thinking to calm things down, so he wouldn't move too fast with her. So that he could keep his promise of making love to her for hours. To his own amazement, he felt ready to go again, a reaction no longer familiar to him.

He'd wanted her from the instant he saw her. Only years of rigid self-discipline had kept him from thinking about that nonstop. But today had stunned him more than he wanted to admit.

Had he put Allison in danger because of his desire for her? Because maybe he hadn't been thinking as clearly as he should have?

Though he would never let Allison know, that shot at her had shaken him. Yes, he knew perfectly well that the shooter hadn't meant to hit her. That was obvious from the sightline and the height of the mark on the tree. But it remained he could have missed and hit her by pure chance.

Then there was his own thinking over the past couple of weeks. How much of it had been clouded by his need to be with her? He was appalled in retrospect at how quickly he had assumed she was the one at risk. He knew his own past well enough to realize that someone might be after him even now. There were some cultures in which a vendetta never died. Unfortunately, he'd given a few people cause.

While it seemed unlikely that anyone could have tracked him given the way his identity had been concealed, he knew better. A friend of his had run into it just a couple of years ago when someone with a grudge against him had landed at a nearby airport to come after him. Only face recognition software had saved him.

So why should he be exempt?

It didn't matter now. He'd been a fool and had endangered Allison. He could deal with the guilt later. Right now he had a warm and partially satisfied woman resting on him, and he'd made her a promise. However long or short the rest of his days might be, he was going to make sure he kept this promise: to love her until she no longer doubted that she was a good lover.

He had no doubts. He'd never had any about her, but the past few minutes had certainly proved him right. She had given herself freely to the moment, and that was absolutely the best starting point on earth.

She stirred against him. "Tell me we're not done," she said, her voice rusty.

"No way." He rubbed her back and stroked her hair. "I just wanted to calm things down a bit so I'd be able to take my time with you."

"You doubted it?"

"Hell, yeah. I've been hard for you for two weeks now. You can tell how well I was able to restrain myself."

To his pleasure, he heard a tiny laugh escape her. "I thought you were very restrained."

"Then you didn't catch on to what was happening here. This was an appetizer. Being a little less ravenous will allow me to devour you more slowly."

"Damn, you talk sexy."

"I act sexy, too. So do you." He tightened his hold on her. "Since I have a lot of plans for the rest of the night, how would you like to eat a little more? I want your batteries fully topped off."

Another little laugh. "I can barely move."

"My point exactly." He squeezed her. "If you want to stay here, I'll go rustle up something. You sure didn't eat much lunch. Then I'm going to take you to bed and we're going to do this right."

"I didn't notice anything wrong this time."

"Oh, sweetheart, there was nothing wrong. I just want to do better by you."

She pushed herself up slowly then, and he could feel her arms tremble a bit. "Now, I like the sound of that," she said, and gave him a sleepy-happy smile.

* * *

Allison followed him to the kitchen. Almost like a puppy, she thought wryly, but she wasn't the princess sort, anyway. She didn't need to be waited on. But she didn't want to be away from him, not right now. Maybe not ever, as if that would be her choice.

But she firmly brushed the thought aside. Not now. There'd be plenty of time later to deal with fallout. Right now she wanted to live in the magical world he was creating for her.

He insisted she sit while he plundered the fridge for leftovers. A few needed reheating, and he handled the microwave like a pro. Soon they had a smorgasbord spread on the table before them.

Instead of sitting across from her, though, he pulled a chair around until they sat shoulder to shoulder. Each time they brushed, Allison felt an electric spark zap through her, a tingle that headed straight for the apex of her thighs. Man, he got her motor running.

He kissed her, cradling her face, another of those gentle kisses that so moved her. When he lifted his head he said, "Hurry up and eat, woman. The horses are kicking at the stall door."

He made her laugh. He was good at that, and she liked it the same way she liked everything else about him.

She could feel shadows of things to come hovering around them, dark shadows, but he seemed to hold them at bay. As if he had learned over the years how to live in the moment when he wanted to. She could do with a dose of that.

She gave him the other half of her steak sandwich and ate chicken marsala herself along with the remains of the salad. Her senses remained heightened, and everything tasted exquisite. But nothing could compare to the interlude on the sofa. Impatience built in her, but he was determined that she eat.

Caring and loving all in one very special package, she reflected. A pang struck straight at her heart as she thought of him leaving, but that was something else she refused to let enter these hours with him. She might be constructing a glass globe of denial around herself, might be living out a fantasy, but right now that seemed far more important than reality.

At last he rose and swept everything off the table, leaving it beside the sink. Then he reached for her, leaning back against the counter and drawing her against him. His legs were spread, making a natural cradle for her to rest in. One of his hands cupped the back of her head as he kissed her again, this time deeply. His other pressed her hips into him.

"Feel that?" he said when he raised his head. "That's what you do to me."

His frankness delighted her, as did the hardness she felt. Heat trickled through her, then began to rise in a flood. They had begun the second act of his promise to her, and eagerness drenched her. The deep, throbbing ache began anew.

One kiss and her breath sped up, her heart leaped.

"Easy," he whispered, trailing kisses over her face, scattering them like rose petals. "We have all the time in the world."

If only that was true. She sighed, leaning more toward him, wanting everything she had once dreamed that making love could be. "Jerrod..."

"Yes, sweetheart?"

Her hands roamed his back, his shoulders, his chest,

drawing every sensation and line of him into her memory, trying to etch it forever so that not a detail would ever be lost. The power in this man took her breath away, and feeling it this way filled her with wonderment that he could be so gentle. Always gentle with her. Like petting a lion, she thought hazily. Petting one with utter trust.

An inkling of her own power filled her, amazing her. Beneath her hands, he became as gentle as a lamb, yet she could feel his raging hunger pressed hard against her, a hunger to equal her own.

Blood hammered mindlessly in her now, demanding more and yet more. Her breasts swelled until they ached. Each movement of fabric against her skin had become a sweet torment, adding to the growing fires within her.

Any remaining inhibitions began to desert her. Growing desperate, she reached for the buttons of his shirt, pulling them open. At last, at long last, she felt the heat of his smooth skin beneath her palms, the twin peaks of his nipples, felt him shudder as she ran her hands over them. She wanted him to lose his control. Now.

Slow? Forget slow. She didn't have time for slow.

But when she reached for the button on his jeans, his hands grabbed hers, stopping them.

"Jerrod!" She almost stamped her foot in frustration. He couldn't stop now. Now, now.

But he pushed her away just a bit. Then he circled her waist with one arm and began to lead and push her toward her bedroom.

"Easy," he said again.

She was well past easy. The only thing that kept her in line was the realization that her bed was only a short distance away.

Need thundered through her like galloping horses;

pounding blood awakened every cell and nerve ending. Desire pierced her core, nearly painful in its intensity.

Only when they crossed the threshold of her room did he stop and face her again. Then, a crooked smile on his face, he reached for his shirt, shrugging it off.

An absolutely perfect chest filled her gaze. She drank him in, hardly noticing the small scars that dotted his landscape. Powerful chest, a belly so flat it amazed her, and all of that above the waistband that rode narrow hips.

Still smiling, he reached for the button he had recently denied her. She held her breath, staring, as he released it and tugged the zipper down. Couldn't he move any faster?

When he bent to push his jeans down, he took them along with his briefs in one smooth movement, then kicked them aside. All that remained were his socks, and he got rid of them fast, revealing feet that struck her as beautiful as the rest of him.

Fully naked now, he straightened. His staff was hard, a small bead on its tip. Ready. A work of manly art.

"Now you," he said hoarsely.

At that moment a flutter of anxiety hit her. She wasn't ashamed of her body, but Lance had left her uncertain about its appeal. For an instant, just an instant, she slipped out of the moment.

"Oh, no, you don't," he said quietly.

Before she could react, he stepped toward her and pulled her shirt over her head. Chilly air hit her skin, a surprisingly erotic sensation, almost like the whisper of cool lips. He reached around behind her, twisting the clasp, and her bra fell away. Her breasts, freed, felt as if they were reaching out to him.

"You're beautiful. Perfect."

Then his hands closed on those mounds and the last of her disquiet fled. Powerful hands kneaded her, and she couldn't help looking down. Big hands that nearly swallowed her. Thumbs that began to flick back and forth across her engorged nipples until they pulled a moan from her.

He bent, closing his mouth over one breast, sucking her into that warm cavern, running his tongue over and around the nipple until she had to grab his shoulders for support. The world spun around her and passion lifted her to new heights of need. Clenching, clenching, deep inside she clenched with each movement of his mouth and tongue.

Never had she felt so utterly possessed.

His hands found her hips, but she was almost past noticing when he dragged her pants down. Then the world tipped crazily and she was on her bed.

He tugged her pants the rest of the way off. Then he stood at the foot of the bed, looking at her just as she had looked at him. A fleeting need to cover herself vanished half born as he reached down and pushed her ankles apart.

"Spread for me," he whispered. "Let me see all your beauty."

Only then did she realize that she had been resisting. With effort she forced her muscles to relax, even though that was the last thing they wanted to do. They wanted to clamp together in answer to the throbbing at her center, as if that could ease it. Opening to him was at once difficult and thrilling.

No man had ever looked at her this way, taking in every inch. The touch of his eyes felt almost like tongues of fire, ramping up her passion even more. When he knelt between her parted legs, she instinctively lifted her arms, reaching for him.

But he evaded her, instead pulling her knees up and spreading her even wider. So utterly exposed now, and helpless, in thrall to the delicious sensations that were zinging through her, making her heart pound, making her ache.

She gasped as he touched her petals with his fingers, running them lightly over her, so lightly that the demand for more flared instantly in her. Dimly she heard herself call his name, but he didn't stop this exquisite torment, those gentle caresses that promised ecstasy but refused to deliver.

Then, slowly, he slipped his finger between them, finding the knot of nerves, so swollen and sensitive now that she cried out. Then as he rubbed it gently, causing her to roll her hips with need, he slipped a finger inside her. She felt caught on his hand, needing more and more but getting only a hint of things to come.

Hours of this? She was going to go out of her mind. She was nearly out of it already.

Suddenly his hand was gone. She snapped her eyes open in dismay in time to see him lie beside her.

"Your turn," he said.

To her amazement, he lifted her as if she weighed nothing at all until she straddled him again, but over his legs this time.

"Anything you want. Any way you want."

He looked like a meal to a starving person. She wanted to learn every inch of him, but first, first…

She closed her hand around his staff, felt its silken steel, felt it jerk under her touch, listened to his groan with immense satisfaction.

"How...?" she asked.

Reaching down, he helped her roll a condom on him, then he showed her how he liked to be touched. He kept no secrets from her, letting her watch his responses, letting her hear them. She felt the power again, the power of holding a lion in thrall to her least touches.

Leaning forward, she propped herself on her arms and sprinkled kisses on his chest until at last she had the courage to take one of his small nipples in her mouth.

He swore, but it was a good swearing, she could tell by the way his hand suddenly gripped her, holding her closer, and the way his entire body jerked, nearly rising from the bed.

Emboldened, she sucked on him and even nipped a bit, enjoying the pleasure she could give him, feeling as if his pleasure fueled hers until the intensity between them became almost beyond enduring.

Then he slipped one hand down between them, finding her sensitive nub, stroking it and finally pinching it.

The pinch did her in. She arched backward and one pleading word escaped her.

"Please...." It was a drawn-out moan.

Finally he obliged. Lifting her, he settled her on his staff. He felt so huge, sliding into her, but the stretching of muscles answered another need, and when he had entered her completely, she froze, savoring it.

"However you like," he murmured. "However."

She took him at his word, riding him desperately toward culmination. Riding him hard, letting sensation guide her. She flew. She flew to regions she had never imagined, goaded by the demanding hammering in her body, by an ache that needed to be quenched as surely as any wildfire.

The climb was fraught with peril. At some level she feared it would all pop like a soap bubble. But it didn't. Higher and higher she went until she exploded in a shower of blazing embers. Moments later she felt him follow her.

She was still sweat slicked but just beginning to feel a bit chilly when he slipped from the bed. She groaned a protest, but still felt too weak to do more than that. A minute later he returned from the bathroom, climbed back into the bed and pulled the coverlet over them. She crawled back into his arms as if she belonged there. He welcomed her with the same ease.

"You," he said, brushing her damp hair back from her forehead, "are one hell of a lover."

"Really?" She felt suddenly shy.

"I'm not kidding. I'd never lie about that. I wouldn't say anything at all if I felt otherwise. Not only have I been crazed with desire for you, but you just set me off twice like a string of firecrackers. You're gorgeous, you're giving and…"

Suddenly, he threw the covers back, "We still haven't gotten to what pleases you."

"What makes you think I wasn't pleased?" The thought astonished her.

He smiled at her in the dim light from the hallway. "Lady, we've just begun. But first, a shower."

She learned something then, too. Her shower was tiny, meant only to hold one person, but he squeezed in with her anyway, and beneath the hot spray he soaped every inch of her he could reach, then passed her the bar of soap.

She knew a moment of hesitation as shyness rose

again, but the truth was, she wanted to touch this man all over, learn how he felt everywhere. The freedom to do so had just been handed to her, and she wasn't going to pass it up. No way.

She began at his neck and shoulders, then slowly moved down to his chest. Each touch she gave him seemed to renew the longing inside her. She would never get enough of him. Never.

She learned every plane and hollow, loved the way his muscles quivered beneath her touches. When she tried to reach his back, he obligingly turned and gave her complete access.

The scars she had barely noticed earlier caught her attention now. His front, his back, slashing scars as if something had cut him, and a few deeper hollows near his spine. The marks of stitches. Some scars had faded; some were still slightly red.

She couldn't imagine what he had endured, but she gentled her touches even more, trying to convey that she cared. Then she reached his sculpted butt. She bit her lip, then slipped her soapy hand between his cheeks.

His flanks quivered, a quiet groan escaped him then he suddenly pivoted. "Now you're in for it," he growled.

"In for what?" Teasing overcame her. Then a giggle followed as he poked her stomach with his hardened staff.

"You didn't think you were going to get away from the havoc you've created, did you?"

Another laugh followed the first, and soon they were laughing almost like kids, slipping around each other, the soap like a lubricant, making their skin slide so easily. But gradually the shower spray washed it away, the sliding became less easy, and his arms locked around her.

"I've always wanted to wash a woman's hair," he said, his eyes as dark as night. "But I'm not sure I have the patience for that right now."

"I'm in no mood for patience," she agreed, closing her hand around his staff.

"You'll pay for that," he said.

She shrieked then laughed as he abruptly lifted her from her feet and put her on the mat outside the shower. He paused just long enough to turn off the water, then grabbed some towels.

He started drying her. She grabbed a towel and reciprocated. And somewhere they went from laughing to quiet sighs and moans.

When he passed the towel between her legs, she grabbed his shoulders for support, afraid she would suddenly collapse into a puddle.

When he returned her to the bed, he propped himself over her. "Now," he said, "I'm going to learn every single thing that pleases you."

"I thought you already had," she said, as her body melted into a pool of hot honey.

"We've only just begun."

He proved it, too, learning every inch of her with his tongue and mouth and not quitting until she was helplessly begging.

Her imaginings hadn't even come close.

Across the street, the hunter waited. The house was under surveillance, which meant, as he had hoped, Marquette was under suspicion for the shooting in the woods today. The cops weren't sure he'd meant to hurt the woman, but that didn't matter as long as Marquette didn't wind up in a cell.

He probably looked pretty damn suspicious, the hunter thought with satisfaction. He was the only one they knew was out there with her, and he'd been careful to cover his tracks.

So they'd think it was a setup by Marquette, and his explanations of everything that was wrong with the nest would only make him look more suspicious.

So he was being watched.

Perfect. And while he didn't know Marquette personally, he knew enough about him and his kind of training to know the guy wouldn't leave it like this. No, he'd lay low for a day, maybe two, letting the heat cool down a bit, and then he'd come hunting the hunter.

Which was exactly what the hunter wanted. They had a score to settle, a big one. Since the hunter knew everything he needed to, and would be staging the ambush, he had no doubt about how this would all come out. Marquette would be at a complete disadvantage, because he had no idea who might be setting him up or why. Intel was always important, and Marquette had very little.

And because of the setup, he'd peeled the woman away. Marquette wouldn't allow her to come along. When Marquette disappeared, the cops would be sure he was on the lam.

Perfect.

Satisfied, the hunter shifted back into the shadows and headed for the mountains. He'd be ready whenever that bastard showed up. Tomorrow, even, although he suspected it might be a day or two. And it would be at night, because not even Marquette could slip that police noose in broad daylight.

Soon. Very soon.

Chapter 11

Allison awoke in the early hours while the outside world remained dark. She wanted to luxuriate in the way her body felt, so well loved from tip to toe, pleasured so well that she ached in delicious ways in delicious places. Instinctively, she turned on her side, longing to wrap herself around Jerrod, and found him gone.

Her heart nearly stopped. Had he left already? Jumping up, she scrambled for her robe and slippers without turning on the light. The whole house was dark. Not even a light from the kitchen or hallway.

Frightened, even a little angry that he could have left without at least saying goodbye, she hurried down the hall, glancing into her office where only the red glow of a digital clock provided illumination. A peek in the kitchen showed her the indicator on the coffeepot glowed. He'd made coffee.

Hope leaped into her throat, then seemed to stick there as she saw him at last, a dark shadow at her front window, staring out into a world not yet ready to stir to life.

She stood in the doorway, uncertain whether to disturb him. He stood as still as a statue, but even so she could feel his alertness. Maybe she shouldn't bother him.

Then, without turning, he held out an arm, inviting her closer. She tentatively eased over to him until his arm snaked around her and pulled her close to his warm side. He was dressed again, although his shirt hung open, and he even wore his boots.

When he said nothing, she finally whispered, "What are you doing?"

"Thinking. Waiting for you to wake up. Let's get you some coffee."

"Not yet." She stood with him, enjoying the weight of his arm around her. "Do you see something out there?"

"Only one of the poor cops who's been assigned to watch this house."

"Why are they watching you?"

"Not me. You. They're here to protect you in case we figured this all wrong. Don't worry, I'm sure we didn't."

"How can you be so sure?"

"Experience." He sighed quietly, then fell silent.

"Just a little while ago you thought the opposite."

"I know. I'm sorry for putting you at risk."

She leaned against him, staring through the sheers at the patrol car parked out front. "They're pretty obvious out there."

"That's the idea. There's somebody in the alley, too, with a clear view of the back of the house. Sometimes you want obvious."

"I suppose." But a chill crept through her as reality

returned after last night. She hoped their lovemaking didn't turn into a treasured memory, a bubble out of time that never happened again.

"Are you up for good?"

"Wide-awake."

"Then let's get some coffee," he said.

Jerrod was thinking, all right. He'd spent time ransacking his memory, trying to come up with any idea of who might be after him. A few faces popped up, but they seemed so unlikely. Then he'd spent more time chewing over the night he and Allison had just shared. Without a doubt it had been the best sex of his life. Maybe more than sex, but he didn't want to think about that right now, not with what he was facing. He couldn't allow himself to be distracted, not by anything, and the focus had already started to tighten.

He talked the talk and walked the walk, and did a damn fine job of it, but if he'd ever thought he was absolutely secure in his skills, he had plenty of scars to prove he was mortal. He knew with certainty that he might not survive this hunt.

That didn't frighten him. He and the possibility of death had been close acquaintances for a long time now. Every twinge of his back reminded him of how close he had come. So he wasn't at all worried about what he might face, not for himself. In fact, he was almost eager to be at it. His only disadvantage might come if his back decided to spasm hard on him, but he thought he could keep on going through that, no matter what.

No, he was thinking and worrying about Allison, probably more than he should, given what he faced. He felt a new admiration for his teammates who seemed to have been able to cut off all concerns about their families once they became mission focused. But they all understood something: any distraction might be deadly. Total focus was a must.

He figured it would take over completely once he set out, but right now he sat with a woman in a darkened kitchen, his eyes night adjusted enough that he could see her clearly in the little bit of illumination that filtered in through the window from the streetlamp down the street.

He thought of how she had looked last night and hated himself for the tension he saw in her now. He wanted to erase it with one sweep of his hand. He supposed he could. He could carry her back to bed right now and make them both forget for a while, but then reality would return. Inevitably.

Maybe he shouldn't have loved her last night. Maybe he'd made things worse for her. He'd wanted her to understand that her old boyfriend was wrong. He'd wanted to give her back that part of herself.

But what if he took away something equally important when he walked out of here?

The thought pierced him, hurting almost like the shrapnel that had once slashed him. He hadn't wanted to hurt her, not at all. Not even in the least way.

Instead, he'd mucked up her life, caused her a scare she'd probably never forget and now was about to go out the door on a mission that would leave her waiting, frightened to death.

He'd ripped a hole right through the center of her life. He looked back at the past two weeks and wondered why he hadn't just kept his distance. Why had he felt so compelled to insert himself? For God's sake, he'd even been wrong about the threat she faced…which had likely been none until he walked into the middle of things.

All he could do now was mentally kick himself for being so dull witted. He'd formed the wrong shape in his head, and there was no excuse for that. He knew better than to settle on a single outline until he had a lot more information.

But out here in this bucolic county, he'd felt so far from his own past. No reason to think it could have followed him here, certainly not so swiftly. Instead, in the stupidest way imaginable, he'd allowed events to mislead him. *He* had been the danger to her, not some shadowy poisoner.

She had tried to tell him that no one had anything to fear from her, but he hadn't heeded her. In his world, a paranoid world to be sure, there was something to fear from everyone. Eventually, she had concluded the same herself. Only yesterday she had said, "What if he's still using the poison?"

But had she thought of that because of his insistence all week that she could be in danger?

God, he nearly despised himself. Why couldn't he be like other people? Why wasn't he in bed with her right now, whispering the sweet nothings she deserved, holding her and caressing her and helping her to appreciate the incredible gift she had given him?

Instead, he was prowling the dark, thinking about equally dark things and ready to dive into business again even though it was still too soon.

"I'm broken," he announced.

Her head jerked a little. "Your back?"

"No, me. I'm broken. I can't squeeze myself back into regular life."

"I think you're doing okay, but aside from that, why should you?"

That startled him. "Why should I?"

"You are who you are. I think the world can make some room for you, Jerrod. It makes room for a lot of different types of people. Besides, I don't think there's any real state called normal. Everything's relative."

"Well, I'm so lost right now that I seriously screwed up, scared you, put you at risk… I shouldn't have done that."

"Oh, I don't know. You perceived a threat. One that fit with the situation. Why would you think it was anything else?"

"Because there *are* people with a reason to want my hide."

"That would be the first thing to occur to you when I was tracking a poison and my car window was smashed. Yup, that rises right to the front of the brain, doesn't it?"

Despite himself, he felt his lips twitch at her sarcasm. He couldn't believe she was making light of the situation he'd led her into. A situation that had gotten her shot at and probably left her sense of security in a shambles.

She amazed him.

She sighed and rested her chin in her hand. "Don't beat yourself up. You're sure now it isn't just the guy with the hideous poison. You've got a handle on it. So isn't this when you put on your game face?"

"Soon."

"As for the rest." She paused a long time. "In case you think your white-knight self-image has been tarnished, it hasn't with me. Last night… Last night…" Her voice thickened a bit. "Let's just say you helped me consign an idiot to a pit he should have been in a long time ago."

Happiness struck him then, a feeling so rare he almost didn't recognize it. Real happiness. "Thank you."

"No, thank *you*."

He shook his head quickly. "You gave me something precious, Allison. Don't ever think otherwise. Nobody's given me the gift you gave me last night, the gift of your trust when you were so afraid. But as for the white-knight thing... I'm nobody's knight."

"You're mine," she said quietly. "Hardly surprising since you've spent years in the shadows protecting people who will never know who you are. That boggles my mind, frankly. Then you protected me. More, you *rescued* me. So please, just don't be hard on yourself. You did the best you could with the information you had at hand. Just tell me one thing."

"If I can."

"If you were so sure someone was after me, why did you walk around me rather than with me yesterday?"

"Because I was starting to have doubts."

"About me being the target?"

"Yes. A couple of times this week, the shape shifted. Just a little. It arrested me. Other possibilities began to bother me."

"Like what?"

"Like being watched in town and out there both. Like the fact that I couldn't find any sign of this watcher. That indicates a certain level of training. Not impossible in the folks you have living here, but I was starting to consider other things. You're not going to like this."

"Like what?"

"I figured yesterday would settle the shape in my head. It did. I saw what I needed to see, and somebody took a scare shot at you. And it *was* a scare shot. I was never more than twenty yards from you. If someone was after you, that would have made them unlikely to act. You were safe."

"Except from a guy who was after *you*. Did it occur to you that you could get killed?" Her voice grew sharp.

"Of course."

She swore and jumped up from the table. When she reached the counter and stared out the window at the night, he followed and wrapped his arms around her.

"Just tell me," she said, her voice tight and thin. "What if he had been after me? What if he'd shot me? Twenty yards wasn't close enough."

"If he'd hurt you, I'd have been after him so fast and so hard that he never would have gotten away."

"Too late."

"No, I don't think so. By that point I was pretty sure that if the guy was worried about you, he wasn't out to kill. He'd had plenty of opportunity before that."

"Damn you," she said quietly. "You used me as bait."

He couldn't explain. How could you possibly explain to someone who had never been where he'd been about how things worked, how they measured out, how rarely you were wrong if you survived? He couldn't afford mistakes, and his only mistake here had been taking too long to figure it out.

"You were never bait. By the time we came down that mountain on Saturday, I was reasonably certain no one wanted to hurt you. Not seriously. That's all I can say."

"So what was chapping you? Why did you insist we break off early and come home?"

"Because I needed to reevaluate and plan."

"And your planning included me being on that mountain with you so you could get this creep's measure. Thank you very much."

He couldn't blame her for her anger. He wouldn't have blamed her if she hauled off and socked him. She couldn't possibly begin to see it all the ways he saw it.

"I had very little to go on," he said finally, painfully aware of how she had stiffened in his arms. "I screwed up, I admit it. But I'd been in this town just two weeks when the stuff about the poison began to happen. I got really concerned when your car window was broken. But I sure as hell didn't think anyone could have found me this fast. So I focused on you and the toxin. Then over the past week, a couple of things made me start to reconsider. You kept insisting the poisoner couldn't be caught unless he was caught red-handed somehow. I was thinking he might not know that."

"It was possible," she admitted grudgingly.

"Of course it was. Few bad guys are actual masterminds. But why would this guy watch you in town? You weren't taking samples here."

"No." But she didn't relax at all.

"Then I sensed him out there Saturday morning. We only had a few hours of light left, and I wanted to rethink things. Plan differently. Make *myself* bait."

She sucked an audible breath at that. "But you took me out there."

"Yes." He wasn't going to deny it even if she consigned him to hell, a more painful prospect than he wanted to imagine.

"Why?" she repeated.

"Why? Because you wouldn't have stayed here even if I'd told you. You were hell-bent on doing your job, and none of my concerns or cautions had slowed you down.

If I had gone out there alone, you would have been right on my heels." There, he'd said it. He suspected that being right about her wasn't going to soften her any, though. No, she'd probably just get madder.

"You're right," she said finally, her voice still tight. "You're absolutely right. I had a job to do, and you weren't going to stop me. Maybe I'm hopelessly naive, but I didn't see how my samples should make anyone want to kill *me*. Not even when the worst possibilities occurred to me. So yes, I would have gone."

Then she turned, shrugging away his arms. "Unless," she said, her voice like steel now, "you had told me what you were really thinking."

Now the ache in him began to give way to a simmering anger. "Even if I *had* told you this guy might be after me, that wouldn't have stopped you. You wouldn't have seen how you could have possibly made things any worse. You'd have tried to tell me not to go with you but you'd have gone up there, anyway."

She opened her mouth, then closed it. Then opened it again.

"Some truth would have been nice," she said finally. "Very nice."

"I was figuring it out as I went."

"Sure. All wrong, apparently. Well, go on your damn hunt. Stay alive. Don't get hurt. And don't come back."

He watched her storm out of the kitchen, listened to the bedroom door slam. He felt as if he had just been skinned alive.

Oddly, though, even as he wanted to roar at the universe, he realized something: the two of them were more alike than either of them had guessed. Now he knew.

* * *

Allison stared up at the ceiling in her dark bedroom. Her eyes burned like hot coals, although no tears fell. She felt as if she had been lied to, yet as she replayed the past two weeks in her mind, she couldn't find a single lie.

Jerrod had been trying to figure it out. He knew something wasn't right. Was it so surprising that he had settled on the poison and that the car window had seemed like a red flag to him?

Maybe it was a flag, but it had been misread. So what had sundered her, seemed to cleave her heart in two? That he had gone out there with her today not telling her that he might be at risk?

He wasn't absolutely certain of that, either. He *did* seem certain that nothing bad was going to happen to her.

She actually felt a pang for him through her own pain. How must he have felt when he heard that shot and come racing her way? She hated to imagine. Then he had stayed with her to make her feel safe, when she was absolutely certain he'd wanted nothing more than to race up that mountain. But no, he had stayed, losing his chance at the shooter until he'd felt sure she was calm enough. Only then had he crept off into the brush.

Now he had to go face that again, and he was planning to do it alone.

She had known from the start that he was different, but she hadn't guessed just how different. He was right about one thing. If he'd explained his suspicions to her this morning, she wouldn't have stayed home. She'd have gone out there anyway, because she had a duty to her community to find out how much toxin they were facing. Plus, said that little voice that never quite left her alone, she wouldn't have wanted him to be out there alone facing whatever he expected. Yeah, she would have gone, little use though she would have been.

So what was galling her? That he hadn't shared his tidbit with her? He hadn't even been sure at that point. What was more, this was a guy whose lips had been sealed by years of training, duty and loyalty. Operational secrecy probably pervaded his bones.

She rolled on her side, staring at the closed door, wishing he'd barge through it and sweep her away to that Eden they had visited in the hours past. Wishing he'd just ignore her childish dismissal of him and take her to where she really wanted to be.

God, had she ever been so confused in her life? Wounded before, but never this confused. Saturday had torn open old wounds. Yesterday in the woods she had been stripped of the innate, and probably blind, belief in her own security, one shared by most of the people around her. Last night he had opened her like a treasure and remade her in a new way.

Then, in the minutes just past, he had managed to make her feel... What? Betrayed? He hadn't betrayed her. Hurt? Why? He was so right that she would have climbed that mountain, no matter what he might have told her.

Which revealed something else about her, and she looked it straight in the eye. She could be a stubborn fool, but no way would she have let Jerrod go up there alone if he felt at risk.

Really stupid, considering how little help she would be. What did she know about this kind of thing? Nothing. Absolutely nothing in her life had prepared her for the kind of fight he was facing. She had her father's shotgun in her attic, one that she hadn't fired since the last time her dad had dragged her hunting while she was still in high school. She'd cleaned it a few times, but for all she knew it was utterly useless now.

So what earthly good could she be, except to call for help if he got hurt?

God! She pounded her fist in the pillow, frustrated by her own limitations and uncomfortable with her new self-knowledge. Jerrod had been giving her a lot of that. Allison today was not Allison from two weeks ago. He'd brought all that about.

Maybe that was why she was mad at him. She'd buried herself in a safe little cocoon in a safe little world, and he had ripped all that away like the illusion it was.

Why had she told him not to come back? Because she thought she could rebuild her cocoon? Hah!

Shoving out of bed, she grabbed her clothes and put them on quickly. She needed to talk to him, to tell him she hadn't meant that, that she was just upset.

That much had to be clear. She didn't want him to go out of here thinking she never wanted to see him again.

On stocking feet, she hurried to the kitchen. He wasn't there. Over to the living room. No sign.

Oh, damn, damn, damn, he'd left with those last words of hers ringing in his ears. Maybe he didn't care, but she did. She had sent a man she cared about off into a dangerous situation with the words, "Don't come back."

God, she *hated* herself.

She almost went to open the front door, but remembered the watcher might be out there.

So she went to the back door and found it unlocked. He'd left that way. Stepping out onto the back stoop, heedless of the icy cold, she tried to see if any lights were on at his place. None.

"Allison?" It was one of the city officers, a young

man who had been in one of her classes only a couple of years ago.

"Where'd he go?" she asked without preamble, keeping her voice low.

He answered so quietly she almost didn't hear him. "Over to his place first."

"Is he still there?"

"No. He left on foot about twenty minutes ago."

"On foot?"

"That's all I know."

On foot. Leaving no sign to a watcher that he'd gone. She almost panicked, wondering how he was going to get to the mountains, then wondering if Gage Dalton might be in on this somehow. He seemed to be more in on it now than she was.

"Rob?"

"Yes, ma'am."

"I need you to do me a favor. Would you get in trouble for coming inside?"

Her mind was made up. And she didn't care who didn't like it. She knew one thing for certain. Foolish or not, she couldn't endure another round of survivor guilt. She was not going to let that man face this alone.

"I don't think so, ma'am. I'm supposed to be watching *you*."

"Then come on in. I need some help."

Jerrod made it to the edge of town and a little beyond about the time the first gray light showed from the east. Still dark, but not for long. A minute later he heard a truck approaching. He ducked down into the ditch, in tall, dry grasses and snow, until he was certain it was Jake Madison. Then he stood up and the truck stopped for him. He climbed in, putting his rifle bag between them, barrel pointed downward.

Madison passed him a bag. "Breakfast and coffee. What the hell are you up to?"

"You really don't want to know."

"So Gage tells me, but he was awful insistent." Jake looked at the gun tote. "Loaded?"

"Not yet."

"Good. Too dangerous in a vehicle."

"Thanks for breakfast."

"I had to have some reason for going to town." He patted another bag on the seat beside him. "Nora will be surprised."

Jerrod swallowed a mouthful of egg and English muffin, washing it down with hot, strong coffee. "I met Nora's father."

"Quite an experience, isn't he?"

"Even in a very small dose. Nate Tate doesn't think he'd have had anything to do with your livestock being poisoned. From what little I saw, I got the same read on him."

"I don't think it was him. He's got too much to lose. But I wouldn't put it past one of those zombies of his."

Jerrod nearly choked on muffin. He laughed. "Zombies?"

"Not a very kind way to speak of some of my neighbors, I know. Most of the folks who go to that church are a little on the far side for my taste, but they're okay. There's a small handful, though... Well, let's just say there are a few of them who would drink the Jim Jones poison brew, if you get me."

Jerrod got him, loud and clear. "So he might have told one of them to do it?"

"Probably not. But one of them might have done it on his own, all whipped up by Loftis's rants about sin and so on. All it takes is one nut who believes he has a cause. Anyway, there are maybe a half dozen of them I keep a close eye on. So does the sheriff. They have the potential to slip a cog. The nice thing about a small town is that sooner or later you know everything. We'll hear if one of them put that bait out because sooner or later someone's going to be bursting and just not able to hold it in any longer."

"Seems to be a common trait."

"Except among folks with your training."

Jerrod played dumb. "My training?"

"I may be just a rancher, but I can read it all over you sometimes. It's okay. There are things we don't talk about around here. Nate, Gage and I aren't going to blow your cover."

Jerrod snorted. "I'm supposed to be a civilian now."

"I hear it takes some getting used to. So Gage said I was to take you to my barn, right? Then what?"

"I'll hide out there until it gets dark again."

"You could hide in my house. It's more comfortable."

"I've caused enough trouble. I don't want to be bringing you any."

"Some of us out here might like to help you out."

"Some of you already have. I'm better off solo on this one. Believe me."

He was relieved when Jake dropped the subject. Unfortunately, he still had a whole lot of hours left before nightfall. He hoped he could focus his attention where it needed to be, but he figured he was going to spend an awful lot of those hours thinking about Allison.

Last night. Her final words to him. They had penetrated his armor in ways it had never been penetrated before.

Well, he'd take care of this problem, then move on. He'd caused enough trouble already.

Allison sat at her kitchen table with Rob. She'd pumped him full of coffee and made him some toast and eggs. He seemed grateful to be inside with her, and didn't raise any objection when she climbed into her attic and reappeared with her dad's shotgun.

"Thinking about hunting?" he asked, carrying his plate to the sink and pouring more coffee.

"Hunting," she repeated. "Yes. But it's been a long time since I used this and I wondered if you could help me out."

"Help you how?" He returned to the table and sat, running his hands over the sleek barrel and stock, where gun oil still gleamed, although it was a bit marred by dust.

"Well, I need to make sure it's clean and safe to use."

"Oh, I can help with that. You have a cleaning kit?"

She did, indeed, and as she opened it the odor of gun oil stung her nostrils and carried her back in time. Her dad sitting across the table from her when she was twelve, teaching her gun safety and gun care all at the same time as they prepared to hunt together for the first time. She remembered being excited and nervous about it all at once. Now she looked at the gun and wanted to cry. She missed them, would always miss them.

She could still hear him saying, "First we'll get you some target practice, though." She had gotten to be a good shot. Very good.

But she'd never developed a taste for hunting. She guessed that was about to change.

She sat back, watching attentively, listening as Rob explained what he was doing. He first checked to be sure there were no shells in the gun.

"This is a nice piece," he said. "Six shots. I wouldn't mind one of these myself."

"My dad liked the best equipment for what he did. Always."

Rob laughed. "Smart man."

She noted that he seemed pleased with himself to be able to help her with this. Role reversal, with him being the teacher this time. It had to be good for his ego.

"I have some shells from years ago," she said. "Are they still safe to use?"

"I'd get fresh, myself. You don't want to take a chance."

"Then I'll do that."

But having his ego stroked didn't make Rob stupid. When he'd finished up and went to resume his post, he rose, then paused to look at her. "You wouldn't be thinking of doing something idiotic, Allison?"

Her heart stopped. Then she managed to shake her head. "I might carry it with me. You know I got shot at yesterday, Rob. I'm not feeling exactly safe."

"We're watching you."

"I know. But it's my feelings we're talking about here." Which was true, if misleading.

"All right, then. If it will make you feel safer. Just don't carry it loaded in the car. It's dangerous. Wait until you have both feet on the ground, okay?"

"Is that what you do?"

"In my own car. In the patrol car I have a dash lock for my shotgun. If it goes off, the worst it can do is give me a sunroof, okay?"

"Got it." She gave him a wan smile.

He shook his head a little, as if none of this was quite adding up for him, but finally he just left.

Relief filled her. If he'd kept questioning her, she wasn't sure what she might have said, simply because her own determination hadn't yielded a useful plan yet.

All she thought she knew was that Jerrod was probably going to head up into the mountains after dark. And she intended to be there in case he needed help.

She had a gun now. She also had a sheriff's radio keyed to the emergency frequency. If nothing else, she could call for the cavalry.

What she could not do, no matter how much common sense argued with it, was wash away the guilt over having sent him off with those words. Since he'd already left, she had no other choice.

She had hurt him, she was sure. If she died in the attempt to make up for it, so be it. She just couldn't leave it this way.

Foolish, aching heart overrode sensible mind. She knew it. She just didn't care.

Chapter 12

The snow complicated matters. Jerrod stood at a barn window, watching night settle over the world. There was no moon, the snow wasn't deep enough yet to cover the taller thatches of grass and the occasional tumbleweed that seemed frozen in time, but it still made for a difficult situation. He needed to get across a lot of open ground without being spotted. Once in the woods, blending in would be a whole lot easier.

The barn door opened and he turned. Jake stood there. "I can help."

"Jake…"

"Just wait. I have some cattle at the western edge of my property, near a river crossing. I'll drive out that way and drop you off. You can't possibly cross all that open ground without being spotted."

"I don't want you dragged into this."

"Sometimes life just drags us in. You're not going to tell me to stand aside, are you?"

"Are all you locals so stubborn?"

"Stubbornness is required for ranching out here. Look, I don't know what you have in the way of gear."

"I'm going black, and I've got an AR and a couple of good knives."

"Heavy weaponry. You know black will stand out on that snow. Once you get into the woods it might cover you, but not on my range. I'll drop you in my herd and you can use them for cover. With any luck, the clouds will move in and cut the light to nothing. They're sure trying to. And," he added, reaching for a dull gray blanket hanging over the edge of the stall, "take this. It won't stand out as much."

So Jerrod added a blanket to his gear and finally agreed to let Jake drive him. "Allison's stubborn, too," he remarked.

"How's that going?" Jake asked as he threw the truck into gear and they began to jolt across the open ground.

"Not well. She told me not to come back."

Jake ruminated for a few minutes, then remarked, "I know that woman. She didn't mean it."

"She did when she said it."

"Well, she's a stubborn cuss like all the rest of us out here."

"That's what worries me." And it did. He'd spent most of the day flipping between attention to the night that approached and memories of Allison. "You know, most women—hell, most people—would have backed off when I suggested that taking those soil samples could be dangerous."

"You told her that?"

"Repeatedly. That was before I realized anybody might have an interest in me. I was afraid the guy who did the poisoning might want to stop her. She refused to believe it, mostly, and she kept right on taking samples. Frankly, most people would have washed their hands and said somebody else could take the samples."

"Maybe so." Jake fell quiet for a few minutes. "I wonder if she would come out here tonight?"

"I'm hoping like hell she won't. Then I met you. You're not backing off, either."

"That will complicate things." Jake sighed. "I'll tell you, I've got a fiancée who is a tigress when it comes to protecting those she cares about."

"I'm pretty sure Allison is a tigress, too. I just hope she uses her head."

"I'll do what I can on my end. I'll watch for her vehicle up the road a bit toward town, and I'll have my hired hand ride around a bit."

"Thanks. I just hope she hasn't already come out here."

With a fresh hunting license tacked to her vest and a shotgun filled with ammunition, Allison had donned her orange gear and set out in the midafternoon. A little late for a hunting trip, but not too late. She'd managed to get away by lying to the cops, too. She had claimed she needed to work late on the samples. That had caused some rearranging in her keepers, and during it she had managed to slip the noose. So far she hadn't seen any flashing lights behind her, or anyone else for that matter.

Her cell phone rang before she got too far out of town and she answered it only because it was the sheriff. "Hey," he said, "how's it going?"

"I'm going to be stuck in my office grading papers until hell freezes over," she lied gamely. "What's up?"

"I thought you should know we have a confession about the poisoning."

She perked up instantly, and pulled her car over to the side of the road so she wouldn't lose the connection. "Really? Who? Why?"

"It was funny. I wish you'd been here. Fred Loftis all but dragged this skinny kid in by his ear. It seemed the kid was striking out for truth, justice and not living in sin. Unfortunately, he bragged about taking action."

"What in the world did he hope to achieve?"

"Brownie points with Loftis, as near as I can figure. It backfired."

"I guess so."

"Allison?"

"Yes?"

"You wouldn't do anything unwise, would you?"

"Since when has grading papers become unwise?"

A pause, as if he didn't quite believe her. "Sometimes," he said quietly, "it's better to stand aside."

"I'm grading papers," she repeated.

"Let's keep it that way."

She was relieved to disconnect. Lying wasn't easy for her.

She hiked in from quite a distance away, but she had made good time. She didn't know exactly where this was going to play out, but she suspected it would be somewhere around the area where earlier events had happened. It was the likeliest place for Jerrod to go, and thus the likeliest place for someone to look for him.

Just what she hoped to accomplish, she didn't know.

All she knew for certain was that her heart wouldn't rest unless she did this.

Her parting words to him thundered in her ears and heart. Yes, she'd told him to stay safe but she'd also told him not to come back. She had rejected him in lesser ways before, and she had seen his reaction, almost as if he closed in on himself. And she had sent him off on a deadly mission with a rejection like that on his brain.

Maybe he didn't care. Maybe he didn't care in the least what she said or thought. Maybe she was just a cipher for him, a woman he had loved for one night and would leave behind.

None of that mattered against her own sense of iniquity. That she could have said something like that to anyone made her feel loathsome. Despicable. It was even worse than not meeting her parents in Minneapolis. She *should* have been on that plane with them. She could have saved at least her mom. Well, she wasn't going there again, not going to live with regrets, especially one so ugly.

Following what her dad had taught her so long ago, she paused from time to time, as if she was looking for nibbled plants. When she reached the right area, she climbed a tree to keep watch. Just like a hunter, with her shotgun ready, her orange cap and vest identifying her.

She released the safety lock and prayed that a deer wouldn't cross her path. If one did, she'd have to shoot it to carry out her ruse, and she didn't want to. Not at all.

Once she felt watched, but only briefly. The feeling was ephemeral, possibly imagined. But if it wasn't her imagination, then the attention had moved on, dismissing her.

Sitting still as the day waned, she grew chillier but ignored it. At sunset, hunting ended for the day. The only question was how she was going to manage it. Leave and start walking away? Ditch her safety gear? She didn't know.

So she sat there pondering as the light began to fade, wondering if she had totally lost her mind.

She certainly seemed to have lost something else.

The hunter saw the woman with the gun. At first he was annoyed and considered removing her from the picture. But then he remembered he didn't want to leave a trail. When she climbed the tree and settled in, blazing orange, he concluded that she really *was* there to hunt. And she was most definitely alone.

He dismissed her. She'd leave at sunset and be out of the picture completely. He'd seen other hunters on the mountain over the past week, and while she had been hanging with Jerrod, she wasn't with him now. Apparently Jerrod hadn't been able to slip the leash the cops had on him. The woman alone presented no threat whatsoever. He'd just check back at nightfall to make sure she was gone.

Then he'd wait for Jerrod Marquette, who would definitely come by night.

The blanket and the cattle proved to be nearly perfect cover. Keeping low, Jerrod moved among the herd. He didn't seem to disturb them at all. Steers and cows grazed placidly together, or just ruminated while they stared off into space with an almost dreamy look. They huddled fairly closely, probably for warmth, but a few wandered away, looking for more to nibble on. A big bale of hay had been broken up not far away, and that drew a few more of them.

He wished he'd had cover this good on some of his past missions. As cold as it was, with the blanket over him he doubted he was casting enough of a heat signature to stand out from the warm-bodied animals. He also soon discovered an interesting tendency: when he moved toward the stream, a lot of them edged along with him.

He wondered if he was wearing eau de cow or something.

Finally he was at the river's edge. He shucked the blanket, leaving it in some snow. He waited, allowing himself to cool down more to reduce his heat signature in case his foe was using infrared goggles. He had a pair himself and slipped them on, scanning the far bank. Nothing. Nothing at all.

Pulling them off, because he preferred his own night vision under most circumstances and the infrared emitted light that would worsen it, he waded across the water, wincing once when some sloshed into his boot. It wasn't much, but a trickle of ice ran down his calf to the bottom of his foot. It didn't take long for it to warm up to his body temperature.

On the far side, he melted quickly into the woods. The promised clouds had begun to move in, turning the night to near pitch as he moved deeper into the trees.

Every now and then he looked through his infrared sensor, but saw nothing bigger than a raccoon. The guy was probably waiting farther upslope. That was what he would have done. He'd have found a place to make a kill box, and a way to lure his quarry into it, but he'd want it to be far enough out of the way that it wouldn't be found soon.

Then he heard a twig crack.

Spinning and crouching in one smooth movement, he brought the infrared to his eyes again. This time he made out a human figure working its way slowly through the woods.

Damn, could this guy be that stupid? He waited, watching, then realized this was no trained person. A lost hunter?

Not a good place for him to be right now. He debated whether to scare the guy off or let him be.

He put his infrared away and pulled out his night-vision goggles. He needed more detail.

He got it. And what he saw made his heart stop in his chest.

Allison winced as the twig cracked beneath her boot. The whole world out here was soft with pine needles and snow, but she had managed to find the dry twig to step on. She froze, listening, but the night remained silent, except for a quiet murmur of wind in the tops of the tallest trees.

She had hidden her orange gear after making a big show of heading out of the woods. She hadn't felt watched since then, but all of a sudden she felt watched again.

Damn! What now? A thousand not-so-nice self-criticisms flitted rapidly across her brain. Stupid was the kindest of them. Stubbornness, guilt and an aching heart had driven her out here with only the slightest plan of what she might do.

Had she checked her brain into storage or something? She prided herself on being reasonably intelligent, but she had proved today that she might be the world's biggest fool. What did she hope to accomplish? Hear a gun report and call the cops on the radio she still had? Maybe. But as the darkness deepened, she knew beyond a shadow of a doubt that she wasn't going to find anyone who didn't make some noise out here.

But she'd just given her own presence and position away. *Damn it, Jerrod,* she thought as she crouched down. *Why didn't you at least wait until I could apologize?*

But would that have made any difference? She knew her own stubbornness, her own willfulness, and this time she had let them rule her, all because a man she cared about was out here facing a deadly enemy.

But the best thing she could have done for him was stay at home. Now she might turn everything into a mess for him.

Utterly without warning, a gloved hand clamped over her mouth and nose, and another arm locked around her shoulders, pinning her. She tried to draw a breath, but the hand prevented it. This was it, the fruit of her folly.

"Shh," came a sharp whisper in her ear. "It's Jerrod. Don't make a sound."

She closed her eyes, managed a nod and felt the hand drop away. Air at last. She tried to draw it quietly, but the hammering of her heart made that difficult.

He didn't release her shoulders. "What the hell are you doing?"

Good question. For once she didn't have a ready answer. "I was worried."

"This helps how?" He spoke so quietly she was sure the whispering pines were louder.

His hold on her eased a bit, becoming gentler, but the question still hung in the air. She had no answer that didn't involve a whole lot of mixed-up emotions and confused thinking that she couldn't imagine explaining under these circumstances.

"I said something awful to you," she whispered. "And I didn't mean it. I really didn't mean it."

"I'll survive."

The coldness of his tone seemed to pour through her like an icy river. She couldn't blame him, but it hurt so badly to feel it. He had cut her out of his life, and now he was probably furious with her.

"I was crazed," she admitted finally, the words barely passing her lips. But he heard them.

"Clearly," he murmured in her ear. "We'll discuss it later. Right now I have to figure out how to get you out of here before that creep sees you."

"He saw me already. I think it was him. I was sitting in a tree wearing my orange vest and hat, like I was hunting. I felt someone watching, then it went away and didn't come back."

He swore. The word managed to sound savage, even though it couldn't have been heard two inches farther away. "Then?"

"When it started to get dark, I headed back out of the woods toward the road. I got behind some rocks, stuffed the vest and cap inside my jacket and came this way. Then you found me."

Jerrod didn't say anything right away. She felt his head swiveling, so she tipped hers so she could see him. He was wearing some kind of goggles.

She touched them, whispering, "Infrared?"

"Light amplification. Infrared creates light and would kill my night vision completely. These woods are too damn empty and quiet. A dead giveaway. He's out there, probably upslope in a kill box. What the hell am I going to do with you?"

"There must be some way I can help."

"Why?" The coldness remained in his voice.

"Because I need to. Because I give a damn what happens to you."

"You being here doesn't help anything."

No, she admitted to herself. Driven by her heart instead of her mind, she had merely complicated everything for him. Now he had something else to worry about. But she hadn't expected him to even know she was there. She'd underestimated him, and overestimated herself. What *had* she thought she would accomplish? Had she even had a sensible thought at all? Driven by guilt, she had acted like an idiot. Another insight from this emotional ride with Jerrod: she could be an idiot. She swallowed that self-knowledge, but it tasted bitter. Her stomach turned over.

"I'm sorry. I'll head back to my car."

"Like hell. I can't have you wandering around out here with that guy on the loose. I found you, didn't I?"

Yes, he had. In the dark. While she was trying to be surreptitious. It didn't bode well at all. She wished the ground would open and swallow her. The sting of humiliation began to build beside the guilt. This was, bar none, the most foolish thing she had done in her life.

"Okay," he murmured in her ear. "You had the best of intentions. I get it. I'm even touched. But now the only thing that matters is skill."

But she had none. Her heart sank like a stone all over again. Her stomach seemed to turn to lead.

It seemed forever before he spoke. "So you looked like you were out here hunting?"

"Just like I used to do with my dad."

"It's time for you to get lost."

Her mouth turned dry as the prairie in August. "I'll go."

"No, that's not what I meant. You're here. I'm fairly certain he doesn't want to take you out. Either he has an ounce of humanity somewhere in him, or he figures it'll make a bigger mess than he wants. If you disappear, there's going to be hell to pay. I can vanish with hardly a question."

Her chest tightened. "So?"

"So we're going to move you upslope a ways. Not a whole lot. Then you're going to hunker down wearing your orange, and you're going to pretend you're lost. You wander a bit around an area, then just settle and get out your survival stuff, like you figure you'll stay put until morning. You can do that, right?"

"Of course."

"If he sees you at all, and we don't get you too close to the kill box, he won't care. What he wants is to lure me into a trap. Well, I'm going to quit being so damn covert. I'm going to act like I'm looking for you. Because you didn't come back."

"Wouldn't you bring the sheriff out here?"

"How many S and Rs do you run at night out here?"

"S and R?"

"Search and rescue."

She thought that over and got his point. "None, unless it's a little kid. It's too dangerous. They always start at dawn."

"Good. So that's the scenario. You're lost, nobody will get out here before morning. Except me. Clearly, I'm going to look for you tonight in case you need real help.

I'm not going to call out loudly for you, because he suspects I know he's here. But I'll make a show of tracking you. In theory, he'll find a way to guide me toward his kill box, or take me at some other point."

"I don't like the sound of this."

"This was always the sound of this. I should have realized it earlier."

"Why?" But she didn't argue. There wasn't time, and it would make too much noise.

"Anyway, I'm going to pretend to have more than ordinary trouble trying to track you in the dark. I'll keep well away from you. His interest should be on me alone." His hand gripped her shoulder. "I'm going to use you, Allison."

She swallowed hard. "I trust you."

"Just so we're clear. You put yourself here, and now that you're here I'm going to take advantage of it. It's what I do."

This time she got it, with core-deep understanding. "What if…" She couldn't bring herself to finish.

"If you see anyone but me, use that damn shotgun. You brought it for a reason, didn't you?"

That chilled her most of all.

Jerrod was furious, but he cleared his mind as quickly as he could. While he thought the danger to her was minimal, probably nonexistent, it remained she had changed everything and put a new problem on his plate.

Along with fury, worry for Allison reached new heights. Whatever happened now, he had to keep her safe. He didn't care if he died in the attempt, but her safety came first. She had certainly planted herself in the midst of a dangerous situation.

However, he could use it to his advantage if he was careful. If he weren't silently stalking the woods, but clearly looking for someone, that might cause the creep to lower his guard a bit. That always helped. He'd make himself look like easier prey, maybe bring this thing to a head sooner.

And he'd make sure to draw the guy away from Allison. In fact, it might well work. He'd been off active duty for half a year now. He just needed to look rusty. Lull the guy and drag him away. He had a pretty good idea of where he was supposed to be led. He'd seen the nearly invisible markers the guy had left, markers that should be visible only to him. If he messed up some of those markers he'd send exactly the signal he wanted: that he wasn't fine-tuned and on high alert.

"This can work," he whispered to Allison. "Let's go."

This can work. Allison tried to take some comfort from that as she settled in among protective boulders. Jerrod had slipped away into the night ten minutes ago. She wandered, as he had told her, then made a show out of cussing and pulling out her survival gear. Surrounded by three big boulders that provided a windbreak from the stiffening breeze, she covered herself in her survival blanket, hoping it would prevent her from being visible to infrared, assuming the hunter was using it. Finally she pulled it up until it covered everything except her eyes. Her gloved hands rested atop it, cradling her shotgun.

Use it? As much as the words had chilled her, she had to accept that she had brought it with her for exactly that purpose. Not to pretend to be a hunter, but for protection if needed, whether for herself or Jerrod.

She wasn't used to thinking in these terms. They

seemed alien, from another world. But facing the fact that she had been an idiot because she was worried about Jerrod had changed more than one thing inside her. She had come out here prepared to do what she could, what might be needed. What she hadn't wanted to face was that she might actually have to do it.

Plenty of time over the past few days, and now as minutes dragged by, to look at herself and wonder who she was and if she'd been living in some kind of bubble of denial. Her reaction to seeing Jerrod armed that first time. Her own self-doubts, her blossoming sexuality and then those cruel words. She winced every time she remembered them. So much she hadn't thought herself capable of.

Gripping the shotgun, she now had a new dimension to face. Who was the real Allison? Apparently not the subdued teacher who had been trying to skim over life's surface since her breakup with Lance and her parents' deaths. No, she was a woman who had inserted herself into a life-and-death situation without proper thought. A woman who had insisted on coming out here even when she had thought it possible that she might be the target of some crazy poisoner.

Apparently she had a steel core she had forgotten about. And equally apparent that she wasn't as smart as she had thought. Smart would have kept her home.

But her heart had dragged her out here. So many things she had put on hold since Lance had welled up, demanding their due. You couldn't skim through life indefinitely. Sooner or later you had to commit to something.

Well, she had committed. She guessed she could debate her folly for years, but now she sat here, and she was going to do as told.

Unless something happened. Deep inside her grew a core certainty that she would act if necessary. What that action might be, she couldn't imagine; she just knew that if the moment came, she would do what was necessary.

For herself. But mostly for Jerrod.

Jerrod slipped quietly back downslope. This time as he resumed his climb, he trampled some of the signs that had been meant to guide him to his quarry. Set there by the hunter, knowing Jerrod had the training to spot them and would follow them.

This time he acted like that was the last thought on his mind. He scuffed through a few, and used a high-intensity penlight to scan the woods around. A man on a search for a woman, not a covert operative on a mission.

A couple of times he called Allison's name, though not too loudly. He didn't want his enemy to wonder why Allison didn't answer.

In short, he made the most ham-footed, ham-handed hike through the woods of his entire adult life. He wandered away from the trail that had been set for him, adding to the guy's confusion about what was going on here. And each time he wandered, he wandered farther from Allison.

He crunched sticks. He kicked rocks. Not overdoing it, but looking like he felt he had no need to be secretive. He paused again, calling Allison's name.

Then he felt it. The hunter had found him. A grim satisfaction came over him. Who was the hunter and who was the prey? He guessed they would soon find out. One thing for sure, he wasn't walking into the kill box. The guy was going to have to figure out how to deal with this.

He didn't expect to be shot. A gunshot on the night air

would be too audible. Allison's presence on this mountain had brought that benefit. If the guy left her alone so he wouldn't leave too big a mess behind him, then Allison would report she had heard gunfire.

So it was going to be up close and personal. Silent and deadly.

He continued another few paces, then paused. He shone his light around as if looking for something, but he was straining his ears to hear the slightest sound. A man could be nearly silent if well trained, but few achieved total silence. Something would give away the man's location sooner or later.

Then he heard it. If he hadn't been waiting for it, the sound would have been lost in the sighing of the breeze in the treetops.

Game on, he thought.

Allison wished the survival blanket made less noise. Every time she stirred, it rustled. Finally she cast it aside and waited. She had heard Jerrod calling in the distance, and the calls seemed to be moving farther away from her. He was doing what he had promised, drawing this threat away.

But at what risk to himself?

This, she thought, was every bit as bad as sitting at home worrying, helpless and wondering if he would come back. So he was out there alone in the darkness, and he seemed to think this guy had training like his own. An even matchup?

Thoughts of Jerrod's back began to plague her, the pain she had seen whisper across his face a couple of times. It couldn't possibly be an even matchup.

But she had promised to stay here. She'd been castigating herself for her own stupidity in getting in the way, of involving herself and making things more difficult for Jerrod.

Was she going to be a fool again?

No, of course not. She had learned her lesson.

At least until she heard voices in the distance. The two had met.

She pulled off the hat and vest again and stood, releasing the safety on her shotgun.

After this, he'd probably never speak to her again, she thought as she started to mimic the way Jerrod moved and began to cross the slope as quietly as she could. But she'd never forgive herself if she might have helped him. Or saved him.

The guy who was after Jerrod wouldn't be expecting her. And maybe that was the best help she could offer.

Jerrod turned toward the sound. "Let's have it out here," he said.

A shadow emerged from the trees. Something about it rang the bell of familiarity.

"Drop your gun and I'll drop mine," came the answer. "*Mano a mano,* Major Marquette."

Good, Jerrod thought. So the guy didn't want Allison to hear a gunshot. Finally he'd gotten the shape of this right. He dropped his rifle. The other guy followed suit.

"Do I know you?"

"Not really. But you knew my brother. Dave Sorenson."

Understanding crashed through Jerrod. His team member, the one who had died a few weeks ago. Now it all made sense. He was being held responsible for a command decision that had cost one man his life. Yes, he took responsibility, just as he took responsibility for every decision, for every life under his command.

But taking responsibility wasn't the same thing as having done something wrong. "I'm sorry about your brother. He was a good man."

"Better than you."

How the hell was he supposed to answer that? Jerrod wondered as he watched the guy slowly move closer. Given what he wanted, he'd pull a knife soon. Jerrod had unzipped his jacket when he'd started this pretend search, and his own knife was in easy reach.

"We don't have to do this," Jerrod said. "We can talk about it, every detail of it. You're special ops, aren't you? You know the risks we take. You know that things go bad sometimes."

"But you're here and he's not. You didn't even come to his funeral."

"I didn't hear about it until two weeks later. Sorry, but you only get one chance to go to a funeral. If I'd known, I'd have been there. I'd have liked to tell everyone what a good soldier your brother was. The best."

"Exactly. The best. And you got him killed."

This conversation was going nowhere fast. Sorenson had his mind made up. He wanted someone to pay for his brother's death, and Jerrod was it.

"Well, then, let's do this."

"The sad part is," Sorenson said, "I heard about your back. This is going to be like taking candy from a baby."

He was in for a shock, Jerrod thought. "So take it," he said. "I'm not all that thrilled about surviving."

That stopped Sorenson between one step and the next. "Why not?"

"You think I don't care? Of course I care. I care about

your brother and everyone else who's been wounded or killed on my watch. It's like carrying a ball and chain of guilt and grief. So just do it."

Allison heard that last bit as she drew close. The men were so focused on one another they apparently hadn't heard her inexpert attempts to be quiet. She squatted down to be sure she had a load in the chamber, then straightened again.

A ball and chain of grief? God, she hadn't even begun to consider the burden Jerrod must carry in his heart.

Easing closer, she heard a grunt. She guessed the battle was on, and this wouldn't be a good time to hold back. She hurried as fast as she dared over the rough ground, trying not to fall with a ready weapon in her hands.

At last she reached the point where she could see the shadows of two men locked in struggle. Just enough light poured through the trees that she caught the flash of a knife. One knife? Who? Jerrod? The other guy?

Why hadn't he pulled his knife? Did he have a death wish?

But they were so close together, slinging punches, that she didn't know what she could do.

Then they broke apart a little and she saw the knife raise. Now she knew who was who, and the other guy was preparing to stab Jerrod.

But Jerrod's arm shot up and caught the one holding the raised knife. "I don't want to hurt you," Jerrod grunted. "Damn it, hasn't your family lost enough?"

"My family wants payback." The arm holding the knife swung to the side, breaking Jerrod's grip, but only briefly. Once again, his arm shot out like a striking snake and caught the guy.

Then she saw something that nearly froze her heart in her mouth. The other guy used his free hand to pull out another knife. In a second he'd stab Jerrod under the ribs.

But just then Jerrod, who seemed to have sensed or seen the threat, whirled away beyond reach. Now he faced two knives and he was moving in again.

Allison couldn't stand another minute, another second. She pointed her shotgun well above them and pulled the trigger. The deafening blast froze everyone in place.

"I'll shoot you," she said, hoping her voice didn't quiver as much as her insides did.

It was a moment of distraction, just what Jerrod needed. He leaped into hyperdrive, calling on reserves of speed he hadn't needed in a long time. Sorenson, in that moment of shock, lost his edge.

A punch to the gut. A roundhouse kick to the knees and Sorenson fell to the ground. "Shoot him if he moves," Jerrod said to Allison. His back had seized, but he couldn't afford that right now. He pushed down his awareness of the pain.

"He's in my sights," she said coolly. God, what a magnificent woman.

Limping now, he went to grab his own rifle. Soon he was aiming it at Sorenson. "I don't want to kill you, son, but I can't let you go, either. We're not going to play this game again."

Sorenson swore at him but didn't move.

"Allison, approach him from his head and kick the knives away. If he twitches he's going to have a fist-size hole in his chest."

She did as asked, moving cautiously, keeping her own

shotgun on the guy. She reached out carefully with her foot, kicking each knife well away.

"Now get his rifle. It's over there. Do you know how to pull out a firing pin?"

"I can try."   •

"It doesn't matter. Bring it to me. Then, for the love of heaven, please call for help."

It took an hour for the sheriff and his deputies to find them. By then, Jerrod was propped against a tree trunk, knees slightly bent to ease his back. Sorenson, with two guns on him, had the sense not to move.

Once the sheriff had Sorenson thoroughly cuffed and under control, Gage came over to them.

"You can tell me all about it in the morning," he said, looking from one to the other. "This is a story I've got to hear. Especially what the hell Allison is doing here. But tomorrow's soon enough. Get home and get warm."

Jerrod slid down until he sat on the ground with his knees up. He had turned over Sorenson's rifle, and now held only his own AR-15.

Allison, still waiting for her heart and stomach to settle, squatted beside him. "Can you make it?"

"In a minute. It's easing up."

He reached for her hand and tugged her down beside him. "Thank you. You turned out to be a great help."

She began to warm inside at last. The fears started easing, and she didn't care who saw her rest her head on his shoulder. "I was a fool, but I'm glad I was a fool."

"So am I." He snaked an arm out until it wound around her shoulders. In front of them, the forest remained busy. And now they were bringing up floodlights. "We'd better go before we're blinded."

"Can you walk?"

"I can sure as hell limp."

"Lean on me if you need to."

His arm squeezed her. "I already leaned on you a whole lot tonight. You were magnificent."

Her heart nearly exploded with joy at that. It might have been a gross exaggeration on his part, but it felt good.

She'd have felt a whole lot better if he had ever suggested he might hang around. Not after what she'd said to him. As they made their way down the mountain, a heaviness filled her heart. She couldn't think of one good reason why he'd want to stay here. Not one.

No apology could make up for the words she had thrown at him.

Chapter 13

They arrived home well after midnight. They'd shared few words, and that might have bothered Allison except she could tell from the way Jerrod kept shifting in his seat that he was hurting badly. He was a man to whom stillness seemed to come as naturally as moving but right then he just couldn't hold still.

"Are you going to be okay?" she asked finally. "Do you need to go to the E.R.?"

"It was that damn kick that did me in. I'll be fine."

She wasn't exactly doing well herself. The adrenaline that had buoyed her for hours was now exacting its toll in extreme fatigue. She wanted her bed, and wanted it desperately. The whirling mass of thoughts and impressions in her head were just going to have to wait. She felt as if she could have conked out on a bed of nails.

Jerrod eased out of the car in a way that made her wince for him.

"I'm getting some fresh clothes," he remarked. "I need to clean up."

She watched him limp toward his house, then went inside. She might be exhausted, but she wasn't past feeling. She didn't expect him to come back. In fact, she wondered if she would ever see him again.

She'd been a fool, and his saying she had been magnificent didn't make up for the fact that she'd let her feelings take charge from her brain.

Idiot.

Too late, she told herself. Too late. She'd said horrible things, then she'd done stupid things. She couldn't take any of it back and… Oh, God, losing him was going to hurt beyond belief. The pain was already settling into her heart, constricting her breathing, feeling like the worst of toothaches with each breath she drew.

She wanted to curl up in a ball and just sob, but first she made herself shower and change into a drab flannel nightgown. Only then did she crawl under the covers, resisting the urge to pull them over her head like a child.

The sobs came at last, and tears were still pouring down her cheeks as sleep stole her away.

She awoke from a disturbing, mixed-up dream to the darkness and a realization that she wasn't alone. She caught her breath and froze. There couldn't be another threat, could there?

"It's just me," Jerrod said. His voice came from the floor beside her.

Startled, she sat up and looked over the edge of the

bed. She could barely make him out in the dark. "What are you doing down there?"

"Two things. Trying not to wake you up and trying to get my back to settle. I must have dislodged the shrapnel a bit."

"You need a doctor!"

"No, I'll be fine. They told me what to watch out for. It just needs to settle down."

"Can I get you anything? Can you get on the bed?"

"I'd like to get on that bed with you, but right now…" He drew a deep breath, sat up and cussed. "Right now I think a chair might be best. One that isn't padded."

"I'll take the pillows off my rocker. Do you need help getting up?" Concern for him overrode her absolute relief that he was here. Part of her stubbornly wanted to rejoice, but most of her was focused on one thing: helping Jerrod.

"I can get up on my own. I just won't like it."

She hurried out to the living room to remove the pillows from her rocker. It would give him a hard, straight back to lean against. She heard him limp as he approached, then watched with nails biting into her hands as he lowered himself gingerly into it.

"Thanks," he said.

"Do you want some coffee? Ibuprofen? Food?"

"Haven't you done enough tonight already?"

Her heart sank, and the incipient sense of joy over him being here felt like a balloon that had just been pricked. She could feel her whole body sag as a renewed sense of impending grief rolled through her. "You're right," she said in a small voice.

"Oh, hell, I didn't mean that the way it sounded. You must be exhausted. You don't need to take care of me."

Her heart lifted, but just a tiny bit. "What if I want

to do something for you?" She waited, hoping he didn't reject her simple offer. If he did, she was going to lock herself in her bedroom with her own misery until he left.

She was so tired of the roller coaster she had been on the past few days that she didn't think she could stand another dip or plunge.

"Coffee would be great. Anything to eat would be great. But it's still the middle of the night, you need your rest and I don't want you running around like my nanny."

A solo birdcall penetrated the house.

"Not quite the middle of the night. The birds are waking. Jerrod, just let me do this. Then we can have it out, or you can try to sleep sitting up or whatever."

"Have it out?" he repeated. At last his dark eyes met hers. "Oh, woman, we have some talking to do."

"But not right now."

She flew to the kitchen, afraid of his coming words, afraid that she would once again be shredded by a man she cared about. And this time there'd be a whole lot of good reason for it.

She wondered if she would ever come to terms with what she had done last night. The rest of her self-discoveries seemed minor by comparison. Each beat of her heart pained her. Each breath seemed almost impossible to draw against the weight in her chest.

She made the coffee, trying to gird herself emotionally. He had brought her walls down, though, and she couldn't seem to erect them again. Against him she was defenseless.

She made him a ham sandwich from a thick slice she had bought to use for breakfasts. Keeping busy suddenly seemed as important as sleep had just a few hours ago. Thoughts raced around inside her head like mice scurrying for cover. She couldn't seem to light on a single one. The overwhelming sense of doom was the only thing that remained stable.

Well, she'd asked for this. All of this. She was out of her cocoon, back in the real world and probably about to be reminded why she had built that cocoon in the first place.

He thanked her for the sandwich and coffee as she set them beside him. "This chair is great," he remarked. "I guess I should get one."

His face looked more relaxed, she thought, not as tight as earlier. As if the pain was easing.

"Aren't you eating?" he asked.

She shook her head and folded herself into a corner of the couch. She couldn't have eaten to save her life. Not the way she felt then.

He washed down a big bite of sandwich with coffee, then gave her one of his patented half smiles. "Perfect," he said.

"I'm glad." As if she could be glad of anything at the moment except that he was still alive and still talking to her. Well, talking for now, at least.

"We've got to get one thing straight now," he said.

She braced. Here it came. "What's that?" she asked, hoping her voice didn't sound as small as she felt.

"Don't ever, ever scare me like that again."

Surprise lifted her head a notch. "Scare you?"

"Fear comes in all shapes and sizes. I thought I knew them all until last night. I swear to you, I was never as scared as I was when I found you in those woods. You could have been killed."

"So could you," she argued. That was worth arguing about, no matter what.

He waved his hand as if that didn't matter a bit. "We're not talking about me. I didn't choose for that guy to come after me. I didn't set this mess up. But you *chose* to walk right in the middle of it when I'd done everything possible to keep you out of it. You terrified me, and I don't like that. Don't ever do that again."

Her back stiffened a bit. She didn't like being given orders, however justified. But then it struck her: he was talking as if he was going to be around. Her heart began to rise, and butterflies went crazy in her stomach. "I'm sorry," she said on a breath. Her gaze was fastened to him now, unable to even glance away.

"Don't be sorry, just promise me."

"I promise. As much as I can, anyway."

Astonishingly, he laughed. It was a free and easy sound, music to her ears. "That's the best I guess I can expect from a stubborn woman."

Some vitality began to return to her, as she realized this conversation sounded more and more like he wasn't planning to go away. That didn't necessarily mean a whole lot, but at least she'd have him for a while. "I was wrong to go out there last night," she admitted. "I tried to talk myself out of it."

"What happened?"

"I kept hearing myself tell you to never come back. I was hating myself and feeling guilty and terrified for you…." She trailed off.

"Your heart drowned out your head."

"Basically," she agreed. Nothing basic about it.

"That's never a good thing," he said seriously. "Not when it comes to something like last night. But at other times…" Again he smiled, that breathtaking smile she could never get enough of. "Well, I've never had anyone like you ride to my rescue before."

"You probably wanted to kill me yourself."

He shook his head. "All I wanted was to make you safe. Then you couldn't even stay where I planted you."

She bit her lip. "No. I figured I could stay out of sight, but I heard you arguing and I was scared for you. I needed to be there. I *needed* it."

He sighed, closed his eyes and tipped his head back. "It's letting go." Then his eyes snapped open and pinioned her. "I get it. I understand it. I'd have done the same thing."

"Wow. Really?" For the first time it occurred to her that she might not have been a total fool.

"Allison, your reactions were right. Your instincts are the kind that my life has depended on. Buddies are there for buddies. So except for your lack of training, I can't really criticize you. You had all the right reasons. I get it."

Buddies? She didn't want to be his buddy, but she wasn't immune to the high compliment he was paying her. "Thank you."

"I mean it. I found myself thinking last night that you and I are more alike than we probably realize. You've got the heart of a warrior. The part that matters most. And in the end you were awesome. Magnificent. Fantastic. So I'm not mad at you at all. I'm just wondering how many more times I can take a scare like that without having a heart attack."

She felt a silly smile tip up the corners of her mouth as she began to realize things were far from over. He was talking like there was a future for them, for crying out loud. At this point maybe only a few weeks or months, but she'd take every minute she could get. "I'm not planning to scare you again."

"It's unlikely you'll have to. But on the off chance, just promise me you'll let me know next time you think I need a teammate."

"You weren't here," she reminded him. Then the silly smile turned into an equally silly giggle.

He tilted his head, still smiling. "Maybe I need to hang a radio around your neck so you can let me know next time you want to go haring off."

Her smile grew so broad her cheeks began to hurt. "That sounds more like a promise than a threat."

"It's not a threat." His voice changed, growing even deeper. "Allison, sweetheart, you scared me so much last night that I realized something."

She held her breath. Her heart skipped, then began to hammer. "What?"

"That I love you. More than I've ever loved in my life. I know it's early days yet. I get that you hardly know me, but you stole my heart. Maybe you don't want me around. Maybe it's too soon. Either way, I can't take back my heart. It's yours."

Joy exploded in her, nearly blinding her with its intensity. Her answer was already there, hiding in plain sight. "I love you, too, Jerrod. It's been killing me, thinking you'd go away."

"I'm not going anywhere. Not for long, anyway, and only if I get called away. Take your time. The past few days have been hard on you. I need you to be very, very sure of this."

She'd never been surer of anything in her life.

"Damn," he said, "I wish I could take you to bed right

now. All I want is to love you, to erase last night with something good and beautiful."

She rose and went to him, reaching for his hands, speaking with utter certainty. "We're going to have a whole lot of time for that. The rest of our lives."

The expression on his face stole her breath once again. She'd never dreamed this man could look so happy. He tugged her hands until she perched on his lap.

"Seal it with a kiss," he demanded. Their lips met, a gentle kiss at first that steadily grew hungrier. She was gasping when she pulled her mouth back, her entire body aching with freshened need.

"Sweetheart," he said, "you are about to learn just how much I can ravish you while you sit on my lap."

He laughed, and she laughed with him, until the laughter dissolved into sighs, and the sighs into moans.

Everything could be worked out with time. But happiness was here, now, forever.

* * * * *

A sneaky peek at next month...

INTRIGUE...

BREATHTAKING ROMANTIC SUSPENSE

My wish list for next month's titles...

In stores from 21st March 2014:

❏ Josh – Delores Fossen

& The Bridge – Carol Ericson

❏ The Legend of Smuggler's Cave – Paula Graves

& Primal Instinct – Janie Crouch

❏ Diagnosis: Attraction – Rebecca York

& Relentless – HelenKay Dimon

Romantic Suspense

❏ Defending the Eyewitness – Rachel Lee

Available at WHSmith, Tesco, Asda, Eason, Amazon and Apple

Just can't wait?

0314/46

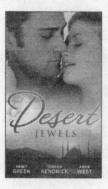
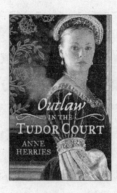

The World of Mills & Boon®

There's a Mills & Boon® series that's perfec
for you. We publish ten series and, with ne
titles every month, you never have to wait
long for your favourite to come along.

By Request
Relive the romance with the best of the best
12 stories every month

Cherish™
Experience the ultimate rus
of falling in love
12 new stories every month

Desire™
Passionate and dramatic love stories
6 new stories every month

nocturne™
An exhilarating underworld of dark desires
Up to 3 new stories every m

M&B/WORLD4a

Discover more romance at

www.millsandboon.co.uk

- ❤ WIN great prizes in our exclusive competitions
- ❤ BUY new titles before they hit the shops
- ❤ BROWSE new books and REVIEW your favourites
- ❤ SAVE on new books with the Mills & Boon® Bookclub™
- ❤ DISCOVER new authors

PLUS, to chat about your favourite reads, get the latest news and find special offers:

- Find us on facebook.com/millsandboon
- Follow us on twitter.com/millsandboonuk
- ❤ Sign up to our newsletter at millsandboon.co.uk